SAVED BY THE DARK

Dark Sons Motorcycle Club - Book One

ANN JENSEN

Published by Blushing Books
An Imprint of
ABCD Graphics and Design, Inc.
A Virginia Corporation
977 Seminole Trail #233
Charlottesville, VA 22901

Ann Jensen
Saved by the Dark

eBook ISBN: 978-1-64563-838-4
Print ISBN: 978-1-64563-839-1
v3

Cover Art by ABCD Graphics & Design
This book contains fantasy themes appropriate for mature readers only. Nothing in this book should be interpreted as Blushing Books' or the author's advocating any non-consensual sexual activity.

Acknowledgments

Thank you for reading my book. I hope you enjoyed this first look into the sexy and protective men of the Dark Sons Motorcycle Club. This was the completion of a dream to become a published author and only the first of many books to come.

I would like to thank my family who has always been supportive of every dream I've ever had and been there for me all the days of my life. There are so many people who made this dream a reality. My best friend of over twenty years, Mike who listened and sparked so many of my ideas. Lisen, your humor and encouragement helped me not give up. Stephanie, your comments and suggestions made this a book I am proud of. Nina, the fun tales of how this book spiced up your life still make me smile. To all my beta readers I say thank you.

Thank you Blushing Books for taking a chance on me and especially Sandra for your great editing and support for a nervous author.

Thank you readers! I would love to hear from you. Find me at:

www.annjensenwrites.com
   @annjensenbooks
   AnnJensenWrites@gmail.com

Can't wait to share more stories with you.

Chapter 1

If my options are to jump off a cliff or get eaten by a bear, I'll leap and hope I learn to fly on the way down...

The late afternoon crowd of rowdy and rough-looking men at the aging roadside bar might have scared a normal traveler. To Phoebe, though, the over-the-top laughter and the smell of old beer and fried food was like a sweet memory that helped her remember life hadn't always been a nightmare. Hell, a year ago she would have fit in perfectly. Working under the table at a dive bar for tips was probably the most respectable way she had ever earned money. She didn't need much, four walls and a moderately clean bed. Back then her clothes were cheap and her housing erratic, but she had been happy and understood how to survive. She believed being completely homeless was as low as a person could drop and took pride in the fact she only slept on the streets a few weeks a year.

The past six months of hell proved how naïve she was. She might be wearing a linen pantsuit and flashy jewelry, but she would gladly sleep on a cement street corner every night in winter if it meant escaping her current situation. The man sitting next to her in the tailored suit was worse than a drug-dealing pimp. He was a violent nightmare who trained and sold women like expensive, broken pets. Phoebe hadn't been a saint, but she tried to cling to the thought that she was worth more than a dog. Actually, people probably would have cared more if a dog was treated the same way he treated women. The men at the twisted sex auctions and parties that 'Master' hosted laughed and joined in the abuse of the female party favors he provided.

Phoebe ground her teeth and mentally reviewed the image of his driver's license. He was Mitchel Thomas, not Master. Blond hair, blue eyes, 5'10" and selfishly not an organ donor. Her eidetic memory meant whether she wanted to or not, she remembered every little detail of each horrifying minute. Phoebe tried to focus on useful things, but with each hour that passed her dreams changed from escaping to finally ending the nightmare. Being taken out of the training center and away from the hallways that echoed night and day with women's screams and whimpers was a rare treat. The sights of human depravity and cruelty she'd witnessed during her time there would forever haunt her nights. The public surroundings were new and should have comforted her, but dread built inside her each moment she spent in the fake freedom.

Phoebe would give anything to be sitting with the other customers instead of trapped at this table. The woman she used to be, would have flirted with the men, distracting them as she emptied their pockets, her small stature and elfin look fooling almost everyone into believing she was an innocent. Hell, looking back, she was an innocent. Life on her own on the streets couldn't compare to the horrors of her current life. Maybe it was time to give up and seek a way to end everything.

Did these strangers know how lucky they were to be drinking and joking with friends? She clenched her fists and used the pricks of pain her nails caused to focus and lock down her spiraling feelings. Envy and hope were emotions Phoebe couldn't afford.

Nothing made sense. If they were going to spend the afternoon at a dimly lit bar, why had Mitchel insisted the stylist use makeup to cover up her sallow skin and gaunt looks and put hair products on her blonde curls? He reveled in showing her off as his broken pet. After accepting a drink from the wrong guy and waking up chained in this new reality, she had tried to figure out how to escape and survive. But the beatings, drugs and chaos meant that every time she thought she understood the rules of this horrifying world, something changed and had her struggling to hold on to a single scrap of her sanity.

Phoebe shifted slightly, trying to ease the discomfort caused by the fresh cuts and bruises on her back and legs. Doing her best not to draw her captor's attention, she let the pain wash over her, focusing on the adrenaline and the wonderful rush of chemicals her body produced.

"Where are you?" Mitchel's cultured voice held iced impatience as he spoke to someone on the phone. "I'm here at the god-awful pit in the middle of nowhere because you insisted we had to meet tonight. The product better be worth my time."

A shiver ran down Phoebe's spine. The product Mitchel dealt in was exclusively unwilling women. Sitting here quietly, listening to arrangements for the pickup of girls about to be dragged into slavery, made her ill. Would they be like she had been: twenty, living on the streets, and stupid enough to take the wrong guy up on the offer to party? How many of them would survive even a week at the training center with their minds still intact?

"If you aren't here in five minutes, I will find another source for the low-class trash you provide."

She had been a piece of low-class trash. Phoebe had watched dozens of girls pass in and out of Mitchel's 'training center'. Most of them sold after a month, already broken and ready to do anything for their new owners. Yet she was still there, Mitchel's personal whipping post. A durable toy he wanted to break before letting it go. A week ago, she had swallowed her pride and pretended to give up, continuing the fight inside her mind while clinging to her sanity by her fingernails. Was that why they were here? Could he finally be selling her?

Would that be a good or bad thing? Escape from the training center was impossible, but her new owner might be less vigilant. Her pessimistic side said her new owner was just as likely to kill her. A small part of her soul crumpled at the knowledge that both options appealed equally.

Loud laughter erupted from the other part of the bar as a group of ten rough-looking men flirted with their waitress. From her seat across the room, Phoebe swore she could smell the savory mix of cheese and bacon emanating from the fries they were eating. Her stomach cramped remembering the single protein bar they had allowed her earlier that morning. The clock on the wall showed it was after six, nearly ten hours since her meager meal. Phoebe had noticed a row of beautiful motorcycles lined up outside on her way into the bar and guessed, by the matching black leather vests the men wore, the bikes belonged to them.

Every man in the group was tall, muscled, and tattooed, advertising to anyone with eyes they were dangerous. Phoebe's gaze was drawn like fire on a dark night to the man at the head of the table. With deep brown eyes and hair, and a scruffy jawline, he had a face that would melt any woman's panties. More reserved than his companions, he leaned back in his chair like a king on his throne, taking everything in. Phoebe's breath caught in her throat as his predatory gaze caught hers, locking all her muscles like a rabbit trying to hide on a mowed lawn. He smirked when he noticed her attention and winked.

Pain seared through her as Mitchel's hand closed around the cuts and bruises lining the back of her neck.

"Eyes down, slut. Don't you look at them."

"Sorry, Master." Phoebe dropped her gaze, her whole-body trembling at what he might do next. Being in public should mean safety, but Mitchel was unpredictable. When no blow or further words followed, she relaxed a little, keeping her gaze on the dirty stained wood in front of her.

The quiet click of his ever-present switchblade made her stomach turn. He ran the edge lightly along her thigh, the scrape of the material of her pants against the metal causing her to flinch. "I can force your attention if you can't focus on your own. What would those men think if they knew you were a dirty little pain slut? That you love being hurt?"

Shame swamped Phoebe as it always did when Mitchel taunted her with her body's responses to pain. She tried to remember when her love of rough sex with a large bite of pain was a quirk rather than a weakness. Mitchel could make her body respond even when her mind was quivering in fear and she hated it. It was that mental torture that had broken her more than the physical. Her sanity only held in place by being able to transform pain to pleasure and disconnect into her vivid pleasant memories, but she now believed it might have been better if she had broken long ago like the countless women who came through the training center. It had to be easier being a shattered, mindless drone than being aware and hating yourself.

"What's with the piece of ass?"

Mitchel pulled the knife away as two men joined them at the secluded table. Phoebe lifted her gaze long enough to notice the two men were also bikers like the other customers, but they wore slightly different leather vests than the men across the bar. They also seemed oilier somehow, without the powerful aura of strength and violence.

"Caravaggio finally made me an offer I couldn't pass up. I'm delivering her to him personally after we finish this meeting."

Caravaggio. The name echoed inside her head. He was one of Mitchel's frequent customers. Half of the scars on her back were from his cruel attentions. Too many times she had listened through the walls as the screams of his recent purchase faded into whimpers and eventually silence, signaling the death of his victim. So, when he had paid for the privilege of helping Mitchel break her, she had found comfort in refusing to scream for him. Able to disassociate since childhood, she knew that within the limits Mitchel set for him, she could remain blessedly quiet. That act of defiance made him want her with an obsession that bordered on mania. Tears would burn in her eyes, but she would fight them back. If given complete freedom without consequence or witness, that psycho would make her scream. She would end up unrecognizable, buried in some unmarked grave in the forest.

"This bar is neutral territory. No trading of goods here."

"I'm not meeting Caravaggio *here*." Mitchel said the word as if this bar was a cesspit.

"Just saying. Taking her out in public takes balls, man."

"My little slut knows better than to cause trouble, don't you?" Mitchel squeezed Phoebe's neck, and the pain pulled her out of her spiraling thoughts.

"Yes, Master." Her voice shook. She should run and take her chances. Even if it got her killed, anything would be better than ending up raped while bleeding to death by Caravaggio. Mitchel chuckled, probably loving both her fear and obedience.

"Drinks before we talk, though I doubt they have any good scotch in this place." Mitchel turned his head as if looking around for the server. Through her lashes, Phoebe took in the room. The single waitress in the place was still flirting with the table of bikers and unlikely to pause any time soon. "The service is appalling here." He raised a hand, trying to attract her attention, but she smirked and pointedly ignored him. Anger darkened Mitchel's face. "Screw this. Slut, get us three glasses of scotch, neat."

Phoebe stood, at first hesitating, not believing Mitchel would let her out of his grasp for even a second. Surprised, she kept her face neutral and slid out of the booth. She turned towards the bar to get their drinks and realized this was her chance. Running was a possibility, maybe she actually could escape the hell that was her life. Mitchel's bodyguards were outside, but if she surprised them...

No, making a scene wouldn't work. Who would help a stranger, a girl like her? Phoebe racked her brain for some plan that might save her from her fate. Mitchel always had a gun in the small of his back. She could easily lift it with a slight distraction. Killing him would be satisfying if she could, but even the worst-case scenario gave her comfort. She could use it to kill herself. Hundreds of ideas swirled through her mind on how to get the gun, every one of them bringing her one step closer to a shallow grave.

And she was okay with that.

Chapter 2

I train for the impossible because crazy shit happens every day and there ain't no way I'm backing down.

Sharp looked at his Brothers relaxing and enjoying their dinner after a long ride. They were a few hours from home, and he wanted to get there tonight and spend at least a few hours in his bed before heading back out. Some of his lucky Brothers would be staying at the Clubhouse, but others like him were heading right back out in the morning for another three days' ride to set up an escort for the next shipment of guns. Back-to-back jobs were a nightmare, but when you were the local chapter VP of the Dark Sons, one of the largest MCs in the country, you couldn't turn away from a big-ticket job because it was inconvenient.

HRs Bar was on the outskirts of Cheyenne, making it a convenient stop for them. Pops, the owner and current bartender, was a vet and respected by everyone because he kept his place neutral. The beer was cold, and the food wouldn't kill you, which was more than you could say about a lot of road-houses. Most nights, this place was packed with loose women and road-hardened men, but this early on a Sunday, the sole eye candy in the bar was Trix, the waitress, and she was currently entertaining Grinder and the prospect, Kickstand.

Well, there was the little slip of a thing hiding out in the corner. Her kind of beauty didn't belong in a place like this. She belonged somewhere fancy where her china-like skin could glow under the lights, and everyone would stand back for the sole purpose of admiring her long, golden hair. It reminded Sharp of that annoying kid's movie about the princess stuck in a tower. She was so far outside his usual tastes even thinking about her was ridiculous. Who wears a white outfit to a biker bar? Her man must be a complete moron to bring someone as special as her to a place like this.

Something about the two of them bothered Sharp. The way she curled up on herself any time the slick prick looked at her made his instincts tingle. Add that to the fact the two guys who joined them were low-level players in the Bloody Blades Club and the whole situation felt off. The BBs were a small motorcycle club that mostly ran girls and heroine in Utah and Wyoming. If this suit was tight with those psychos, he definitely didn't deserve a quality girl like her.

The object of his fantasies got up and his dick stirred as her delicate body was finally fully on display as she walked toward the bar. She was much thinner than he usually liked, but something about her just did it for him. She was so small, maybe 5'2" and light enough that she might have trouble on windy days. Still, he could imagine pinning her against the wall and fucking her for hours as she screamed out his name. It would be exciting to find out all the dirty fantasies hidden deep in her proper little mind. He would be happy to act each one out until she was addicted to his cock. Damn, she did more for him all buttoned up in her upper-class armor than any of the scantily dressed sluts ever had.

Deciding to have a little fun, he stood. Max, the ever-vigilant Dark Sons Road Captain, raised an eyebrow. Sharp shrugged and gave his friend a small smile. It had been a dull few months. If a little flirting landed them in a fistfight, well, that would be the icing on the cake. His Brothers would have his back and probably thank him for the exercise.

The vision in white stood in front of the bar, giving Pops her order. She trembled, her delicate hands clenching nervously. Was she afraid of being in a biker bar or was it something else? Her face was masked by beautiful blonde curls as she kept her gaze down. Sharp wanted a close-up look at the woman triggering all sorts of wild thoughts in his mind.

"Hey, beautiful. Why don't you let me buy you a drink?"

She mumbled something, but her voice was like a quiet breeze, and the words were lost in the noise of the bar. Sharp reached up and tucked her hair behind her shoulder.

"What was that, darling?" Sharp's hand froze as his eyes caught on the skin he had revealed. Tiny scars ran up and down her neck, but it was the purple and black marks, poorly concealed by makeup, covering her neck and shoulder that had his muscles locking and a fine tremor of adrenaline firing through his veins. Emerald green eyes that sparkled with tears looked up at him.

"Please. Help me." Her words were strangled and so quiet, he wondered if he'd imagined them.

"Get the fuck away from her, asshole." The suit-wearing prick had noticed what was going on and stormed over towards them. Instinctively, Sharp stepped between the woman and the furious pansy who seemed bent on dragging her away.

The bar went silent as all ten of his fellow Dark Sons stood. The dick stepped closer, getting up in his face. At 6'4", Sharp didn't often encounter people stupid enough to try and face off with him. Eight years in the SEALs had honed his body into perfect condition, and he hadn't let up on his training during the ten years he'd been out. Add that to the biker leathers and weapons he wore, and people rarely even had the guts to look him in the eye.

"Get your ass over here, bitch!" The man was at least smart enough not to try to push through Sharp, but still seemed oblivious to the danger that built around him. The woman didn't move.

"Doesn't look like she wants to go with you." Sharp did his best to keep his voice level, but his hands ached to beat the crap out of a scumbag who left marks like the ones he had glimpsed. He glanced over at the BBs flanking the prick, assessing any consequences that might come from them. The BBs didn't usually deal in high-class women, but she might be one of their whores in dress up. Did that matter to him? No, it didn't. She had asked for help, and he was going to fucking help.

"Do you know who I am?" The suit puffed himself up as if that would add another four inches to his height.

"No, and I don't give a shit."

The two men glared at each other, with neither backing off in the now quiet bar. Pops cleared his throat. "If you're going to get messy, Sharp, you take this piece of garbage outside." With the casual comment, the aging bartender had unofficially declared sides, letting Sharp know everything he needed to know. This guy wasn't welcome.

"I'll do my best, Pops."

The little twit looked around and finally realized he wasn't in the power position. Outnumbered and drastically outgunned, he stepped back a pace, changing his tone to one of annoyed, but reasonable. "That is my property. How much is it going to take for you to step aside?"

His use of the word 'property' made Sharp's lip curl. Bikers claimed their women as property, but for him, it was a term of respect. This guy talked as if the woman was a jacket he had misplaced. Probably used to his money buying him out of any situation, he didn't seem to fully comprehend this wasn't a negotiation. One of the BBs stepped up and tried to clue in the pretty boy. "Mitchel, this guy's a Dark Son. Just let the snatch go."

"I am not telling Caravaggio I gave his new toy away to some biker boy." Mitchel huffed like he didn't know he dug his grave deeper with every word. "Now, how much is it going to take?" he repeated.

Sharp recognized the name Caravaggio and wanted to spit. That sick fuck had been banished to the Midwest, in the hopes his twisted shit would stop blowing back on his Mafia family. Sharp wouldn't let any woman get sent off to spend time with that fucker, especially not this beauty who had his dick rising for attention. Her hands brushed at his back and he enjoyed the caress for a brief moment, thinking she held onto him for protection. His gentle thoughts scattered when the fabric of his jeans tugged against his stomach as his gun was removed from his waistband.

"Don't come near me!"

Sharp spun to see her shaking hand pointing the gun in the general direction of the suited prick. He watched the untrained way the girl held his gun and came to the easy conclusion that she had no idea what to do with the weapon. His Beretta had a very handy and engaged safety and her clenched trembling fingers were nowhere near it. He would remember this the next time his Brothers razzed him about his backup weapon. He carried a Sig in a holster under his arm for when he needed to fire quickly but anything he put in his pants was going to have more than a trigger lock to keep it from firing.

"Now darlin'," Sharp began, trying to talk the shaking beauty down, "give me the gun. I've got you covered."

For a second, it seemed she might hand it over, but then Mitchel laughed. "She won't fire. The little slut wants me to

Saved by the Dark

hurt her some more." The asshole smirked down at the terrified woman. "Don't worry, whore. You'll get what you want."

Tears streamed out of emerald eyes and Sharp swore he could feel something break inside her. She turned the gun up and into her chin and declared, "Never again." For a moment he saw the reality of what could have been. This delicate star's light had extinguished because the dark had become too much for her. He had seen enough death that his mind filled in the gory picture as he watched her finger contract on the trigger. The silence seemed to stretch as he stepped forward, pulling the gun from now unresisting hands, and hugged the surprised but undamaged woman against his chest for a moment. His spine tingled as he imagined how things might have been different, had she known to disengage the safety.

Sharp didn't want to think about how bad this woman's life must have been that she chose death over another minute with this asshole. Her defeated sobs as she fell against his chest were the last straw.

"Max, settle up. We are out of here." His Road Captain threw money down on the table, which more than covered their tab. Mitchel smirked and stepped forward as if to grab the sobbing girl. Sharp used his thumb to disengage the safety and pointed the barrel right at the idiot, stopping his forward momentum. Sharp took a moment to enjoy the warmth of her body against his own, seemingly pulling strength from him. "Now, little bird, you have a choice to make." Sharp tipped her face up to him, putting his free hand on her shoulder and giving it a squeeze. "I got a long ride ahead of me that would be made much nicer with you at my back, or we can keep your friends here busy for a little bit, and you can make your own way out of here. What's it gonna be?"

One of his Brothers chuckled a curse under his breath. Sharp didn't want to let this beauty go. He wanted to feel her body wrapped around him while he rode and, maybe later, he

13

would give her a much more intimate ride. The disbelief and hope in her eyes tore him up.

"She's going nowhere." Mitchel reached toward the small of his back but halted as the sound of nine other guns being unnecessarily cocked was evident over the background music of the bar.

The two BBs had stepped back, hands away from their bodies, clearly indicating they weren't willing to fight. With his Brothers at his back, Sharp felt safe enough to put his own gun away. He cupped the girl's face and brushed her silent tears away.

"There are two more guys outside, and they're dangerous." Her voice was like gentle music, slightly harshened by the tears.

"Make your choice, darlin'." Their eyes locked and Sharp swore his battered soul warmed at the exchange.

"You. I choose you."

Their moment of connection was broken by Mitchel's angry voice. "I'll find you, bitch. I'll find all of you."

Sharp and all his Brothers laughed. "Your buddies know right where to find me if you are dumb enough to try."

Chapter 3

You never know how strong you are until life bitch-slaps you and you slap it right back.

Several hours later, after the girl's grip around his waist had gone from just clutching to a firm hold, Sharp realized he had never even asked her name. The long drive through small mountains and long stretches of highway passed quickly as he enjoyed her warm little body wrapped up against his back. The two couldn't talk but their bodies communicated perfectly and his started to get impatient to have her at his front. Hours of riding wasn't easy for inexperienced riders, but she hadn't moved or complained. She just tucked her head down against his back like she was going to sleep with her favorite teddy bear.

Sharp was in for a rash of shit when they got back to the Clubhouse, but from the smirks and grins his Brothers were wearing it would be all good natured. Every one of the guys with him was ex-military and, while they were rough and wild, choosing the life of an outlaw biker over the comfy middle-class, none of them would have turned their backs on this woman. What could have made her so desperate that death was the preferred option to going home with the man who had brought her?

The whole situation bothered him. Sharp was going to have to get some answers, find out exactly what he had dragged his Brothers into. He patted her knee to let her know they were close and couldn't help but linger for a moment, enjoying the silky feel of her pants under his hand. His time was limited with this beauty since he had to head back out before lunch, but he figured there wasn't any question that couldn't wait until the morning.

It was almost midnight when they pulled through the gates of the Dark Sons' compound just outside of Denver. Loud music played, and a few people milled around the Clubhouse. Late night parties weren't unusual on any night, but the numbers were small since it was Sunday. Sharp expected it was the younger single Brothers and dedicated hangers-on enjoying themselves. Concern raced through him when the girl against his back didn't even move when he backed his Harley into place. Had she somehow fallen asleep?

"Come on, darlin'. We're here." Sharp patted her leg but only a small moan came from behind him.

"Shit, Sharp. What the fuck happened to her back?" Razor's voice came from his right.

Sharp reached behind him and easily pulled her around in front of him. Once she relaxed her grip, her whole body went limp in his arms. His hands were damp, and when he pulled one away, even in the dim illumination of the outdoor lights, he could see they were peppered with blood.

"Fuck, get Doc!" He scooped her into his arms and practically sprinted for the back room of the Clubhouse and the medical supplies it held.

He knocked into a few people on his way and didn't bother to apologize. He hit the lights with his elbow and brought her over to the table they used whenever Doc had to stitch someone up or deal with more serious injuries. In the bright lights of the room, he could see the back of her white linen outfit was almost completely stained with blood. The majority of it looked dried, but a few spots were still damp.

At least she wasn't going to bleed out before Doc showed up. He sat her down in front of him with her legs dangling off the edge, while he held her head up so she didn't fall.

"Come on, darlin'. I need you to wake up. Tell me what hurts." He tapped her face lightly.

She moaned, and her eyes fluttered halfway open. "I'm awake, Master." Her words were slightly slurred. That combined with her condition told him just how fucked up her situation must have been.

"Seriously, I need you to wake up now."

She leaned back, her eyes still not focusing. Sharp let her lie down and groaned as she spread her legs as if inviting him in. God, he was going to Hell because even hurt as she was, her movement had his dick jumping to attention. It took all his willpower to grip her thighs and start to push her knees together.

He must have hit a bad spot though because her eyes fully opened and she swallowed down a scream as she lurched up, barely avoiding knocking heads with him.

"Where am I?"

Thank fuck, she was back with them. "You're safe at our compound, darlin'."

The sound of several people behind him made Sharp turn to see Doc striding through the door with Hawk, the President of the Dark Sons, right behind him. At 5'10" you wouldn't think the man could fill a room but his presence alone could intimidate even the most hardened soldier. His black hair was peppered with grey and it looked like fire was about to leap out of his brown eyes. Things tended to go sideways when the man was pissed. The two of them had been friends for years, both before joining the Dark Sons and after forming this chapter together, but Hawk was the one in charge and had the final say on all things.

Doc stepped up to the table. "What is she on, Sharp?"

"If she's on something, she took it over five hours ago."

"No drugs, I'm fine." Her voice trembled and she started to pull her knees up to her chest but stopped the motion with a wince.

"They told me you had a girl passed out. I thought this was an OD," Doc grumbled. The man was in his late sixties and had been an Army field medic. For the last 30 years, he had been with the Dark Sons and had chosen to move with them when they formed the Colorado chapter. His gray beard hung down past his waist giving him a gruff look, but inside he was a marshmallow to the women, which was why the sweetbutts still took him out for a ride on a regular basis. And why he was probably still here at this hour. Doc moved to the other side of the table and took in a breath through his teeth.

"I'm fine, really. A few bruises. All I need is a shower, and I'll be fine."

"Hell, you will. Everyone who doesn't have to be here, out!" Doc's bark, when he used it, got results. Everyone except Sharp and Hawk cleared out. The President pulled his VP to a corner of the room, leaving Doc to talk quietly with the girl.

"What the hell is this?"

"It's a long story." Sharp gave a short version of what happened, and Hawk's eyes softened a bit.

"Damn it, Brother. Pussy is supposed to be uncomplicated, no matter how pretty. Why did you have to bring home a stray?"

"There's something about her. Thought she'd be grateful for the white knight routine and go home to her picket fence after a few hours on the wild side, but something is way off."

Sharp knew he'd colored the truth. He didn't like the idea of her taking off. She called to the protective side of his nature, and he wouldn't be happy until she was safe.

"If you ladies are done gossiping, I need some help here. Get some water and a knife. We're going to have to cut this shirt off to see what we're dealing with."

The girl clutched at her top, hysteria adding an edge to her voice. "I'm okay, really. I've had worse. The ride was long, and the pain just got to me for a few minutes. That's all."

"And I told you, girl, with that much bleeding, something needs stitching. I can't know what, until I see. I've seen plenty of tits before and so have these boys, so no need to be shy."

Hawk handed Doc a gallon of distilled water, and Sharp stepped in front of the girl. He caught her eyes and held them. "What's your name, darlin'?"

"Phoebe."

"Beautiful name. Phoebe, you asked for my help." He reached up and gently took her cheek in his palm. "I need you to let Doc do his job. He was a combat medic. Whatever is under there, I promise you, we've seen worse. Do you trust me?"

She took a deep breath and nodded. Within five minutes, they had her face down on the table and naked. For a solid minute, his body reacted to her beautiful tits with their ripe raspberry nipples, all his blood rushing south and nearly blinding him with fantasies. His eyes quickly refocused and his brain caught up and catalogued what he saw on her back. Sharp had seen battle wounds and missing limbs. Men bruised and bloody from fights and women with black eyes and broken limbs from abuse. None of that compared to the story her skin told. Sharp knew now he had lied to her. He may have seen more deadly wounds in the past but, fighting this nauseous feeling, he had to admit he had never seen anything worse than the long-term horrors this girl must have suffered.

Bruises from black to yellow-green covered the backside of her body. Welts, scars and slashes peppered her back and most of her thighs. He didn't see any burn marks, but that was a small mercy. How could she even move? He had seen men with half that much bruising from a fight laid up for days. Yet somehow, this little wisp of a girl had managed to ride five hours without complaint.

He couldn't even imagine what had made some of the marks on her. Red tinged his vision and the urge to ride and hunt down the fucker responsible for her pain was nearly uncontrollable. God knew how long she had been trapped with that sorry excuse for a man. He wouldn't even use his favorite guns, which had earned him his sharpshooter nickname. Instead, he would use his hands, slowly breaking every joint in the asshole's body.

Doc leaned over her, putting stitches in a few of the longer cuts. She had refused any painkillers stronger than aspirin and Sharp had wanted to step in to override her choice. But before he could he noticed the pills Doc gave her weren't aspirin as he'd claimed, but some of their strongest Oxy. After a few minutes, little Phoebe slept through the process.

"You didn't kill him?" Hawk's face showed the same cold rage Sharp felt. Dark Sons weren't known as boy scouts. Hell, no one who lived the outlaw lifestyle cared one bit about laws made by the government. But some things you just didn't do. Some things were evil.

"Had I known. I would have."

Hawk closed his ice blue eyes as if thinking and shook his head. "I wish I could free you up, but I need you on that ride tomorrow. That little nutcase arms dealer won't sell to anyone else."

His President's words were right, but that didn't mean he was happy. The guy they were meeting was a paranoid freak, but he had some of the best custom refitted weapons around. "I understand."

"Tell Kickstand and Puck they share guard duty until you get back. I'll get Dozer's Old Lady to check on her as well." Hawk took another look at Phoebe's mangled body and growled. "If that fucker shows up here, I want him to be vulture bait."

Sharp considered the plan. Dozer's Old Lady, Val, was a nurse, so it was a good call, and the guys he had picked were solid prospects who had been with them for over a year. Hawk often appeared heartless but by using Club resources to protect Phoebe he gave a firm declaration of his intent to back Sharp's play.

"Will do."

"Your instincts are always solid. Don't let worrying about this girl trip you up."

Sharp chuckled. "No worries. I'm on target."

Chapter 4

There's no place like home... but I'd rather be in Vegas.

L ike every other day of her life, Phoebe woke in pain. Something was different this time. It took her a minute to figure out what it was. Instead of a cold floor, she was prone on a comfortable surface. Stretching aching muscles, she realized she wasn't cuffed and chained. She was also wearing a soft, black cotton shirt. Memories from the day before rushed back to her. Had she really gotten away? Sitting up a little too fast the skin on her back was tight and spasmed with pinpricks of pain.

"Careful, darlin', or you'll pull the stitches." Her head whipped in the direction of the voice and she wanted to sob in relief. Sitting in a chair in the corner of the tiny room was her savior. What was his name? The man called Doc had said it last night; she searched back through her memory.

"Thank you for saving me... Mark?"

"Sharp." He was a giant of a man, but his amazing smile and warm eyes comforted Phoebe. He pointed to a patch on his leather vest.

She blushed. "You go to all the trouble of getting it embroidered on your vest and I still get it wrong."

He chuckled. "It's called a cut, darlin'. Not a vest."

It looked like a vest to her but if he wanted to call it a cut then who was she to argue? "Oh, um, well it's a cool name." What did you say to the man who saved your life?

"It's not my real name. I got it when I was a sniper in the SEALs. I won every sharpshooter award they had, so my buddies called me Sharp. The name stuck."

"What's your real name?"

His eyes crinkled as he studied her, before answering, "Sean Oliver, but I'm not that boy anymore."

She liked the idea of being able to become a new person with the simple act of changing a name. She shifted on the bed, turning to put her back to the wall so she could look right at him. She pulled her knees up to her chest, ignoring the pain and letting it roll through her. As usual, she enjoyed the endorphin rush, instead of avoiding it. Glad now for the ability to absorb and enjoy pain, something she had learned as a kid in a particularly bad foster home.

She had always felt abnormal being the child nobody wanted. When she had started seeking out pain to find a bit of pleasure it had put the cherry on top of the 'no-one-wants-me' sundae. Not all of her foster parents had been bad. Some had even tried to get her professional help. At age fourteen she had been forced to talk to a state psychiatrist. He diagnosed her with sexual masochistic disorder. The man definitely liked using fancy words to describe a survival mechanism. One that had barely been enough to protect her from her latest nightmare.

Mitchel had loved finding new and horrible ways to torture her far beyond her ability to enjoy. He would spend hours with his knife cutting away bits of her skin. When that didn't work, he would use a whip or his fists until he discovered her weakness. Waterboarding had cut right through her ability to disassociate, tapping into a primal survival instinct that left her vulnerable to even the mildest forms of torture. Only when she cried, hoarse from screaming, would he find his satisfaction in her bloody body. Phoebe's stomach churned as she closed her eyes, trying to push him from her thoughts.

"What is today's date?" She needed to know how much time had been stolen from her.

"April second." Sharp's voice was deep. She let it seep inside her like a warm wave.

She held her breath as she did the math she had avoided before. Shaking her head, she opened her eyes. "Six months? Was it really only six months?" An odd thought struck her, and she giggled. "I'll be twenty-one in four weeks." That age had seemed important to her before but with how she felt inside the number didn't really matter. She noticed his gaze had gone hot staring at her legs. Phoebe took in her position and realized the single piece of clothing she had on was an over large t-shirt that was rucked up and just covered her upper half. The way she sat put her pussy on full display between her ankles.

The old her would have stayed put. Enjoyed the effect she had on him. But even though she was grateful and wanted to find some way to pay her savior back Phoebe wasn't quite ready to play the vixen. She pulled up the sheet that was right by her hand and laid it lightly across her legs. Sharp's broad shoulders, muscles and dark good looks alone had her heart racing, but she wasn't completely sure if it was because of attraction or fear. Phoebe should never want anything to do with men ever again, and yet here she was, hours after escaping Hell, almost wishing for this rough man's touch.

Could she be what people called 'normal'? The rest of the bikers had made her nervous and not even slightly aroused. Even the gentle, gruff Doc had made her skin crawl when he touched her, but for some reason, Sharp made her feel safe.

Emotions rarely made sense, at least not hers, so she decided to not look too closely at her feelings yet.

Sharp's eyes snapped up to her face as he took in her statement. "You were with that asshole for six months? Why did you stay with him?"

Phoebe dropped her head back against the wall and studied the ceiling. Could Sharp think she would willingly stay in an abusive situation? The idea hurt. It shouldn't; they didn't know each other, but again emotions did not equal logic. The embarrassing truth wasn't much better. One stupid choice had led to months of hell.

"I wanted to party to forget how much life sucked, so I said yes to a drink from a guy I had just met. I woke up chained in Mitchel's basement."

"For six months?"

She really didn't feel like reviewing the activities that had made up the last few months of her life, but she owed him something. "Not solely in his basement but, until yesterday, I had never been in public or even allowed outside unguarded."

"You were alone with that psycho for six months?" Sharp's harsh voice caused her to look back at him, and she couldn't understand the intense emotions reflected in his eyes.

"I wish we had been alone." Phoebe's throat closed up, and she couldn't make herself talk about it anymore. Fear and terrible memories were pushing at the barriers she kept up around her sanity. Faces of the women who had died in or passed through the training center or were still trapped in slavery threatened to overwhelm her. Phoebe pushed her back against the wall and let the spike of pain roll through her, and she moaned as it turned into a pleasant burn, sparking a flame of desire that for once she might be able to satisfy.

Chapter 5

Being a gentleman sucks... If you're lucky.

Sharp did his best not to stare at Phoebe's pussy, but her bare, pink, lush lips were like a siren call. The sheet she had pulled up around her had slipped back down as they talked, and he was pretty sure it wasn't on purpose. This tiny woman had been through more than he could imagine and didn't need him rubbing up against her like a puppy. Trying not to think of how wonderful she would feel wrapped around his cock, Sharp tried to remember what they had been saying. She hadn't answered his last question.

He tore his eyes away from the inadvertent peep show and realized she was pressed up against the wall and groaning with pain. Fuck. He shouldn't have questioned her when she was in so much pain. Letting her know she was safe was the priority, not dragging her through the muck of her past. He moved over to the bed and gathered her up into his lap. Phoebe needed to know he was leaving soon, but that she was safe and welcome. He had barely slept last night so he could make all the arrangements while she slept off the painkillers.

Sharp looked down at her with the intent of saying all of that, but when he caught sight of her deep emerald eyes and sleep-mussed hair, all that came out was, "Fuck, you're gorgeous."

When she smiled and leaned in, their mouths were drawn together like two magnets. Sharp tried to keep the kiss gentle, but the sounds she made had him devouring her like his favorite dessert. She was like a drug and he lost himself in her, forgetting all his good intentions, his dick pounding against his zipper as she ground into him.

Phoebe slipped down through his arms like a little eel, breaking their kiss. "Phoebe... What are you... Oh *fuck*."

The girl was a fucking magician. Somehow, she had undone his pants, freed his cock and swallowed it down in fewer seconds than it took him to realize what she was doing. He groaned as her tongue massaged the underside, then swirled up over the tip.

"Baby, you don't have to do this, but damn, it feels amazing."

Sharp was far from a small man. Hell, he had women who couldn't take all of him in their pussy without whining about pain, and this little minx swallowed him down like it was nothing. She looked so innocent, but her mouth proved it was the furthest thing from the truth. When her throat swallowed around his dick, he almost came apart. "You do that again, baby, and I'm going to come straight down your throat."

She pulled back a little, her moan vibrating up his cock, then she was back with her nose against his body, with one hand stroking his balls through his jeans and her tight as fuck throat milking the tip of his dick over and over. The orgasm hit him like a fucking train, and he shouted his pleasure into the room.

Phoebe licked her way up Sharp's dick like it was her favorite lollipop, the salty taste pleasant on her tongue. Powerful emotions surged through her body and tightened her nipples in arousal. This wasn't healthy but having the choice made her able to forget the past and live in the now. She didn't want to be a victim, she wanted to be the one in control. She had made this overwhelming man lose control. Before she had been taken she had been the aggressor, and it was amazing. As she licked the slit, trying to get the last drop out of his slowly softening cock, her body trembled as Sharp's growl flowed down her skin.

Suddenly she was airborne, terror causing her pulse to race. Phoebe's back slammed into the bed, causing tears of pain to leak out of her eyes. Then he was on top of her, pinning her down. Panicking she tried to break free, but he was too strong.

"My turn."

She tried to squirm away but he locked onto her legs, all rational thought fleeing before the pleasure of her endorphins and his touch. Sharp's tongue found her clit like it was meant to be there. She had never, in her many experiences, had a man go down on her for more than a few seconds. The directed assault of his mouth was amazing. This wild man didn't just lick her clit, he devoured her pussy like it was his mission.

The pain of her body mingled with the sweet ecstasy of his mouth and her pending orgasm threatening to crush her.

"You're so fucking wet. You taste like sweet clover honey."

His fingers drove into her and brushed against that sweet spot deep inside and everything inside her exploded as she came, screaming his name. Every muscle hurt as it contracted, pushing the orgasm higher. He pumped his fingers harder, rubbing relentlessly against her walls.

"That was so fucking beautiful. I want to see it again but look at me this time."

She bit her lip as she opened her eyes and his dark gaze locked with hers. They were midnight pools of black with a hint of shimmering moonlight peeking through the treetops. He held her gaze as he lowered his mouth, sucking her clit with fast, sharp movements. Unbelievably, she was already hanging right on the edge, her body so close, but not falling over. She whined in frustration, wanting to lose herself in him, in this moment.

On his next suck, he pulled her clit hard into his mouth. Phoebe held her breath in anticipation. He bit down the slightest bit, and her body exploded. She lost his gaze, no longer able to control her muscles. Tremors took over her body and she floated in the sweet bliss of the best orgasm she had ever experienced.

A loud knock on the door pierced her haze. "Ten minutes, Sharp. Finished checking on your girl or do you need help?"

Sharp's head hit the bed. He shouted a muffled, "Fuck off."

Someone laughed on the other side of the door, followed by footsteps as the person walked away. Sharp scooted up the bed until they were eye to eye. He used a hand to brush the hair off her face. "You've got some kind of spell over me, darlin'." He looked down at his undone belt and pants. "How do you do that so quick?"

Phoebe blushed, wiggling her hands. "Nimble fingers are important if you want to eat when you live on the street." Pick-pocketing had been her main source of income most months.

Sharp shook his head. "You know I came up here to check on you and let you know you were safe."

She should be scared, and when her brain finally fully engaged, she probably would be, but something about Sharp made all the other shit in her past just melt away. "I didn't mean to distract you." She hated how weak her voice sounded. She sounded like a victim, instead of a lifelong survivor.

"Darlin', you can distract me that way anytime, I fucking loved it. But it does mean I'm out of time."

Phoebe pulled in on herself, knowing she wasn't going to like what he said next. "Okay."

"I have to go. I'm going to be gone for a few days. Kickstand and Puck are going to watch over you while I'm gone. They're prospects but still solid men. Dozer's Old Lady is a nurse. She's going to check in on you, too. Let her know if you need anything."

Prospects? The majority of what he'd said made little sense. "Where are you going?"

"Club business. Don't worry about anything. You're safe here."

Phoebe wasn't sure she believed that. Sharp might be willing to protect her because he wanted her, but what about the other guys? She shivered a bit. As a child, she had learned that nothing in life was free, even if the cost was hidden. She couldn't stop him from leaving so like always she would survive and hope the price was something she could afford to pay.

"Fuck, I don't want to leave." Sharp gave her a gentle kiss that was cut short by the sound of several motorcycles roaring to life. "I gotta go, darlin'. Be safe."

Sharp stood up, tucking his dick back into his jeans and left without another word. Dazed, Phoebe looked around the room, really taking it in. A full-sized bed, a single old wooden chair, and a nightstand were all that she could see. She checked the nightstand. It contained a few boxes of condoms and some lube with several dust bunnies.

This small room was her life for now. What were the rules she would be expected to follow? There was another door to the room, so she checked it out. A small private bathroom with a shower stall, sink, and toilet was a pleasant surprise. She took advantage of the facilities and tried finger combing her hair into some semblance of normal.

The woman in the mirror was a stranger. Her green eyes and blonde hair were passingly familiar yet almost felt wrong. The training center didn't have mirrors, so it had been months since she had looked at herself. She had always been small compared to others, but now she looked gaunt, her cheekbones too sharp and every one of her ribs visible under the colorful bruising. Phoebe hated the physical evidence of the starvation and torture she had been through and wanted to cover it all up. Try to forget.

Sharp hadn't left her any clothes but the over-large tee shirt. The baggy shirt did hang like a dress but left her vulnerable and she didn't want to risk bumping into any of his Brothers while looking for more clothes or food. She made a few faces at the girl in the mirror, trying to accept that this was her. A muscle in her back twitched, shooting pain across her nerves. She lifted up the back of her shirt and got a glimpse of the roadmap of her life.

Mitchel had always saved the worst of his tortures for her back, preferring to keep one side of her pretty. The whole image was surreal, like she was gazing at an intricate piece of modern art in mottled colors, instead of the evidence of her torture.

A loud voice from behind startled her out of her thoughts. "Jesus Christ on a cracker! Mother Mary and all her tiny little babies! Get me my shotgun 'cause I am going to turn whatever man made you look like that into swamp chum!"

Chapter 6

If at first you don't succeed... Ask a southern woman, she'll know what to do.

Phoebe dropped her hold on the shirt and spun to face a woman who looked like she could win a Dolly Parton lookalike contest. That was if Dolly was in her late twenties and had fire engine red hair that gave her close to a foot of extra height.

A man ran in behind her looking around like he expected an attack. He had shaved blond hair and features that would have sold hundreds if not thousands of Ken dolls. His arms were so big Phoebe wondered if he benched pressed small cars for fun. She tried to back further into the bathroom so he wouldn't see her half-dressed, but her movement caught his attention and his gaze trapped her like a deer in headlights. Fear shot through her. She vaguely recognized him from the group of men who had been at the bar with Sharp but that didn't calm her nerves at all.

"Puck, you stop lookin' at that girl's legs like they're covered in gravy and being served for Sunday dinner! Geet." The other woman made a shooing motion towards the door.

"I am not..." His voice choked for a second and he tried to pull himself together. "You were shouting, Val. I thought something was wrong. Sharp has me watching out for her."

"I was not shouting!" She was definitely shouting now. "I was being southern and enthusiastic. Now shoo before I call Sharp and he decides to cancel your birth certificate for oglin' his woman."

"I wasn't..." Val stomped her foot and the smart man turned and walked out of the room.

Val fluffed up her hair and ample cleavage in her rhine-stone-covered shirt with a sigh. Should she hide or burst into giggles?

"Those prospects are worse than tomcats in July. Remember that and keep them in line."

Phoebe couldn't help it, she laughed. The laughter led to hysterical giggles, then tears as if letting any emotion through had broken the walls she had tried to keep around her. Sobs shook her body as Val led her over to the bed and cradled her. The woman was at least 5'10" without the hair. Compared to her own 5'2" it felt like she was a kid again crying on a mother's shoulder. One who actually cared.

"There, there child. You gotta let all that rain out so the sun can come on in."

"I'm sorry, I don't even know you and I'm crying all over you."

"Honey, tears dry. My old man told me some of your story and your back showed me some more. Let's save the talking for outside. Sunshine helps push away all those shadows. I brought you some clothes, though my man told me small when he should have said tiny, so hopefully they'll stay up. I'll run into town later and get you some things your actual size. Oh, I almost forgot." Val pulled a plain black phone out of her back pocket. "Sharp gave this to me on his way out. Said he's going to call you tonight."

Phoebe took the phone and bag of clothes from Val. The single item of clothing that looked decent on her was a lemon-yellow sundress that she belted up with a black neckerchief that had skulls printed all over it. The clothes covered less than the shirt had but for the first time in a long time, Phoebe felt comfortable. Val pulled her hair back in a ponytail and declared her prettier than a posy in a field of dandelions and gave her a pair of flip-flops before dragging her outside.

The wonderfully crazy woman was right: the sun was like a healing touch on her skin. The place really was a compound with the Clubhouse situated as the closest building to the gate. Several concrete buildings flanked the main warehouse-style building with what looked to be a motel further back on the property and several small farmhouses in the distance.

The fenced-in property extended well beyond what she could see, and a forest of trees seemed to fill the back end with a road that disappeared into its shadows. A large field was behind the Clubhouse and held lots of picnic tables and a play-ground. She might have believed it was a state park if it wasn't for all the bikers. Val and Phoebe avoided the few men who were wandering around and the two settled at an out of the way picnic table.

"I've heard you recently came out of a bad time. What was life like before that?"

Phoebe leaned back, letting the sun soak into every pore. As with Sharp, she had an easy connection with the wild woman. After so many years of silence, when she made the decision to talk the floodgates opened and Phoebe found herself babbling. "Mom OD'd when I was four. I don't know who my dad was. From there I bounced around Denver's foster care system and got labeled as a troubled kid by age six, so I never got placed in homes looking to adopt. Ran away at sixteen because of a handsy 'dad' and spent a few years on the streets before getting drugged and sold into hell."

Val started a bit at the terse recitation. "Child, most girls with that story would have dead eyes and broken spirits but I look in your eyes and still see light. You are so strong." She reached over and squeezed Phoebe's hand.

This woman was so open and honest. She was like the sun washing away all doubt and fear with her crazy southern accent and wild sayings. Phoebe had to share, or things were going to tear her up inside.

"I don't feel strong. I feel shattered and jagged. When any man but Sharp comes near me it's like I want to cower in a corner. Something's wired wrong in me. I like things I shouldn't—that's why the bastard kept me to himself for so long. If I would have broken for him, he would have sold me off like all the others. Why can't I just be normal?"

"Now that's like a rooster asking why it's a cock. You are you because that is the way it was meant to be. Don't listen to no Baptist preachers, God don't make mistakes. We don't have to understand his plan, we only need to know he has one."

"You don't understand."

"Then explain it plain and thank the Lord we are women who can talk about everything from the size and talent of our man's cock to the politics of the day."

Phoebe burst out laughing and a wonderful warmth began growing inside her. It was a tiny seed, but it was something. She wasn't ready to really share more. Her enjoyment of pain was too much to burden this wonderful woman with.

After a few minutes of silence, Val spoke. "All right. I am not one to pry a virgin's knees apart. Why don't you ask me questions? I know you have them."

Phoebe did have one question that had been digging at the back of her brain. "Sharp called you Dozer's Old Lady. I was kinda expecting someone old."

Val cackled with laughter, her eyes bright. "Oh, my stars. With all the TV shows and romance books out there, I guess he assumed you knew about biker life."

Phoebe blushed, wishing she had kept her mouth shut.

"Now don't go blooming like a tomato." She sighed. "Dark Sons is a one-percenter biker Club. They live by their own laws, free of society's expectations. That can mean different things to different Clubs but there are some common ways between them. 'Brothers first' is sometimes the hardest rule for a woman to accept."

"How do you mean?"

"Let's say you plan for months a special anniversary dinner with lingerie for dessert. Five minutes before the meal hits the table your man gets a call for an emergency church meeting. I don't mean the godly type, that's what they call their Club meetings. Guess where your man will be?"

"That happened to you?"

"Oh dear, yes. And he came home to find the food and lingerie burning on the front lawn and him on the couch for a spell, but it didn't matter to him."

"But you forgave him?"

"I realized it might be 'Brothers first' but for all of them it's 'family next'. If my car breaks down or I need something, every one of those boys will treat me like I am a princess. They'll drop everything to help out family and take or deliver a bullet if necessary. For that, I am willing to put up with the secrets and give up a piece of my man to them."

"There are no women in the Club?"

"Oh, there are women. But they aren't in the Club and they ain't family. That's the third thing that's hard to accept."

"What's the second?"

"Respect. To get it, you have to give it. Lord knows there are times my man barks an order at me, and I want to strip him down to gator bait. But you don't do that in public and you don't do it in front of the Brothers. If your man gives you an actual order, don't matter if it's to fetch him a beer or strip down and do the cha-cha on the pool table, you do it. They have to show they have control and respect and sometimes that can come at the cost of a bit of your pride."

"I'm guessing there's a trade-off for that too?"

"It's much of the same. But mostly your man will treat you like a queen and if he doesn't then you got the wrong one. Which is where the women come in. Old Ladies are the wives, part of the family. Some are actually married like Dozer and I but it's more serious to them than simply being married. Some of the guys marry their baby mamas to make them happy but won't make them an Old Lady."

"Sounds backward."

"A tree is a tree, no point calling it a bush. The rest of the women are either sweetbutts, whores, or civilians. It's the last two you have to worry about. They hang around looking for good times; the main difference between the two is a whore is looking to hang around and freeload while a civilian is looking for a cheap thrill."

"I can only imagine what a sweetbutt is."

"Nah, don't let the name fool you. On the whole those girls are looking for the safety and protection being associated with the Club gives. They give back the ways they know how. Fucking, cleaning up after the boys, they might cook meals or tend bar when the prospects can't. They usually hook up with one Brother at a time but most of them have been with many different Brothers at one time or another."

The Club needed women to cook and clean for them? That made sense, though from the look of the place the sweetbutts weren't very good at the cleaning part. She could do that. She loved to clean—it was the one thing she could do that would make almost any foster parent happy. Plus, she got a sense of accomplishment seeing chaos turned into order.

"What does that make me?"

Val seemed to think it over a bit before she answered. "Sharp told his Brothers you're his and Hawk gave you Club protection." She nodded over at Puck who did his best to stay out of the way but close enough to watch them. "If I had to put a label on it, I would say you're a sweetbutt who is dating a Brother. So, you're off limits."

Something settled inside her. "So, no other Brother will touch me as long as Sharp says I'm his?"

"Not in the trailers-rocking sort of way but you best stay away when they're drinking if he's not around. A few of them get beer blind and can be a bit grabby."

"I can do that." Her nerves settled with the knowledge of what was expected of her. She would be the best fucking sweet-butt these boys ever saw.

"Don't go settling for scraps girl. I like you and we need another hen in this farmhouse."

Phoebe didn't really understand what she meant but knew she would clean, cook, fuck, or kill for almost anyone if it meant she could hold on to this safe feeling.

Chapter 7

No matter how tempting, the way to a man's heart isn't through his ribcage. It's through his stomach.

Phoebe explored the Clubhouse trying to avoid bumping into any Brothers and ignoring her constant tail. The Clubhouse was bigger than she first imagined, more like a small warehouse. The main part, a bar area and pool hall, took up maybe half the building. Off the back was a commercial kitchen that made her shudder a bit for the level of dirt and mysterious substances coating the surfaces. There was a small room that was obviously used for medical and another room filled with rows of chairs: probably held meetings of some sort. The doors to the basement and offices were locked so she ignored them. Upstairs held lots of bedrooms, most of them laid out like the one she was staying in, but some were larger. A few held nothing more than several stained mattresses strewn across the floor. Phoebe didn't even want to think about what went on in those rooms.

She turned to head back downstairs and the room seemed to sway a bit. Shaking her head, she focused and knew the dizziness was because she hadn't eaten since breakfast the previous day. There hadn't been any food in the kitchen, only beer. Hoping she'd missed something, Phoebe turned back towards the large kitchen to find something to eat. Poking around the large space, she found a closet of cleaning supplies she had missed, but still no food. The clock on the wall said it was ten o'clock—much earlier than she had assumed.

She rested her hands on the counter trying to pull herself together. She had the things to clean and all the cookware she needed to cook but not the food. Did the sweetbutts cook at home and bring the finished food here? Movement at the door reminded her she didn't have to figure everything out herself.

"Puck?" Her voice echoed in the empty kitchen.

He stepped fully into the room. "Yeah, Pixie?"

"Pixie?"

He laughed. "Sorry, my little sister collected those Rainbow Brite dolls when she was growing up. You're so tiny and with the yellow dress and ponytail, you remind me of one of those dolls. I won't call you it again if it bothers you."

Phoebe considered it for a moment. "I think I like it." It was so different from who and what she had been. It felt like her own fresh start.

His eyes twinkled and her fear of the blond man began easing away. "I'm glad. So, what did you need?"

"Where do you guys keep the food?"

"I can send someone out to grab you some drive through if you're hungry."

Phoebe bit her lip. It had been years since she had eaten more than protein bars, oatmeal, broth, or ice-cold fast food. She had dreamed of home cooked meals like the ones she'd made for herself since she was ten. Her foster mother at the time had been a crazy old biddy who insisted she learn to cook by memorizing all the recipes. She said cookbooks were for amateurs. Of course, she also thought if you showed your knees or elbows in public you were a hussy. So, while Phoebe was grateful for her ability to cook lots of meals from scratch, she hadn't been sad to leave that particular foster home.

"I was kinda hoping I could make something. I could cook for you too, and anyone else who wanted."

"You cook?"

Phoebe nodded. "Yeah. I've been dreaming of chicken salad sandwiches and lasagna." She blushed and dropped her head remembering she should be grateful to be alive, not complaining about the food selection. "It's silly. Never mind. I'll take whatever you guys get."

"Nah, Pixie, that sounds amazing. You write down what you need, and we'll get it."

She rummaged through the drawers of the dirty kitchen, pushing aside fast-food menus, old receipts and other junk, finally coming up with an old flyer. Grabbing a pen, she wrote down a list on the back. She looked it over for a second before handing it over to Puck. She was worried she may have gone a bit overboard, listing out ingredients for her four favorite dinners plus several breakfast options. She'd also included the basics to make bread and various fixings for sandwiches. But she couldn't resist. It was stupid, she knew, but after months in captivity and years on and off the street, this sounded like heaven to her.

She handed the list over. "If it's too much, just buy the ingredients for the meals you think people would want."

His eyes went wide as he glanced down at the list and Phoebe's stomach dropped. "Chicken parm, lasagna, chicken pot pie, fettuccine alfredo. You can really make all that stuff? How many people can you feed?"

His tone was so surprised it made her blush. "Yes, and with this kitchen, however many you buy for." The idea of all his Brothers descending on her in the enclosed kitchen caused her to break out in a cold sweat. Strangers closing in, touching her, have to leave can't remember…

"What's wrong, Pixie? You lost what little color you had."

Phoebe gasped and shook her head. "If I cook, can someone else take it out to whoever wants it? I can't." She swallowed. "I'm not ready for a lot of people."

"Pixie, you cook even some of this shit and I will personally guard the door so no one bothers you."

Phoebe smiled at his words, relaxing even more.

By the time the groceries arrived she had scrubbed out the refrigerator, run what dishes she could through the dishwasher, and scoured the floors and counters so clean they truly shined. Puck whistled his admiration. "I barely recognize this place and I was here two hours ago. You got magic in you, Pixie?"

Phoebe felt like she was on cloud nine. She really had done a lot and the feeling of accomplishment was amazing. She jumped when a tall, lean man walked in behind Puck with grocery bags in his arms. She had never met this Brother before, so she carefully moved well out of his way. He had to be close to 6'1" but, instead of the bulky muscles the majority of the men had, he was whipcord and sinew.

"Pixie, this is Kickstand. He was finishing up some things this morning in the city, so I asked him to pick up the groceries on his way in. The two of us are going to be keeping you company till Sharp gets back."

"Hey." Kickstand didn't seem happy about the fact he had to do the grocery shopping. He dropped the bags on the counter.

She nodded, not yet ready to talk with this man she didn't know. Instead, she turned her attention to the grocery bags on the counter. She looked disappointedly at the two bags. There was no way everything she had asked for was in there. Oh well, she would make do with whatever they got.

The back door busted open and men seemed to flood into

the room all carrying bags. Her heart sped into overdrive and her mind tilted sideways. Instinctively, she found herself huddling and shaking in the back corner of the pantry. Men were moving around and talking, but their words didn't register. Eventually the noise died down and with it her heartbeat.

"Shit, Pixie, I'm sorry. I didn't think." Puck leaned in the doorway of the pantry. "It is only me and Kickstand in the kitchen now. So, you can come out if you're ready."

Phoebe wished she could vanish right into the floor, but that wouldn't get her fed or make her look any better to the Brothers. When she stepped out, Puck looked worried and Kickstand stood against the wall looking disgusted. Every surface was covered in grocery bags.

"How much food did you buy?"

Kickstand shrugged. "Just what you had on your list but lots of it. Every Brother we asked wanted in on the meal."

"How many is that?"

"Around twenty-five, but we eat a lot.."

Well, she would make as much as she could and if there were leftovers, she guessed she would have to ask them to get Tupperware. The smell of the Italian spices revitalized a part of her spirit as she diced and chopped, letting the sauce simmer on low. She popped veggies in her mouth, loving the fresh flavor that zipped across her tongue.

A few hours later Phoebe closed her eyes and savored the sweet tang of the tomato. All around her were fresh produce and vegetables as she cooked one meal and prepped several others. Taking just a taste of each item made her want to giggle in disbelief. She had believed that the little things like this had been gone from her life forever. Just outside the window large burly men ate her food and she couldn't help but revel in the pure joy she saw on their faces as they took that first bite.

The only thing that would be better would be to hear them

going silent as they ate, distracted from conversation by wanting another taste. She wasn't ready for that; there were too many of them and, without Sharp by her side, her courage was greatly limited. Puck was a dream, helping her move things around and getting them settled while Kickstand glowered from the corner, standing and eating his food with an almost resentful enjoyment.

When the last dish was stored away, and the final pan washed, Phoebe was surprised by the dark sky outside the window. Rowdy noises of drinking and partying were muffled by the door but obviously coming from the front room. Cold sweat prickled over Phoebe's skin. She couldn't go in there, the Brothers would be drinking and having a good time. She wanted to believe what Val had said: she was safe, but her mind and her heart weren't able to believe it. Sneaking out the side door and up the stairs to her bedroom she let out a breath as she turned the lock, giving her at least the illusion of privacy.

There wasn't any more she could do tonight without risking running into people. Her best option was to try to sleep while they partied. Tomorrow before anyone woke, to show her worth, she would clean up the rest of the rooms. Pacing her private room, Phoebe couldn't get her stomach to settle. Thoughts of the past and what might happen ricocheted through her brain.

Annoyed but unable to stop the horror show of possibilities in her mind she decided to put the chair up against the door for extra security.

Chapter 8

It's good to be... where the hell am I again?

S harp was glad to be pulling into the compound, knowing he wouldn't have to leave again for a while; there weren't any scheduled runs in the next few weeks. Returning to a more normal routine at his garage and getting to know every detail of his little Phoebe was all he had planned. For days, his Brothers had been sending him sexy as fuck candid photos of her and he didn't mind admitting he had been turned on but pissed as hell he couldn't use her to relieve the ache they caused. Tiny ass sundresses showcased legs he wanted wrapped around him. The picture of Val and his woman laid out in the sun in tiny scraps of fabric meant to be a bikini was burned forever into his memory.

Puck had said she was settling in well, but Sharp had an overwhelming need to see her and claim her as his own. Jealousy had never been his thing. Hell, he loved seeing the envy in a man's eyes when they desired the woman he was with. When Brothers had sent texts asking if Phoebe was off-limits, he knew they had been fucking with him, but his rage and, yeah, fucking jealousy, confused him. How could a woman he barely knew make him so possessive?

He ignored the Brothers he passed, simply waving a greeting because he didn't want to stop to talk. All he had been thinking about for the last three days was getting back to those bright emerald eyes and the sweet and sexy woman who owned them. When he stepped inside the Clubhouse what he saw made him pause. It looked completely transformed. Had someone painted the walls and floor? The whole place looked new. The usual scent of stale beer and cigarettes was barely noticeable. Had it even looked this good when they bought the place eight years ago? It was five-thirty and already there were about thirty Brothers lounging around the main room. Unusual for this early in the day. What the hell had happened while he was gone?

"Sharp!" Hawk's voice carried over the bar, which now had shining chrome and cherry colored wood. Had the wood always been that red and hidden under years of dirt? The president sat at the bar with a beer in front of him with Max, the Dark Son's laid back and always cheerful Road Captain, on his left. A large jar sat on the edge of the bar next to them practically overflowing with money. A large white label with the words 'Groceries for Pixie' scrawled in red ink was fixed to the front of the jar. Whoever Pixie was, she was getting a shit ton of groceries because, from this close, he could see all the bills were tens and twenties.

Slightly stunned with all the changes, he exchanged greetings and backslaps with the President and Road Captain, taking another look around the place. "What the hell happened here? You guys spring for Merry Maids?"

Max smiled through the wild brown beard he liked to sport and slapped his arm. "Your woman is magic, VP. She's like Suzie homemaker on crack."

Hawk smirked, his brown eyes sparked with mischief.

"Yeah, you better treat that girl right, man, or you'll have half the Brothers fighting over who gets to take her off your hands. She not only cleaned this place up – while we were all sleeping mind you – she's been feeding every Brother who's here home-cooked meals."

"She makes bread that can make a grown man cry, you lucky fucker. Lunch is sandwiches, which you might say 'big deal', but they are on home-fucking-made bread. Damn, if she didn't run and hide every time I get closer than ten feet, I might try to fight you for her." Max's tone was laughing but his eyes told Sharp he was deadly serious.

Fuck. What had his woman been up to? At best he thought she would have taken a walk or two around the compound. Maybe meet a few Brothers, make a friend. He never imagined she would scrub the place until it shined and seduce his Brothers with food. He scowled wondering if maybe she had found someone else while he was away.

"Don't worry that you're footing the bill," Hawk teased him. "After her lasagna on Monday the boys started this to make sure she had any and all ingredients she needed."

Sharp didn't give a shit about money, he had plenty. He studied the full jar trying to take it in. "Pixie?"

Max shrugged. "It fits. She's so tiny and fucking adorable with everything she touches. Every Brother who has met her can't help but want to keep her safe." The Road Captain clenched his fists as dark thoughts crossed his face. "We've been looking into the dickhead who hurt her. You can bet your ass when the time comes, every man here has your back."

Sharp had never doubted his Brothers' support; being a Dark Son meant you never had to fight alone. Actually knowing his Brothers believed in her cause meant something more. He looked around the room with new understanding of how she had done so much in under seventy-two hours. This chapter had over a hundred members, but some came out solely for church and official gatherings. About twenty lived at the compound. Another twenty floated in and out but didn't usually show up until late at night for drinking and fucking. Homemade meals meant every single man who could, would show up.

"Where's my girl now?"

"Dinner's at six so she is back in the kitchen working her magic. Puck says it is sausage alfredo with, again, home-fuck-ing-made garlic bread." Max rolled his eyes like bread was the equivalent to a good blowjob.

Sharp shook his head and headed off to see what his little Pixie was up to. He liked the name his Brothers had given her. They may have only met days ago and barely spoken, but she definitely had some magic because she haunted his every thought. The small taste of her he had gotten on Monday hadn't been nearly enough. She could finish up dinner but after that, he was taking her back to his place and locking the door until morning.

He lived a few hundred yards away, behind the Clubhouse. The officers each had a small house on the land within over a hundred acres that made up compound grounds. Hell, he should have had her moved in there before he had left but hadn't thought of it. That is until he realized he wanted one on one time with her. Sharp walked through the door and lost his breath at the sight of the woman standing in the kitchen.

Pixie was breathtaking in a white sundress with tiny flowers embroidered on the cloth. The dress hit her around the knees and her hair was up in an innocent ponytail that had blond curls spilling down over her shoulders. Even the mottled bruising and cuts, still clearly visible, did nothing to detract from the angelic picture she made stirring something on the stove.

"No one in the kitchen while Pixie's cooking." Puck's voice was firm but polite. The prospect looked up and recognized

Sharp. He smiled, stepping back. "Hey, Pixie, you got a visitor."

Phoebe turned and he loved the sight of her green eyes as they flashed with joy. Sharp couldn't believe she could get more beautiful but, as she dropped the spoon on the counter and ran towards him, he knew he had been wrong. He caught her as she jumped up, managing to wrap her arms and legs around him.

"I'm so glad you're back," she mumbled into his neck, planting little kisses as she spoke.

Sharp laughed. "I guess you missed me." The feel of her body pressed up against his and the tiny kisses had his cock hard in seconds. He lifted her up until he could tilt his head down and kiss her lips.

Sharp stepped forward, setting Pixie on the counter to free up his hands. He ran them through her hair devouring her sweet taste and silky feel. A loud buzzing sound interrupted his bliss as his little prize cursed under her breath and managed to wiggle down and around him.

Amused, he leaned back crossing his arms as she opened the four different ovens and pulled out tray after tray of garlic bread that filled the room with their heavenly scent. A second buzzer went off and Sharp watched, impressed, as his woman quickly moved across the stove top pulling strainers of pasta out, rinsing them quickly and then spread the noodles out in prepared aluminum serving tins. Sharp exchanged a look of wonder with Puck at the contradiction that was his woman. In less than ten minutes she had fifteen large serving trays filled with alfredo covered pasta and enough sausage to feed a small army.

That miracle of productivity completed, she skipped over to him and wrapped small arms around his waist, a beautiful smile of pride on her lips. Sharp kissed the top of her head. "That smells awesome darlin'."

Puck moved towards the door looking over at them. "You gonna step out, Pixie?"

His woman shook her head, snuggling in close to his side. "No, I'm good."

Puck looked surprised, but swung open the door and shouted, "Foods on!"

In less than a minute, Brothers swarmed the room grabbing trays and taking them outside. The whole thing appeared choreographed and Sharp wondered how so much could have changed in just three days. His growling stomach and hard cock warred in their desires to either try his woman's cooking, or get her back to his place and start showing her all the things he had imagined doing to her.

Hunger barely won out and he wrapped an arm around her shoulders. "Come on, darlin', I can't wait to taste your food."

Chapter 9

My world may look like a peaceful meadow, but the landmines will kill you every time.

Phoebe was filled with a mix of dread and comfort as Sharp sat her down beside him at the picnic table. She had never joined the Brothers for any of the meals she had cooked. Without the comforting presence of Sharp at her side, she wasn't sure she could have. She loved cooking and cleaning; both tasks giving her a sense of accomplishment that had been missing from her life. Each effort had a start and end along with clearly defined success. But seeing these large men enjoying the food and sending compliments her way was like winning the trophy at the end of the race.

Sharp's hand was warm as it whirled circles on her thigh, settling her even more. Phoebe didn't know if he realized he was doing it as he talked and joked with his Brothers, but he was moving her skirt slowly up under the table. The public display and thoughts that he might touch her here in front of all these men had her nipples hardening and her pussy damp.

The tips of his fingers brushed against her panties and she

drew in a sharp breath. Sharp leaned in and bit gently on the top of her ear.

"Are you wet for me, darlin'?" His fingers slid under the silky fabric of her panties. "Damn, you are. I can fucking smell your sweet honey. All I've been able to think about for days is the feeling of those sweet lips wrapped around my cock, and how I was going to work you up so high but wouldn't fuck you until you were begging me for it."

His fingers dipped inside her core and his palm pressed down on her clit, shooting sparks straight to her nipples. She licked her lips, her whole body ready for whatever he asked. Conflicting emotions tore through her at the idea of him doing whatever he wanted right here with all these men watching. The idea turned her on so much she nearly came while shame and fear caused her stomach to roil. She didn't want him to know how much of a freak she was. Her worst fear the past two nights was that Sharp would discover just how fucked up and broken she was and send her back to Mitchel. Or worse, Caravaggio. She liked it here and wanted Sharp's trust and the desire he instantly evoked by being near her.

Somehow she had to find a way to suppress those broken parts of her and be exactly what he needed. Sharp pulled his hand away and up to his mouth, sparking a fresh wave of desire in her as he sucked the taste of her off his fingers. "You have fifteen minutes, little Pixie, to get what you need from the room. Then I am taking you home with me. I need to explore every inch of you and make you scream so loud they'll hear you from across the field."

Sharp nodded to one of the houses she had noticed inside the fenced compound. The one he indicated was maybe five hundred yards away and faced the dirt road that circled the several-acre compound. Phoebe stood, pushing down the disappointment he wasn't going to take her right now in front of everyone. It wouldn't take her long to get all her stuff.

She was back at his side next to his bike in fourteen minutes, with a tote bag slung across her chest filled with some of the clothes Val had gotten her.

On the short ride around the side of the compound, Phoebe boldly let her hands slide down over the front of Sharp's jeans rubbing the very impressive bulge there. It calmed something inside her to know he wanted her as badly as she wanted him. The small two-story house they pulled up in front of was well-maintained but lacked any sort of personality. Probably built in the 1900s, a giant shiny truck and two other Harleys were parked out front. Did Sharp live alone? Were these his? There was so much she didn't know about this man who rescued her.

The moment the bike was parked, Sharp's arm swung around her waist and lifted her so she was facing him on the front of the bike. His lips took hers in a rough, biting kiss. She had to wrap her legs around his waist as he stood up, still kissing her, and got off the bike. His hands were gripping her ass, his cock pushing against her core as he walked them up the stairs and into the house.

They made it a few feet inside the door before he tossed her bag to the side and pulled her dress up over her head. The feel of his rough jeans against her thighs and the leather of his cut and holster against her skin was an intoxicating mix. He pushed her against the wall, the sweet ache of her bruises mixed with the sensation of his lips closing over her braless breasts had her close to coming.

He used one hand to hold her up, pressed against the wall, his mouth doing wonderful things to her breast, while his other hand undid his jeans. She tried to rub against him to get some sort of friction on her clit, but her panties were just enough of a barrier to frustrate her. She moaned, her hands clenching on his shoulders wanting to help but unable to do anything in this position.

Sharp growled pulling back. "You're too fucking hot. I can't wait another minute."

He ripped open a condom and somehow got it on. Her panties were loudly torn off her and then Sharp thrust up into her in one powerful stroke. She was so wet he slid right in, but he was so big her body struggled to adjust, spasming around his length. She screamed in beautiful pain and pleasure.

Her orgasm took her so fast that she thrashed against him out of control, lost in bliss. "Fuck, you are so tight." He slammed into her, his thrusts pushing her back against the wall in a brutal rhythm. She clutched at his hair trying to find some sort of anchor in the tidal wave of sensation. He grabbed her wrists, pinning them in one hand and pushing them up over her head against the wall.

The sensation of something closing around her wrists pulled her out of the pleasure of the moment and into the horrors of the past. Image after image of being chained to a wall while Mitchel and other men humiliated her with her own body's reaction to their torture ripped through her. Memories of Mitchel's twisted game flooded her; being pushed beyond her limits until she was a broken wreck hanging limply by her ever-present cuffs.

With the images came her unyielding thought; no one could want a twisted, broken thing like her. Eventually, they would see beyond the pretty surface to her shattered desperate soul and be sickened. She would never find happiness, a place or people who could accept all of her and she'd be safe. She had to hide what she wanted but it was impossible.

Her mind closed in on itself looping around until it blanked out to preserve her sanity.

Lost in the unbelievable sensations of his woman's body Sharp almost missed what was happening. Phoebe went still and when he looked into her eyes, they were blank. "Shit!"

He pulled out and carried her into the living room, laying her down on the couch. One minute she had been right there with him; the next she was gone. Her blank stare was too close to the ones he had seen on combat vets when they were deep in the grips of a flashback for him not to know what this was.

Damn it! He knew better than to push a victim of trauma. She had made him forget everything with her sexy smile and wild touches. He needed to be gentle with her even though it wasn't in his nature. Years of being responsible for his Brothers in and out of the military had solidified his desire to be in charge. He had dark and brutal needs that he doubted this delicate woman could survive.

He shook her shoulders and she didn't even blink. How could he be with her? Was there anything in his darkness that this brilliant soul needed? Maybe he should let one of his Brothers claim her. They weren't exactly white knights but at least some of them didn't crave the control and violent sex he did. How could this girl who dressed like an angel in sundresses ever enjoy the dirty things he loved so much? After surviving hell, she deserved candlelight and a gentleman.

The idea of another man in her bed enraged him. No matter his good intentions, he could never watch another man claim her. They could watch him, in fact; he loved the idea of claiming her in front of every one of them. She was his for good or evil. He would have to find his softer side. Maybe after she healed, she would be ready for all of him.

Sharp pulled off the condom, tossing it in the trashcan as he tucked himself back in his jeans. He knelt next to her head, speaking to her softly. "Come on, baby. I'm sorry. Come back to me. You're safe."

The darkness lightened at the edges of her vision and she could feel she was wrapped up in a warm fuzzy blanket.

"There you are, darlin'." She focused on Sharp's face and the sensation of his hand brushing back her hair.

Had she really lost it in the middle of some of the best sex she had ever experienced? Her cheeks turned bright red as she realized how pathetic she must have been to end up naked, under a blanket, while he sat there fully dressed. "I'm so sorry, Sharp." She blinked trying to fight the tears that were pooling in her eyes.

"Stop that. You have nothing to be sorry about. Can you tell me what set you off?" She hated the careful tone in his voice, which meant he knew just how fragile she was.

She rubbed her arms, remembering all too well the feeling of numbness that would settle into them when she would be left dangling after the worst of her torture sessions. "My wrists." She brought them out from under the blanket and showed him the solid lines of scars that ringed her hands. "He liked to watch me dangle when I was too weak or too tired to stand upright."

He pulled her up into his lap, cradling her against his broad chest. "I didn't know."

"Of course you didn't." She rolled into his chest, breathing in the scent of leather, sweat, and man that was uniquely him. "Can we talk about something else?" She wanted to move on and find that spark they shared. She needed him to see her as a whole woman, not as some pathetic wimp.

He was silent for a few minutes too long. He petted her hair and she wanted to sob because she had broken the amazing connection they had. She wished she could see his expression and know for sure, but couldn't risk looking up and letting him see the fear in her eyes. Had she screwed this up already? Was dealing with her issues too much for the strong man? If he couldn't handle her weakness, how much more would he despise her if he found out just how twisted she was?

"What's your favorite color?"

The question startled her into sitting up and looking at him. He had a mischievous smile on his face. She wondered what game he was playing. "Sunset purple. Yours?"

"Right now, emerald green." She blushed as he stared down into her eyes like they would reveal the meaning of the universe. "Favorite food?" Phoebe smiled, a glimmer of hope taking root.

He continued on like this for over an hour, his questions getting more ridiculous each round. She was laughing freely by the time he turned the tables on her and said it was her turn to ask questions. His arms had several intricate and colorful tattoos that always drew her attention. She traced her fingers around a beautifully detailed rifle on his arm. "Do your tattoos mean something?"

"Some of them. Others I got because Hannibal and Ink are amazing artists." Phoebe puzzled for a moment then smiled.

"Are they Dark Sons too?"

"Yeah."

"I love that you all choose your names. Makes them more important than something someone stuck on you at birth."

"You don't pick a road name darlin', other people give it to you. Sometimes you go through several before one sticks."

"I still like it."

"Do you now, Pixie?"

"That's just Puck being silly."

"Nope, darlin'. All the Brothers I talked to today are calling you that. I think it fits. Most good names start as a joke. Gives them more meaning."

Phoebe loved the name Pixie, but she couldn't think of

herself that way. There was still so much darkness eating away at her insides that she didn't think something so cute fit her. She covered a yawn. "Can I see your other tattoos?"

"Of course." He leaned in and kissed her on top of the head. He picked up her tote of clothes off the floor. "But let's do that upstairs and I'll tuck you in."

Phoebe knew why she yawned. This was the time she had been going upstairs to sleep in order to avoid contact with any of the men at the compound when they were drunk. But with Sharp in his home, she didn't want to get tucked away like a child. Something about his tone of voice told her he had placed her into a relationship box that at worst was labeled little sister and at best said 'friend'.

Needing to fix that, she stood letting the blanket drop and arched her back, stretching. The motion was delightfully painful and worth every ache because a glint of heat sparked in Sharp's eyes. She put some swing in her step as she walked up the stairs, hoping her bare ass and hips was enough to send his thoughts down the path she wanted.

Chapter 10

If at first you don't succeed... try a different angle

There were several doors on the second floor, but she could see the open one at the end of the hallway had a large bed covered in plain blue blankets. The rest of the room was much like the rest of the house with functional furniture but no personal touches. When Phoebe turned and faced him at the foot of the bed, she was pleased by the hungry look in Sharp's eyes. Although he had complete control over his body, it was comforting to know she could read him even if it were a small hint.

He dropped her tote on the dresser, taking a few breaths, before turning around to face her. Phoebe licked her lips hoping she made a tempting sight. "Can I see your other tattoos now?"

She wanted to see the gorgeous artwork, but it was the idea of finally seeing him without a shirt that had her pulse racing. A sexy smirk tilted Sharp's lips as he pulled off his cut, folding it and placing it carefully on the dresser. His holster and guns were next. He turned his back and with one smooth motion pulled off his shirt. Displayed across his back was a gorgeous motorcycle in a desert sunset background with the words 'Dark Sons' in Gothic script arching over the entire scene.

His perfectly muscled back was a wonderful canvas and, as he turned to face her, she had to suck in a breath at the wonder that was his front. Well defined abs with the all too sexy muscles that formed a V disappearing into his pants were home to a gorgeous dragon that curled around and looked like it was about to blow flames over his heart. The bottom half was vibrant with color while the top was pure black outlines.

Phoebe stepped forward, her hands drawn to the unfinished outlines that covered the upper right of his chest. She petted his pecs as if the dragon were a real animal that would appreciate the contact.

"Why no color?"

His hands settled on her bare hips, the heat of his skin causing her to shudder with chills. "It isn't finished. My Brother, Ink is supposed to work on it some more this week."

"Can I come watch?" Tattoos had always fascinated her, but she had never had the money to spare, so she hadn't looked into the process. His hands gently squeezed her waist, his hips rocking forward, pressing his jean-covered cock against her stomach.

"You like to watch?"

Phoebe gasped as he ground against her. Watching didn't turn her on nearly as much as the man in front of her, but maybe this was a way to get things back on track. "Do you like being watched?" Now that idea did turn her on, and she shivered at the thought.

His expression gentled with what looked like pity entering his eyes, and he cupped her face. "Don't you worry about that, darlin'."

Phoebe wanted to scream in frustration. He totally misread her reaction. She could feel his arousal slipping away like a knife sticking in her heart. She should have known her past would ruin everything. She dropped her head, not wanting to see the look on his face.

"I can go back to the Clubhouse and let you get some sleep." She was proud her voice only wavered a little bit.

"Look at me, Phoebe."

She didn't want to, but the command in his voice was undeniable.

"You stay here with me from now on. I'll sleep in the guest room for a while. Let you have the big bed."

Phoebe couldn't hold in the sob that exploded from her at his words. It was everything she feared. Standing here naked, her body pressed against his, and all he wanted to do was get away from her.

He sat down on the bed and pulled her into his arms. Why did the man feel so good? For once in her life, a man aroused her and made her feel safe. His skin against hers was one of the most beautiful feelings in the world, yet he didn't feel the same.

"Talk to me. Tell me what's wrong."

"Why do I have to stay here?"

His growl sent a zing of excitement through her body. His angry, possessive stare calming rather than scaring her. "You belong to me, Pixie."

"But you don't want m-me!"

"Baby, I want you so bad I am hanging onto sanity by my fingernails."

"Then fuck me." She sounded desperate, but she needed the physical assurance he cared. Words meant little to nothing in her experience. If he would fuck her, she would know he wasn't lying, that she wasn't alone in her feelings. That they were solid, and he would keep her safe.

"Fuck, I want to, but your head isn't in the right place.

Tomorrow, after you've slept, if you still want me, I will fuck you until you're screaming my name."

Phoebe barely resisted the urge to stomp her foot like a toddler denied sweets. Her body longed for his, and she didn't want to accept the logic in his words. She could see he wasn't going to budge, making arguing with him useless.

"Please, stay with me tonight?" The fear and pleading in her voice bothered her, but if he left her alone her doubts and self-loathing would consume her.

"Of course." Sharp kissed her on the forehead.

Before slipping into bed with her, he slipped off his jeans and, much to her dismay, slipped on a pair of sleep shorts that looked like they had never been worn. He slid under the covers and pulled her close so her head rested against his chest.

The way her mind was racing Phoebe didn't think she would ever fall asleep, but the stress of the day and the intoxicating warmth of his body soon had her drifting away with thoughts of what she could do to wake him up.

Sharp had been a light sleeper since BUDs taught his body that danger could happen at any moment. Especially when asleep. So, when Phoebe's small body stirred around five am he was instantly alert. He swore he could feel her eyes studying him. When her tiny hands started exploring down his body, he couldn't help but play along and feign sleep to see how far his little Pixie would take things.

She ran her hands in feather-light circles across his stomach pausing for a few seconds whenever she reached the waistband of his shorts. There was no hiding from her that his dick was awake. The soft feeling of her skin against his sent blood racing to his groin, causing a visible tent in the material.

Phoebe's hands slipped under the soft cotton. Sharp

expected a gentle touch and was ready to continue to feign sleep, but the firm grip and twisting motion had him shouting in shocked pleasure.

"Good morning." Phoebe's voice held mischief and the hint of a laugh. Her hands slowed, gliding over the tip of his dick, spreading the pre-come over the head and gliding down to the base. Pleasure and desire ran through him making him want to roll over on top of the little minx and start the day off right.

"Morning." He looked down into her eyes and the same heat and hunger he felt was reflected in her eyes. He had planned to give her some time to adjust after he had stupidly pushed her too hard the night before. But with her little hand working him like a master he could think of little besides sinking balls deep inside her tight depths. The small taste he had gotten the night before wasn't nearly enough to satisfy him.

Her little body slid down his and dragged his shorts down, freeing his cock to the early morning. Her mouth was like warm velvet as she closed her lips around him. He wrapped his hands in her hair, losing himself in the gentle suction and the feel of her swallowing him down right to the base. How lucky was he that such a tiny thing like her could deepthroat with such skill. The urge to slam up and fuck her face was nearly overwhelming, but he held back. He did not want a repeat of last night.

For the most part, he was willing to let her set the pace, but he needed to get inside her pussy. Sharp reached over, pulling a condom from the side table drawer as he pulled his gorgeous girl up and off his dick. Her whimpers of protest made him grin. Her tongue reached out as if to catch just one more taste. He handed her the condom and loved the eager way she rolled it on and tried to immediately slam herself down. He gripped her hips, easily keeping her still with the tip of him barely inside her.

He needed to change things up if he was going to let her set the pace. If he wasn't going to claim her with brutal strokes, he had to feed his darkness another way. Even in the heat of passion he needed to be the one in control. She might not be able to take him at full force, but he would make sure she knew she wasn't the one calling the shots.

"Tell me what you need, darlin'."

"I need you, Sharp."

"What do you need?" He teased her, sliding in an inch then back out.

"Fuck me! Please, I need your cock deep inside me."

He loved the dirty words coming out of those sweet lips. Sharp lowered his little Pixie slowly down onto his cock, watching her beautiful face as the pleasure echoed across her features. Her hands slid up, cupping her breasts as he moved her slowly up and down.

The muscles of her pussy rippled as she moved, and he enjoyed the teasing pull. Her hands pinched and twisted her nipples, and Sharp groaned as it made her clench harder around his dick. This slow sensual pace would never get him off, but he needed her to find her satisfaction before he took what he needed. Sharp slid one of his hands between them, teasing her little clit as it peeked out of its hood.

"Ride me, darlin'."

As if his words were a starter pistol, Phoebe slammed down onto him, trying to take him in as deep as she could go. She arched her body in waves, always ending in a thrust he could feel echoing in his balls. She looked like a wild woman, glorious in her lust-soaked actions.

He placed his hands on her breasts, gently rolling the nipples between his fingers. Her panting breaths and moans were fuel to his desire. When her rhythm broke tiny quakes of orgasm spasming around his cock, he flipped her up and off him, his control slipping.

He positioned her face down on the bed, her knees against her chest, her ass and pussy tilted up toward him like offerings before the gods. He used his thumb to rim the tiny rosette of her ass wishing he could slam himself home inside that tight nirvana. She shuddered, and he couldn't tell if the action was fear or excitement, but he wouldn't risk fucking up like that again. He would ease her into his primal needs, hoping she wouldn't break along the way.

He straddled her legs, slowly working his cock into the wet depths of her pussy. This position was one of his favorites because the angle allowed for full penetration. He loved the feeling of his cock bottoming out against the cervix. Unfortunately, most women said it was too painful. But a glorious few loved it as much as he did. Sharp prayed that Phoebe would be one of those. He didn't want to have to give it up.

The feeling of his cock meeting her cervix sent a sharp jolt of pleasure right down his spine. Experimentally, he ground into her, pushing against the barrier. Phoebe moaned, pushing back against him. He took a shallow thrust, and she gasped but met his next thrust with more force. With a growl, Sharp pulled out until just the tip of him held her open and slammed back in. On the third thrust, her scream of pleasure made him smile as her orgasm gripped his dick so hard, he saw stars.

He lost himself inside her, slamming with all his force over and over. He gripped her hips and rode her like he was trying to drill through her body with his dick. When the orgasm came, it locked his muscles as he shouted her name to the ceiling.

Their breathing evened out and Sharp watched her eyes come back into focus. He eased his way out of her and went to clean up in the bathroom planning to bring back a warm wet washcloth for her and settle back for another hour of sleep.

When he returned to the room, instead of a sleepy, well-satisfied woman in bed, he found Phoebe rummaging through the bag she had brought.

He leaned against the doorway, frustrated that she appeared to have so much energy. A glance at the clock said it was a little past five. "What are you doing?"

Phoebe turned towards him with a glazed look in her eyes as she took in his naked body. That he could distract her so easily soothed his ego, but he didn't like that she looked ready to bolt out the door.

"I have to shower and get over to the Clubhouse if I'm going to get the cleaning done and breakfast ready before your Brothers wake up." She bit her lip as her gaze caught the sight of his cock, already stirring again at the sight of her standing there naked, her arousal still glistening as it dripped down her thighs.

He walked over and ran his thumb along her lower lip. "Who told you to clean up the Clubhouse?" His Brothers definitely appreciated it, but he would beat the crap out of any man trying to turn her into their personal maid.

"No one. I like to clean and cook. It seemed like so little for everything you all have done." Her body melted against his, leaning in as if drawn to him. He loved that around him she didn't seem the frightened mouse she was around his Brothers. With the exception of his fuck up last night, her complete trust and lack of fear floored him.

"You don't have to do anything. My Brothers protect you because you are mine." Sharp felt his words resound with the absolute truth. Never before had any woman triggered such possessiveness in him. So many women had warmed his bed and fed his needs, but none of them had ever made him think beyond the moment. Phoebe in a few hours meant more to him than all of them combined. If he didn't destroy her with his darkness, this little pixie could be his for life.

"But–" He brushed his lips over hers, quieting her protests.

"You want to cook or clean that's fine, but not because you think you have to. But when you're with me, you don't worry about anyone but us."

His lips covered hers in a claiming kiss that had both of them panting. Sharp nipped at her skin enjoying the salty taste. He was going to make sure she thought of nothing but him for a good long time.

Chapter 11

Sometimes even the littlest of pricks are the biggest assholes.

Sharp was happy to be back in his garage rather than out on the road. Dark Customs Garage was more to him than just a business, it was his passion. Located about a half hour from both Denver and the Clubhouse, it had become famous for custom Harley work and had a waiting list two years long. Every single man who worked at the garage was a Dark Son Brother handpicked by Sharp for their skill. The success of the business meant being able to pick and choose work and offered the flexibility needed to a Brother. That fact meant they could still go on runs or rides whenever they wanted.

Rebuilding and customizing bikes gave Sharp a sense of satisfaction. The side jobs he did for the Club were essential, but here he could relax and do something he loved with some of his Brothers. Gears and Crash were already elbow-deep in their projects, and Rooster and Smoke would be in the office mainlining coffee before they were ready to work.

"Sharp! You're in later than usual," Crash teased him from across the bays.

It was well past eight and Sharp was usually in by seven to try and get the paperwork done before getting his hands dirty. "I ate breakfast at the compound."

The week he had been gone on Club business meant there would be a mess overflowing his desk. Sharp trusted each one of these guys with his life and any bike, but none of them would do an invoice or order parts without the threat of death being involved, and since they were all ex-special forces the danger had to be dire and immediate.

"I heard the new girl is an amazing cook," Crash laughed. "Is that little bit of fluff really your woman?"

Gears sat up from the Harley he was working on, wiping his hands on a rag. "He saved her from some dickhead over at HKs. Sharp is her knight in shining armor."

Sharp flipped off Gears, both of his Brothers teasing him with good-natured laughs.

"She know the shine on your armor is actually blood?"

"Fuck off." He headed to the office, worrying himself. Watching Pixie bustle around like Suzie homemaker this morning cooking eggs and other breakfast foods like it was the highlight of her day was kinda hot, but it made him wonder if she would ever enjoy the things he fantasized about doing to her.

He was a violent man who liked fucking whether it was alone or in front of a crowd. Making a woman scream and beg him to fuck her raw just plain did it for him. He didn't want to break that light in her, and he was afraid that's what he would do. The idea of Virgin Mary turning into Mary Magdalene was the hottest of images, but could any woman be both?

Around lunchtime Puck showed up with a box full of sandwiches.

"Sharp's lady sent over food," he shouted, over the noise of the equipment. Sharp was still straightening out the mess that was his inventory. He needed to put a parts order in by the end of the day.

By the time he got out to the garage, everyone was gathered around the box pulling out chips and sandwiches on thick crusty bread. Sharp grabbed one that was roast beef wrapped in butcher paper and took a bite. The bread was a fantastic wheat that melted like butter but crisp around the edges. Pepper Jack cheese, lettuce, tomato and a spicy mayo were in perfect harmony with the thick cuts of beef.

"Damn. I'll fucking marry the bitch if she makes me sandwiches like this every day," Rooster moaned around a mouthful of food.

"Call my woman a bitch, and you won't have to worry about eating ever again." Sharp was surprised by the violent fury that had come over him at the words of his Brother.

"Nothing but respect man, I swear." Rooster held his hands up in a surrender pose.

Sharp took another bite of the amazing sandwich, choosing to ignore the irrational feelings he was having. The paperwork was slow going because his mind kept drifting to the tiny Pixie back at home. The idea of her small hands on his body sparked fantasies that weren't conducive to work. One particular image of her all sweet and innocent until he lifted that proper little dress to find her soaking wet had replayed several times. He would pin her to the kitchen counter and fuck her until everyone heard her screams of pleasure.

"You expecting someone?" Puck nodded up at the monitor that showed the front parking lot of the garage. Brothers and regular customers knew to come around back, so the two blacked-out SUVs were obviously neither.

Four large and very Italian men stepped out, scanning the parking lot apparently looking for trouble. Sharp got the feeling he wasn't going to enjoy the next fifteen minutes.

"No." Sharp's voice was a growl as he recognized the next man who stepped out. Anthony Caravaggio, exiled nephew of the Minetti family. His oiled back, brown hair and European style suit were out of place in Colorado. City girls probably drooled all over him not knowing the man had no soul behind his dark eyes.

His woman's trouble had found them. Checking his gun, Sharp watched as the slick dick Mitchel started to get out behind the mobster but was sent back into the car with what looked like angry threats. It was a shame there wasn't any sound because it would have been interesting to know what Caravaggio said to earn the homicidal stare.

Without any prompting, Puck, Smoke and Gears headed up the ladders on either side of the garage that led to sniper perches in the rafters. Rooster and Crash checked their weapons before holstering them, taking their lead from Sharp. It was tempting to rush out guns blazing. Scum like these men didn't deserve to breathe the same air as other people.

But a long time in the military had taught Sharp patience, so they waited for the enemy to come to them. When the group of men entered, each was sized up for weaknesses by the bikers. Four of the men were obviously new muscle; they had shoulder holsters but didn't carry themselves like they'd had any training. Good for intimidation; that kind of bulk would cower lesser men. Caravaggio was fit, but it was that soft physique that came from working out for the sole purpose of looking good. His perfectly tailored suit and the hundred-dollar haircut were designed to strengthen that impression.

Sharp had only seen the man once before in passing. The Dark Sons had taken on a job to protect a shipment for the Minetti family. The exiled, spoiled prince had shown up in another designer suit and strutted around like he owned the place. He had been there to make sure 'everything was in order'. Of course he left before any real work had to be done.

Caravaggio believed he was a king in a backwater pond and deserved to be treated as such. The problem was everyone knew the reason the little prick was forced to live in the Midwest rather than on the East Coast with the rest of the Minetti Family: his dates tended to wind up dead.

His sick and often lethal tastes in the bedroom couldn't be covered up when the Feds were watching him closely. So, he had been exiled to live in a mansion far away from the watchful eye of the government and was forced to get his fix by buying girls no one would miss. He was barely smart enough not to get caught even with all those restrictions. Sharp had to take a deep breath and control the rage fueled by the idea of his sweet Phoebe ending up with this monster.

The bastard strode into the open bay, his goons trailing behind him like an over-muscled flock of geese. "I'm looking for Sharp."

Sharp stepped forward, the comfortable weight of his gun at the small of his back. Out of the corner of his eye, he saw Puck and Gears at their posts, guns trained on Caravaggio and his goons. "That's me."

"Good. I'm Anthony Caravaggio." He smirked as if he expected his name alone to strike fear.

"I know who you are." Sharp tried to keep his answers short in the hopes his absolute disdain wouldn't be too obvious. But instinct told him this whole meeting was bound to go sideways.

"Good, that should make this easy. You have something that belongs to me. I want it returned."

It. Not her. The urge to shoot Caravaggio and rid the world of one more asshole was too tempting. This son of a bitch thought he could stride into Dark Sons territory and make demands.

"We have nothing that belongs, or that will ever belong, to you."

The Mafia wannabe's face reddened with anger. "I spoke with Mr. Thomas. He said you stole the package he was supposed to deliver to me."

Sharp smiled, but it wasn't pleasant. Now he had Mitchel's last name, which would make it so much easier to track him down. Sharp found it fascinating that a man this twisted guarded his words as if he were being recorded by the cops.

"If you mean Mitchel, the man you have stashed in the back of your car, then we didn't steal shit from him. He had a very nice girl with him who wanted to come home with me." Sharp smirked as he took in the anger flashing in the psycho's eyes. "Who was I to say no? If your friend was supposed to secure a package for you and lost it, I think you should be talking to him. If you want, I will happily talk to him myself." Sharp hoped he would get another chance to have words with the abusive asshole.

"Look, you little fuck, I paid top dollar for that package. You will return it to me."

The men behind Sharp growled at the insult. It was time to drop the nice guy act. "You pumped up prick. How dare you come onto Dark Sons territory making demands? The only reason you're even breathing is because we respect the Minettis. But that respect only goes so far."

Caravaggio's eyes narrowed and he made a gesture that had his men pulling their guns. Sharp didn't let anything show on his face, knowing his Brothers had done the same.

"You're out numbered, Sharp," the idiot said and smirked, and Sharp knew he thought his four men were enough to kill the three men he could see. "Kill them."

Four guns fired simultaneously, the sound echoing in the garage bay, followed by soft thumps as all four of Caravaggio's men dropped dead. Small holes provided evidence of where bullets had entered the center of their foreheads. Sharp strode forward until he was nose-to-nose with the now confused Italian. He knocked Caravaggio to the ground with a single right hook.

"Dark Sons are never alone and we sure as fuck aren't at a disadvantage when facing off against entitled little pussies who only play at combat." He squatted down using one hand gripped around Anthony's throat to keep him pinned to the ground. "Listen very closely. Phoebe belongs to the Dark Sons now. She is my woman. Anyone who tries to take her is going to discover themselves begging for death long before it comes for them."

"Fifty-thousand dollars."

The number startled and frustrated Sharp. It was a ridiculously high amount. If this scumbag was willing to shell out that much cash, he wasn't going to give Pixie up without a fight. He should kill the fucker, but the Minettis were a powerful family, and as VP he at least had to try to avoid war.

"We don't sell people. There is no price. Do you understand me?"

"I will destroy you."

"Big words from a man on the ground. You only breathe because I respect your uncle. Now get the fuck out of my garage." Sharp let him go before the urge to choke him became too strong.

With a nod, Rooster slipped out the door behind the mobster to make sure he didn't try to make more problems, while Sharp dialed Hawk's cell.

"Hey, Sharp. Pixie is making chicken pot pie from freaking scratch."

Sharp pushed away the image of Phoebe in a frilly white apron. He couldn't let his growing cock interfere with Club business. Not now. "I need Clean here with his crew ASAP."

Hawk's tone lost its lightness. "What happened?"

"Caravaggio showed with some friends. He's on his way home, but we had to make a mess."

"Right. I want details when you get back. I don't want a war if we can avoid it."

"Understood."

Clean had had many nicknames throughout his career in the Rangers and then as a contractor for the Agency. He was a thin, utterly average guy whose face was so nondescript, if you described him you would be looking for words other than normal. He had joined the Dark Sons a few years ago after a few of the active-duty Brothers risked their lives pulling him out of a South American hellhole that he had been left to rot in for months.

He didn't talk about his time in the Agency, but he had an exceptional talent for making anything disappear. The bodies were gone, and the floor power-washed with a chemical mix that was his secret alone in less than twenty minutes. The Brothers had barely finished rubbing the floors down with dirty rags, rolling in some dirt to the concrete, when Sharp's cell rang.

Hawk's voice was tinged with fury when he spoke. "Local PD is on their way over with dogs."

"That fucker called the cops?"

"Anonymous tip said you had dead bodies on the property. Has Clean done his thing?"

"Yeah, but I don't know if it will fool dogs."

Clean grinned, grabbing his heart. "You wound me, man." He then strode over to his bike taking a bag filled with red powder out of the saddlebag. Whistling, he began tossing a small amount of the powder between where the bodies had fallen and where the van had been.

"I stand corrected," said Sharp with a grin into the phone. "Looks like he has dogs covered."

"All right. The lawyer is about five minutes away. Tek already downloaded your security footage and performed a wipe. If they get a warrant, it will look like your system has been glitching for days. I want you here after they're gone." Hawk disconnected.

Clean dropped the bag back in his saddlebags. He glanced toward the road. "Your company is here. Guess I get to stay for the search."

Sharp laughed. "Don't ever say I don't take you to the best parties."

Chapter 12

That shit's going to fester. Fly your freak flag loud and proud.

Phoebe was taking her frustrations out on the pie dough in front of her. Flour was flying, dusting her green sundress in speckles of white, and she didn't care. Last night had been a disaster tainting what she had with Sharp. Stupid fear had fucked up everything. Her attempts at rekindling the fire this morning had barely worked.

Sharp had treated her like a porcelain doll. Sure, he had been attentive, making sure she orgasmed, but they were tiny things in comparison to the heat he could deliver. If he wasn't so big that he bruised her cervix, she doubted her stupid body would have come at all.

Why couldn't she be normal and enjoy the sweet tenderness Sharp offered? Would he leave her if he realized what she wanted? A man that rough and gorgeous probably enjoyed a wild fuck, but if she couldn't show him she was strong enough, would he even be willing to try? She wanted to tell him about her needs but feared he'd think she was broken. He might think she wanted pain because of her history. Would he try to fix her?

She needed a bit of pain with her pleasure, and he gave that to her whether he knew it or not. She feared that bit of bite wasn't enough for her. If she asked for more would he toss her away to be stuck as a Club whore?

Her whole body trembled at the idea of letting any man but Sharp touch her in that way. She slammed the rolling pin into the dough biting back her scream.

"Slap my butt and call me Bessy. It smells like my momma's kitchen in here." Val's southern twang was like a ray of sunshine. Phoebe ran and threw her arms around the woman. Val chuckled, squeezing Phoebe until she squeaked. "Dozer told me you were whipping up chicken pot pie, but I thought he was playin' me a fool."

Phoebe dusted her hands against each other. "Nope, I've almost done the crusts. The gravy is simmering. Potatoes are boiled, and the chicken will be done in a few minutes."

"Well, I stopped by with some news and to drop off some of the cutest sundresses I ever have seen. But if you are makin' chicken pot pie like my momma did, then pet me on the head and call me your kitchen bitch cause Dozer and I are joining y'all for dinner."

"Thank you, Val. You always make the day brighter."

"All right what do ya need?" Val pushed up her sleeves like she was ready for battle.

The friendly and often ludicrous banter soon had Phoebe smiling. When the fifty pie tins were ready for the oven a half hour early, she felt like dancing a jig.

"You never told me what news you had for me." Phoebe washed her hands at the sink.

"Well, I don't know how much you remember of the day you got here, but Doc took some blood to run tests on. Wipe that scared look off your face. I thought you would want to know you're clean of any diseases and not pregnant."

Phoebe tried not to show her surprise that they had gone to the trouble. To her chagrin the idea to get tested had never occurred to her. "That is good news."

"Means you get to start fresh. Nothing hanging over your head."

"As long as you don't count a psycho mobster or a murdering slaver wanting me back, sure let's call it fresh," Phoebe muttered under her breath.

"Honey, that ain't nothin' but mud on a new truck. You let your man wash that clean."

Embarrassed and not wanting to look at Val, Phoebe straightened up the counter. "If he even wants to."

"Now what does that mean? Is Sharp not treating you right?"

Phoebe started to answer, but she caught Kickstand out of the corner of her eye in his protective seat at the kitchen door, pretending to be looking at his phone. "Nothing. Everything is all right."

Val tightened her lips in disapproval. "Kickstand, you take yourself out the door and stop listening to women's talk."

"I'm supposed to watch over Pixie."

"And you can do that just fine from the other side of the door, or you will find out what it's like to be called Shorty." Val held up a meat cleaver to emphasize her point.

Kickstand blanched a bit but took himself out the door.

"Shorty?" Phoebe laughed.

"Well, if I chop off a few inches they won't have reason to call him Kickstand anymore."

Phoebe blushed, realizing that the prospect's nickname had nothing to do with motorcycles. Val pulled her over to the chairs on the other side of the room.

"Now what's going on, precious?"

"It's nothing. I'm being silly."

"Don't you lie to me, sister, or you will find out why they call me Valkyrie." Her friend made what was probably supposed to be a scary face but instead made Phoebe smile.

The new information surprised her out of her sulk. "I thought your name was Valerie."

"No, sweetheart, it's Sue-Anne. But after I reduced some of the Club whores to shivering little messes with nothin' but words, the name Valkyrie stuck."

"I'm still not seeing the name."

Val took on a superior tone that was ridiculous with her southern accent. "I choose what women live and die in this Club based on standards I learned at my momma's knee. I don't let no one hurt one of Dozer's Brothers, and they are too soft on those bitches."

"I guess I can see that."

"Enough stallin'. Now, what did the idiot do?"

Phoebe shook her head. "He isn't an idiot. I had a bit of an episode when he grabbed my wrists."

"And?"

"And now he's treating me like spun glass."

"That's a bad thing?" Val raised an eyebrow.

"I am not fragile!" Phoebe was shocked by how angry her words came out.

"No one who survived what you did is weak. But, honey, you might have a few delicate places, and maybe he's just trying to make sure not to hit any of those spots."

"I don't want him to pity me." Her tone was petulant even to her own ears. "How could a man like him be happy if he has to hold himself back all the time?"

"You let him worry about what he needs. If he pampers and treats you sweet, that doesn't mean he isn't happy."

She understood what Val was trying to say, but her emotions and needs were all a mess. She tried to find the right words to explain what she needed and, of course, her mouth moved before she could stop it. "But I like it rough!" Her hands flew up to her face as if trying to pull the words back in. "I'm sorry, Val, forget I said anything."

Phoebe was afraid she was going to burst into tears as Val's wise eyes roamed over her. How could she have blurted it out like that? Now she was going to lose a friend and a lover to the sick desires of her body.

"Now that is another color of catfish. Why do you look so ashamed? Nothing wrong with liking what you like. Not all ice cream is vanilla."

"You don't think that's sick? Mitchel used to torment me with my body's reactions to pain. I've always been this way. Sweet is nice, but it doesn't do it for me. My body feeds off the pain and turns it to pleasure. Even when I don't want it to."

"Oh, darlin'." Val wrapped her arms around Phoebe, holding her tight as her body shook with sobs. "I am so sorry that evil SOB twisted your mind up so bad. There is nothing wrong with you as long as you find someone who can meet those needs without it crossing into abuse."

"You don't think I'm a freak?"

"Girl, if you knew the sexual kinks the boys around here have, your pretty cheeks would explode. Hell, I love it when Dozer ties me up. Does that make me a freak?"

"No."

"Well then, believe me when I say not only are you not a freak but I think you have the right man. Though be careful if you meet Hannibal. His kink is needle play, and Lord knows I don't want those boys fighting over you."

"You think Sharp will understand?" Phoebe had trouble believing Val no matter how much she wanted to.

"Yes. But you need to be honest with him."

Chapter 13

No one wins in a deal with the Devil except the Devil himself.

Sharp's anger was like a boiling force under his skin as he walked into the Clubhouse. The Dark Sons had all of the local PD on their payroll, but that little fucker had called his tip into not only the local, but also the state police and added the FBI to really spice up the day. Luckily, the locals had given them the heads up and looked the other way while Clean drove away with the few unregistered guns that were peppered throughout the building.

Whatever Clean had done it fooled the dogs and when the cops used their luminol and lights nothing looked out of the ordinary. He was sure either the Staties or feds would be back with warrants for God knew what, if Hawk didn't pull some significant strings.

Max nodded at him from the bar gesturing to the back hall. "He's waiting for you in his office."

"Pixie know what went down?" The last thing he wanted was her worrying about whether she was safe or trying to leave so she wasn't putting them in danger. Caravaggio made his shit list for attempting to shoot him and his Brothers, but the stunt with the anonymous tips was a declaration of war in Sharp's book.

"No. Her and Val have been cooking up what smells like ambrosia for the last two hours. They say it will be served in twenty minutes, so you and Hawk better talk quick, or there will be nothing left."

Sharp wished he could borrow some of Max's calm. The Road Captain never let anything under his skin. Hell, the man rode in some of the wildest motocross races in the country on bikes he designed and never showed the slightest fear. It was how he got his Mad Max nickname, but since he never seemed to get mad, they just called him Max.

Hawk's office was large but filled up with years of Dark Sons paraphernalia. On the wall, behind the desk, hung the Dark Sons flag surrounded by pictures from rallies going back decades. The shelves held mementos from different charity rides they had done as well as the Crest of every branch of the military that a Dark Son had served in.

Hawk sat back in his chair drinking a large glass of Jack. He pushed a matching glass over to Sharp. The VP sat down, taking a large swallow, letting the burn of alcohol cover the taste of bile caused by his anger.

Hawk studied the liquid in his glass. "I just had a very long conversation with Marco."

Marco Minetti was the head of the Minetti family and uncle to the sick piece of work that was Anthony Caravaggio. Like the majority of Mafia families, the Minettis were brutal businessmen who were often unreasonably loyal to their families. Sharp hoped they would see the need to prune this particular branch. "What did he have to say?"

"He wants us to let it go."

"I'm not some Disney princess. That spectacular example

of why cousins shouldn't marry didn't only try to kill me, he called the fucking FBI."

"Marco says he's going to take care of the federal and state cops. He's offering the Club a major marker from the family if we don't retaliate further. He's also offering you and me personal markers as well. I don't have to tell you how valuable that could be."

Sharp hated that even in the MC world compromises were still necessary. Caravaggio was a danger to Phoebe as long as he was still breathing. But going to war was never something to be done lightly. "Is he going to make sure his nephew doesn't pull shit like this ever again? I don't like the idea of my woman having to look over her shoulder for the rest of her life."

"You gonna make her your Old Lady?" Hawk's words were more of a statement than a question.

Sharp hadn't thought that deep or rationally since he met his little Pixie but as the question sunk in, the surer he was. "Yeah. When she's ready."

"Don't know what ready has to do with it. Put your patch on her back; make her family. These conversations get a lot easier if she's family."

"Marco won't guarantee his nephew is going to back off?"

"He said he's going to inform him the woman and Dark Sons territory is off limits." Hawk took a deep drink of his whiskey.

"You think it will work?"

"No, and I don't think Marco does either. If his nephew steps out of line again, he promised not to look too hard at anything that happened to him. But we had better have rock solid proof before taking action. The Minettis can't be seen as weak, but in his words the mountains are wild, and he understands accidents sometimes happen."

"If we can prove Caravaggio made another move against us, he will look the other way as long as we keep it quiet. But until then we have to sit on our dicks for an IOU?" Sharp wanted to punch something. It had been years since anyone had made him suck up even a small insult.

"Or we can go to war with a family that has hundreds of foot soldiers and the money to hire the best mercenaries in the world."

Hawk made a valid point, though it stuck in Sharp's throat like a fishbone. He couldn't say he was okay with it, so he nodded.

"I'll keep the prospects watching out for her. National has our back if we need it."

That was the single good thing Sharp had heard all day.

"National's Officers are conferencing in tonight, so cancel any plans you might have had. I want plans to cover us if either Caravaggio or Mitchel Thomas decides to try and hit us."

His plans for the night included getting to know his woman's sweet body but her safety had to come first, and he had the rest of his life to learn every one of her curves.

Chapter 14

I give you shit because I care.

Phoebe could feel her palms getting clammy. Val had dragged her out to eat with everyone before Sharp was there. She liked Val's husband, or old man, or whatever the term was. Dozer reminded her of a muscular Santa Claus with his big bushy beard, but he didn't make her feel safe. All the men and the few women who had shown up to eat were friendly but being without Sharp in this crowd made her feel like bugs were crawling on her skin.

She needed to get a better grip. Sharp and his protective aura couldn't always be there, and she knew, at least intellectually, not every man wanted to hurt her. She wished she could convince her heart.

Strong arms closed around her, and she screamed. Every head turned her way, and not a small number of guns were drawn. It took a minute for her racing heart to register Sharp's low voice murmuring in her ear.

"It's me, baby. I'm sorry I startled you. Everything's okay."

Her body eased against him. Adrenaline faded as her

embarrassment grew until a flush covered her whole body. Everyone relaxed, and male chuckles filled the silence.

"Sorry, everyone," she stuttered, wishing she could vanish into the big body behind her.

Max lifted a beer in her direction, his smile contagious. "It's okay, little Pixie. Nothing finishes an amazing meal like a little harmless excitement."

Sharp straddled the picnic bench between her and Val. He tilted her face up and claimed her lips in a scorching kiss that let her feel how much he wanted her. He was here and Phoebe's whole body sunk into his embrace, heating up for all new reasons.

"I missed you and those sweet lips, darlin'."

"I missed you, too. I saved you a plate." She pushed over a plate piled high with chicken potpie and cornbread.

"You're lucky she did. These boys descended like the eighth plague on Egypt." Val gave the pair a wink.

"Well then, I'd better eat fast."

Pride surged inside Phoebe as she watched Sharp eat. His expressions were usually hard to read, his eyes the only clue to his emotions. But when he took his first bite, his whole face softened. He let out a groan that sounded more like it belonged in the bedroom.

Val laughed. "Like coming home to a warm fire on a cold night. Wherever did you learn to cook like this, Pixie?"

"Ms. Cramer. She was a bitter old nag who took in foster kids because it was her 'godly duty to help sweep up the dregs'."

"That doesn't sound very Christian." The southern woman rolled her eyes.

"Oh, those are her own words. She wasn't the worst foster parent I had, but there was no love. When she found out I had a photographic memory she had me memorize the bible and every recipe she knew because 'all a woman needs is to love

God and cooking'." Thinking of her past triggered other memories and she shivered as memories of cruelty and pain quickly started swamping her thoughts.

Val snorted. "Sounds like a gem."

With a laugh, Phoebe shook her head, clearing out the past. "Worked against her though when I started quoting scripture back at her."

Sharp looked at her with surprise. "You have a photographic memory? That's amazing."

Phoebe flushed and tried to wave off the compliment. "It's not as useful as you would think. When you know something, it's there right at your fingertips all the time. For me, it's like I have snapshots of everything tucked in my brain. If you ask me a question about, say, history, I can flip through my stored pictures of textbooks and probably find your answer. But that takes time and a lot of headaches."

"Still impressive." Sharp used his cornbread to clean up the last of his gravy.

"Even if it means I know that in the first hundred names in your phone contacts only fifteen of them are male?"

Sharp's jaw dropped, and Dozer burst out in a belly laugh.

"I mean thirty-three women in the A's and C's alone. But only two B's I wonder..."

Sharp grabbed her chin and dropped a scorching kiss onto her lips. Her thoughts shattered and she hummed happily. He pulled back and tapped her nose. "Cheeky. I like it."

Everyone was slowly breaking up, a few carrying the pie tins back to the kitchen. Phoebe couldn't wait to get Sharp alone. Val's earlier words echoed in her head and maybe she might be able to tell Sharp at least some of what she wanted. Maybe if she could get him to let go as he had before her freak out last night, it would be enough. Every woman had fantasies that never got fulfilled. It was a matter of managing expectations.

"We're taking off. Do you need help cleaning up?"

Phoebe bit back on a laugh at the look of aggravation on Dozer's face at his wife's words. He apparently had plans for his woman that didn't include dishes.

"No, we got most of the mess earlier. I just need to drop the pans in the dishwasher."

"Call me tomorrow." Val's voice was a giggle as Dozer hauled her away toward his bike. Phoebe leaned up against Sharp's warmth, enjoying the peace his presence filled her with. Her emotions had been on a roller coaster all day and knowing he chose to be next to her soothed some of her concerns he would avoid her because of all her drama.

He helped her gather up the pans and bring them inside. She was leaning over, loading the dishwasher, when warm hands ran up her thighs under her skirt.

"Have I told you how sexy you are in these pretty little dresses?"

Her body warmed to his light contact and her nipples tightened. They were alone in the kitchen. The idea that anyone could walk in at any moment had her pussy dampening. She pressed back with her hips as she placed the last pans in the dishwasher.

"No, but I'm glad you like them." She rubbed against him, swaying her hips, loving the feel of his hardening dick against her ass. His hands slid up from her hips, tracing along the undersides of her breasts.

"I think my little Pixie is feeling horny." His thumbs brushed over the front of her breasts, catching for a second on her hardened nipples.

She dropped her head back on his chest, arching into his touch. "Yes."

"Are you wet for me? I bet you are. I can almost feel your tight pussy wrapping around my cock, sucking it in like a hungry little mouth." His hands closed around her swollen breasts, sending shivers racing down her spine. People were talking right on the other side of the door. The idea of them knowing what they would be doing caused her thighs to tighten and her core to pulse in excitement.

"Fuck, I can smell your hot little pussy getting ready for me."

Before Phoebe could figure out what was happening, she was upside down over Sharp's shoulder and on her way into the pantry. His hands were up her skirt, resting against her ass, holding her in place. Her excitement was soaking through her panties and starting down her thigh.

Nothing was more empowering than knowing you affected the man you loved so much they gave in to their caveman urges. Loved? She had only known him for a few days, but this strong protective man had become the center of her thoughts. Could this intense attraction be more or was she deluding herself?

He placed her down on the cold, wood counter breaking her train of thought. "You deserve so much better, but I can't wait to get you home. You okay with this? No one will walk in here if they know what's good for them." He cupped her face, searching for agreement.

Phoebe hoped he didn't see the disappointment at not possibly getting caught in her eyes. She tried instead to put all her desire and need into her gaze. "I want you. Anything, anywhere, I need you."

Heat so intense she imagined she might catch fire, blazed in his eyes. "Oh, darlin', you aren't ready for that. You have no idea the dirty things I want. But for you, I can be patient."

She wanted to protest, tell him all the dark fantasies she had. But his hands were pushing down her top and exposing her breasts. When he pulled away, they were cupped by the material, held up like offerings to a dark god. A moment later, his lips were closing on her nipple and any protest she had was lost to moans of pleasure and frustration.

Sharp's gentle touch caused tiny, pleasurable waves to ripple across her body like a still pond tapped by a raindrop. But she needed something more to reignite the flame inside her. Teeth, pressure, something.

"More!" Her hands fisted in his hair.

"Fuck, baby. I need to taste you."

Not what she was thinking but Phoebe wouldn't complain. Sharp's tongue was magic. She licked her lips in anticipation. "Yes. Please."

He chuckled, pulling her swiftly to the edge of the table and flipping up her skirt. He grabbed the material of her panties by the front and pulled up. The action caused the fabric to bunch and pull against her ass and pussy sending a thrill shooting through her core. The cotton rubbed roughly against her clit as he slowly twisted his wrist back and forth, driving her body quickly to the edge of orgasm.

"You're drenched for me, baby. All that honey soaked right through this little cotton." She moaned as he pulled a little harder and squirmed trying to push herself closer to coming. "I don't like that there is something between me and my pussy."

"They keep me from making a mess whenever you're around." Phoebe was barely able to talk when his other hand started gently rolling her nipple between his fingers. She was so close to orgasming, but she couldn't step off that edge. Her back was still colored by bruises but moving barely caused her more than an ache. If he would pinch hard instead of gently rolling, she would fly apart. A small whimper escaped her throat.

"I like messes. I don't want you wearing these." He pulled harder, the sweet ache turning so much sharper. "Understand, Pixie?"

She pressed into his hand, begging for more pressure, anything to let her fly free. Sharp pulled up sharply as he rolled her nipple into a twist.

"Understand?"

Phoebe's whole body shook as the orgasm swept over her. She screamed her agreement to the ceiling, arching her back to increase the pleasure shattering her body.

"God, you are too fucking tempting." Her vision cleared just as he unzipped and pulled out his cock. She licked her lips, wanting to fill the aching between her legs. She watched him as he slid on a condom from his back pocket wishing, though it was stupid, she could feel him bare inside her. Sharp pushed her back down so she was flat on the table and thrust deep into her.

"So fucking perfect. You grip my cock so tight." He thrust and she wrapped her legs around his hips, trying to match his intensity.

"Please, Sharp. Fuck me harder," she screamed, as he slammed into her almost, but not entirely, bottoming out. She didn't care who could hear. All she could think about was the wild rhythm he was setting and trying to pull him deeper.

This position wasn't right for deep penetration, but the force and speed of his hips had the table slamming against the wall. Her orgasm was building hotter, burning her core but frustratingly out of reach.

"Sharp!" She gave a frustrated scream, and her hands came up to her breasts, grabbing and twisting her nipples in desperate need for just a bit more. The pain finally rocketed her over the edge, her growl almost primal in its tone.

The feeling of him slamming into her spasming pussy had lights flickering through her vision. She whimpered in overload, as she felt him thrust one more time into her and then felt his cock jerking from his orgasm inside her.

Sharp got them both cleaned up, marveling at how perfect his little Pixie was. She was still so delicate in so many ways, but when they were alone, she was like a raging bonfire warming the cold parts of his soul. He was pushing her too fast, but he couldn't help himself. Praying wasn't his usual choice of action, but he put a call out to the universe that he wouldn't break that light she held inside with his darker needs.

"With no panties, I am going to make quite a mess of your bike on the way home."

He loved that she called his place home. His stomach turned a bit when he realized he hadn't told Pixie she would be alone that night. Conference calls with national leadership took hours and often led to another few hours with Dozer, Hawk, Highdive, Tek and Max. If he bothered to go home, it would be for less than an hour, then he would have to head back to work at his garage.

"I should have told you earlier, darlin'. I'm not going to be at the house tonight."

"Oh. Okay." The way her voice grew small when seconds before it had been bright and laughing made him want to strangle the fuckers who made this meeting with National necessary.

"Look at me, Pixie." Her emerald green eyes shimmered, making him feel like he had kicked a puppy. No matter how much he wanted to, he didn't have time to comfort her. "You need to trust me to keep you safe. I have Club business tonight. No matter how much I want to be balls deep, making you scream my name, you have to understand the Club comes first."

He hated having to say it, but it was the reality of his world. Most Brothers didn't bother with relationships because it took an extraordinary woman to accept that fundamental truth. Instead of arguing or breaking down as Sharp expected, his words seemed to strengthen Pixie's spine.

"Of course, I know that. It's a few minutes' walk to your house. I'll be okay."

She amazed him again. Unable to resist, he bent down and kissed her, trying to show her with his actions how much her understanding meant to him. He tweaked her nose. "Dragon will be walking you home and staying on the couch. You don't go anywhere, even in the compound, without a prospect I pick or a Brother."

"Dragon?"

"Another prospect, but I've known him since my last year in the SEALs. I trust him, or I wouldn't ask him to watch over you."

Pixie smiled and the sight had his chest tightening. "I trust you."

Chapter 15

When polite fails, try a clue by four.

Sharp's evening was chaotic, but it looked like everyone was slowly working out solid contingencies. It bothered him that no one knew where to find Mitchel Thomas. He was rich, paranoid and, since he sold high-end slaves to the rich and twisted, either none of their contacts knew anything substantial or they were hiding what they knew.

The conference call broke up a little after two in the morning and Hawk had told Sharp and the other officers to give him a half hour. Then they would start making plans for what they could do locally without screwing the deals National had made. Mercenaries coming at them was a distinct possibility with the amount of money Caravaggio and Thomas could access. Hawk wanted to limit the likelihood their Dark Son Brothers could get caught by surprise. Detailed warnings and instructions had to be sent out by morning.

Grabbing a beer from the bar, Sharp noted, for a Thursday night, there were still plenty of Brothers and Club whores partying at such a late hour. Many of his Brothers worked night shifts and used the Clubhouse as a perfect place to wind down. Sharp was tempted to stop over at his house and see if Pixie was awake and find his own stress relief. Unfortunately, that would lead to being late. This was his woman's mess and as the VP he had to show more respect than that.

Sharp took a pull on his drink trying to hide a grimace at the tall, skinny, brunette headed his way. Tina was one of the more popular Club whores because she loved public sex and had a mouth like a vacuum. The woman's exhibitionist nature was the single reason Sharp had hooked up with her regularly before Pixie. He hated the drama she created and was often disgusted by her attempts to set Brothers against each other.

"Hey, Sharp, want me to help you relax?" Tina ran her hands up and down his chest as she rubbed against him.

Her teased up chestnut hair and oversized fake boobs no longer appealed to him. His dick only wanted the tiny Pixie he had at home and she was nowhere near ready for public games. Not wanting to get into it with her he didn't even look at her as he said, "Not tonight, Tina. I've got Club business." That phrase should have warned any Club whore or sweetbutt that the discussion was over.

Tina got a pouty look on her overblown lips, then a calculating look narrowed her eyes. "I know you have yourself a cute little house mouse. She doesn't need to know you're getting your real needs met by me and a few of my friends. I'll fuck you right here like we always do, and you'll be back to Club business in a much better mood."

The pushy slut wrapped herself around him like they were going to fuck with their clothes on. The smell of Tina's cloying perfume made Sharp fight back a gag. The crazy bitch laughed as he pushed her off him. The smug look in her eyes challenged him, as if she had a right to step up to a Brother. Her insulting Pixie had his blood running hot and all his patience evaporating.

Stepping forward quickly he wrapped his hand firmly around her throat and pinned her to the bar. "Club business means you back the fuck off, bitch. And even if I wasn't busy, I don't want your skanky twat or bullshit drama. That house mouse is my fucking woman, you will keep your tone respectful, and your games far away from her, or I will have you fucking banned from this Clubhouse. Are we clear?"

Instead of looking scared or repentant the insane woman smirked. "We'll see."

Infuriated she would outright disrespect him, he tightened his grip until she couldn't breathe. He tried to be as gentle as one could be while strangling another, but he didn't care she would have bruises tomorrow. He held still, not moving until the rebellion in her eyes was replaced by fear, and then terror. She started to fight, clawing at his hand and arm, looking around for help. He made sure to show no emotion. All she could see were his dead eyes that had ended more lives than she dreamed in her tiny little world.

"No one will stop me. None of them will save you. So, I'm going to give you one last chance. Am-I-clear?" He loosened his grip enough to let her breathe.

She gasped out sobs that did nothing to soften Sharp's mood. He shook her, and she shouted in a broken voice, "I understand."

Sharp let go and pushed away from the bar. His temper on the razor edge, he decided to wait out any additional time by Hawk's door. If anyone but his closest friends tried to talk to him right now, he wouldn't be responsible for his actions.

Phoebe weaved her way through the crowded Clubhouse trying her best not to draw attention to herself. Getting away before breaking down was her driving motivation. Why hadn't she stayed at the house? Why had she insisted on picking up the sexy clothes that Val had given her right now? One hour or more in either direction and her dreams and fantasies of being something special to Sharp would still be intact.

If she had just stayed home, happy with things as they were, she wouldn't have overheard what she had or seen them start to fuck right at the bar. A part of her had wanted to stay, rip that woman away, and take her place. The overwhelming shame that filled her was embarrassing.

As soon as she was outside she picked up her pace, heading towards the back of the compound and the privacy the trees would give her. She had been told the Dark Sons owned over a hundred acres of land but hadn't gotten the chance to explore or asked about anything but the main buildings. All that mattered to her now was privacy.

How could she have been so naive? Sharp had made her no promises. To him, what he did with that other woman would have no effect on their relationship, whatever it was. She had been right from the start that there was no way a broken woman like her who enjoyed cooking and cleaning could keep a man like that interested in the long term.

The trees weren't close enough, and Phoebe needed their solitude. She started running, ignoring that her poorly fitted ballet flats fell off her feet. The grass was cold, and she stretched out her stride. Running had been one of her favorite activities growing up. Since it didn't require any fancy equipment, none of her foster parents complained when she asked to join track. Luckily, she hadn't cared about owning the right shoes. The sport had given her freedom, allowing her to leave whatever home she was in for hours and lose herself in the rhythm of her muscles.

But she hadn't run for years, and she could already feel the burn and pull of her legs as they protested her movement. She didn't care, her body could hurt all it wanted, and she would revel in the feeling. The trail up ahead disappeared into the trees as she angled for it, anger and embarrassment pushing her into a sprint.

Not tonight, Tina... Cute little house mouse... Real needs... fuck you right here like we always do...

The words looped in her mind like a crappy song. He said not tonight. Which wasn't yes but it definitely wasn't a no. Tears were blinding Phoebe, and with the dark nighttime sky she could barely make out basic shapes. Rocks and sticks were cutting into her feet, but she didn't care. Within the privacy of the trees, she could cry. The pain in her feet, legs and lungs was punishment and reward. Out here alone she would purge her feelings and when she was done, she'd return home and accept her fate with grace.

She would find a way to accept him sleeping with other women. What other choice did she have? He had saved her and was her protector, not her boyfriend. Somehow, she would accept it. Pain shot through her ankle as she stepped into a ditch she couldn't see. Her whole body flew forward into the unforgiving ground.

Chapter 16

Don't discount friends in low places, they actually know what you are going through.

Before she landed, a strong arm wrapped around her waist pulling her up. She bounced as a large man jogged to a stop with her tucked under his arm like a football. She screamed, flailing out at the unfamiliar shape, trying to get away. He easily pinned her arms to her side as he set her down on her feet.

"Shh, Pixie. It's me. It's Dragon. Come on, Chiquita, I need you to calm down." The rich voice with the beautiful Spanish accent slowly broke through her panic.

She bent over with her hands on her thighs breathing hard from all the exertion. Only shadows were visible in the minimal evening light that filtered through the trees. "How did you find me?" she gasped, taking in deep breaths, trying to calm her racing heart. "How did you catch me so fast?"

Dragon chuckled, walked back a few feet and picked some things off the ground. At over 6'5" the large man was intimidating even when he was far away. His accent said he had grown up speaking Spanish, but his looks were more native American. He dropped the items he retrieved at Phoebe's feet, and she recognized them as her shoes.

"I was with you the whole time, *carina*. I didn't have trouble catching you. You have tiny legs. Adorable and sexy as they are. It was harder not to pass you then it was to keep up."

Phoebe wanted to grumble but, resisting huffing, she said, "My name is Phoebe."

Dragon gave her small smile. "*Carina* is a term of endearment, like sweetheart."

She tried to catch her breath. How could she have been so caught up in her thoughts she hadn't noticed being trailed by this man? She slipped her poor battered feet into the flats. Everyone was taller than she was and sometimes that bothered her. But he wasn't exaggerating, his stride could probably swallow hers. He stood completely unaffected by the run.

"You aren't even breathing hard." She was pouting, and that wasn't what she wanted.

He laughed, and it was a gorgeous sound, deep and unreserved. "Oh, *mamacita*, I have had to run much further with a pack on my back that weighed more than your entire body. I would be a very poor operator if I were winded right now."

She couldn't disagree with him, but her body was still pumping adrenaline, leaving her mind fuzzy. "Why did you follow me?"

"I am your bodyguard tonight, Pixie. Did you forget that when you tried to sneak away?"

Guilt gnawed at her. Phoebe had to admit she hadn't been able to think of much except her jealousy. If she had fallen and gotten hurt or lost, Sharp would have blamed Dragon. The prospect didn't deserve such thoughtlessness after he had been so accommodating to her tonight.

Phoebe hadn't been able to sleep and got the crazy idea to pick up the naughty lingerie Val had given her from the room at the Clubhouse so she could surprise Sharp. When she had asked to go, even though he had been settled in for the night, Dragon had gotten up and walked her to the Clubhouse, without a question or complaint.

"I wasn't sneaking." It wasn't a good excuse, but it was the truth.

Her bodyguard was silent for a few moments. "You really weren't, were you?"

"No."

"Did something upset you in the Clubhouse?"

"I would rather not talk about it." It was silly, and the Dark Son prospect would probably tell her what she already knew. Life wasn't fair, and nothing was free. She would have to accept the situation and find a way to keep her heart to herself or lose the first stable, safe home she had ever had. Was it so awful he wanted other women? Rage and jealousy flared in her stomach, and she had to push her thoughts in another direction.

"Let's get you back to the house, and if you feel you need some more nighttime running, we'll pick up a pair of shoes that won't fall off."

She gave a choked laugh and let him start them back towards Sharp's house. Neither of them speaking, it was too quiet for her to not get sucked back into her thoughts. She searched her mind for something to talk about.

"I've been able to figure out why most of the Brothers were given their road names but I'm curious about yours. Is your name Dragon because of your tattoos or do you have tattoos because of your name?"

In the evening dimness his small smile might have just been a trick of the light. "I have the tattoos because I've always had a fascination with dragons."

"So, you picked your road name?"

"No, but I had the nickname since I was a child. My real name is *Gabor*."

"That's beautiful. What language is it?"

"My mother says we can trace our blood back to ancient Mayan warriors. My name means bravest warrior. But to my sister, I was always *Kukulkan*."

Phoebe found herself relaxing, letting herself get lost in the conversation. "What does that mean?"

"There is a legend of a young boy who turned into a feathered serpent one day. His sister didn't care, she loved him so much she hid him away in a small cave and took care of him. Then one day he grew too big for the cave and had to leave his sister, but every summer he would shake the earth to let her know he was still alive and missed her. The great serpent's name was *Kukulkan*."

"A feathered serpent is a type of dragon?"

"Pretty much."

"I'm guessing the nickname dragon stuck because she took care of you?"

"No, she said I was always so big and clumsy that any time I came near the whole house would shake." Phoebe giggled, unable to help herself. What would it have been like to have siblings who teased and loved you no matter what? That kind of family was so foreign to her it was nearly a fantasy. She had seen glimpses of this within the Dark Sons, and maybe even felt that sense of belonging for a moment or two.

"Did seeing how wild our parties are bother you, Pixie?"

A short laugh exploded out of her lungs. She should have known he wouldn't give up trying to find out why she had run. "You mean the men getting blow jobs that were so bad they could continue to hold conversations? Or the women fucking men like they were one-dollar strippers giving a lap dance at the end of a long shift?"

"Yeah, that." Dragon's strangled, embarrassed tone made Phoebe smirk.

"No. They weren't terribly creative or even enthusiastic. I

have seen much worse. I've learned if something doesn't involve me directly, not to let it bother me."

"I'll let the Brothers know you think they are boring and unenergetic."

"Don't bother. If it makes them happy to have a woman bounce on their lap like a pogo stick, more power to them."

"If not that, what was it?"

Phoebe tried to imagine what she could say to him without opening herself up to ridicule. "Have you ever had instant chemistry with someone? The kind that overrides logic and consumes every image in your head, making clear thought impossible?"

"Once." Dragon's voice was quiet, tinged with sadness.

"What happened?"

"I got deployed. When I got back her phone was disconnected and I couldn't find her. But that has nothing to do with why you ended up running barefoot through the woods at two in the morning."

"Right. Well, Sharp does that to me, and I saw and heard something that shut down my clear thought. I won't do it again. I needed some time to think."

She could see Dragon's nod in the dim light, and she breathed a little easier. They walked for a few more minutes in comfortable silence, her mind trying to process all the possible effects what she saw could have on her life. When they were a few yards from Sharp's house, her subconscious took control of her mouth.

"What's a House Mouse?" Her question surprised her. Of all the different things she was considering, why had she chosen to ask him about that?

Dragon slowed his pace a bit and turned his head. His sharp features silhouetted against the night sky. "Why do you want to know?"

Phoebe waved a hand trying to brush the whole thing off.

"Val explained about Old Ladies, Sweetbutts, Club whores, and stuff; I heard the term and was curious. You don't have to answer. I can ask her."

She got the impression Dragon didn't believe her attempt at nonchalance, but he answered her question. "All those terms can mean slightly different things to different people. House Mouse is another one of those terms."

He was prevaricating which was annoying. "But what does it mean, generally?"

He looked up at the sky as though searching for inspiration. "A house mouse cooks, cleans, fucks, and basically does whatever a biker wants in return for a place to live and protection."

That is what she had signed up for but Dragon saying it made it sound lesser somehow then what she had built up in her mind. "I thought that was a sweetbutt."

"A sweetbutt might help out if asked or if she is hooked up with a specific man but they party with us." Dragon shrugged. "A house mouse is kept separate; she may be shared between a few Brothers, but she wouldn't come to the Clubhouse to party."

Phoebe's chest tightened. The idea she was to be kept away from the Club parties should comfort her, but instead it hurt. Maybe the bitch at the Clubhouse was more honest than she had guessed. They reached the front porch, but Phoebe wasn't ready to head in. She sat down on the steps, leaving Dragon plenty of room to join her if he wanted.

He sat next to her, nudging her knee with his. "I think maybe you're getting too caught up on words, *carina*. If you call a woman a whore, do you always think she gets paid for sex?"

"Of course not."

"*La misma cosa*. Same thing. If you make a woman your Old Lady, she becomes family. But what that means is different to each person." He stared out toward the distant lights of the Clubhouse. "In my experience, everything the Dark Sons do and are is about respect. Respect is a tricky thing. You can earn it through actions but what is more important is you have to give respect to earn it in return."

Phoebe smiled and looked down. "That's deep."

He ruffled her hair like she was a kid. She should be annoyed by the action, but she secretly liked it.

"Well, this wise old man is going to give you one more thing to think about, then you need to try and sleep."

A man who looked to be in his late twenties calling himself old amused her. She knew better than most that age wasn't a matter of how many days one lived, but what those days contained. He turned and looked her straight in the eyes. "Can you respect someone, Pixie, who doesn't respect themselves?"

His words cut right through the happy front and carefree persona she showed to the world to the black shivering freak underneath. Was her self-loathing so apparent to anyone who saw her? She knew she was undeserving of love, but Dragon's words gave her an odd sort of hope. She might not be able to be loved, but maybe she could earn respect.

Chapter 17

Assumptions make an ass out of you, not me.

Sharp ached to fall into bed, curled around Pixie, and get a few hours of sleep. The sky was already starting to lighten, and he needed to head into his shop by ten when it opened in case the Feds or Staties showed up with a warrant. Minetti might have said he was going to take care of it, but Sharp couldn't risk not being there and giving a dirty cop the opportunity to plant evidence. Sharp's nerves were frayed thin by the tense talks with the National officers, losing his temper with Tina, and planning contingencies in case Minetti failed to produce. Having to eat Caravaggio's insult had every Brother pissed.

Dragon was sprawled on Sharp's couch when he walked in. The Prospect's eyes opened at the sound of the front door closing.

"Thanks for watching over her. Puck will switch off with you in the morning."

Sharp continued towards the stairs, but Dragon's words

pulled him up short. "Hey, VP. You should know there's a potential minefield up there."

Sharp ran his hand through his hair, not sure if he could deal with one more thing going wrong. "She pissed I wasn't home by midnight or some shit?" Pixie had seemed to understand and accept he had to stay for Club business, but women were often touchy when they came in second place to the MC.

Dragon looked surprised. "No. I meant whatever happened between you two at the Clubhouse last night freaked her out."

"I haven't seen her since dinner." Sharp ran a hand through his hair again, tired and not needing one more thing to go wrong. "Wait, she was at the Clubhouse last night?"

"Yeah, she asked to pick up some of her shit from the room she had been staying in. I waited by the door for her and when she came out—well I've seen guys shot who looked less wounded."

"Fuck, what did she see? I was planning on warning her before letting her hang out with us after hours."

"I thought that too, but apparently she finds the sexual appetites of the Brothers uninspired." Sharp had to smile at that. His little innocent Pixie had a dirty girl under all that sparkle. "She did ask me what a house mouse was though. Maybe one of the bitches said something to her."

The blood drained out of Sharp's face. As far as he knew none of his Brothers kept a house mouse – the term more an insult than anything else – but he had heard Tina use it last night. "What time was this?"

"Around two. That is a quality woman you have upstairs if you are thinking of making her a house mouse then–"

"She is my woman. And she will be my Old Lady. Fuck, what did you tell her a house mouse was?"

"Well I didn't tell her that it is a bitch not even important enough to meet your Brothers, but with enough skills you keep her locked in your house feeding and fucking her as long as she does whatever you ask." Dragon raised an eyebrow. "Pretty sure that wouldn't have been well received. One of the bitches at the Club must have been taunting her."

With the timing and the questions, Sharp was pretty sure his Pixie had seen his confrontation with Tina. He could imagine how him strangling a woman against a bar must have terrified her. He would like to say he usually had a better temper and the incident was a fluke, but he would be lying. Only his closest friends and family were safe when he lost his shit. Was she upstairs right now, terrified he would hurt her if she said something wrong?

"Tina was playing her usual games last night."

"Pixie saw you fucking her?"

"No. She said some shit, and I lost my temper."

"That makes more sense. Well, that should be easier to explain. Women forgive us when we're stupid, but not if we fuck around."

Sharp nodded his agreement, lacking the energy to finish the conversation. He walked up the stairs, leaving his Brother to get back to sleep. When he opened the door, the sight of Pixie stopped his heart for a minute.

She was curled up like a naked little kitten on top of the covers, right in the center of his king-sized bed. Her pale skin and golden blonde hair looked ethereal in the dim light coming from the window with the dark blue backdrop of his comforter. She had a pillow balled up against her stomach, hiding her beautiful breasts from his eyes. She looked so utterly at peace. Sharp couldn't wake her.

He didn't have the mental or physical energy to reassure her at that moment and figured it would be best if he got at least a few hours' sleep before trying to explain his actions and make sure she understood he would never hurt her.

Sharp could feel someone watching him as his phone alarm dragged him from sleep. Exhausted, he had chosen to sleep in the guest room rather than risk waking her and having to deal with the fallout from last night. Hopefully, the four hours of sleep he had gotten would be enough because Pixie had apparently chosen to make sure he couldn't sneak away without talking.

She sat cross-legged on the floor in a stunning mint green sundress that made her look like the embodiment of spring. Her expression was painfully nervous, and she fiddled with the edges of her skirt. Sharp wanted nothing more than to pull her on top of him and have her ride him until her light erased all the dark places in his mind. Unfortunately, stalling would only drag out the pain, but he could delay a bit.

"Not cooking breakfast at the Clubhouse today?"

Pixie looked confused for a moment then shook her head. "It's nine o'clock. I had breakfast out by seven, and there's plenty of bread and sandwich fixings ready for lunch. Hawk said I should do dinner Monday through Thursday and that breakfast and lunch would be a waste of time on weekends since the Brothers won't be awake and there is the family barbeque on Sundays."

"He's right."

An awkward silence fell between them. Sharp thought he should either speak up or get up and get ready for work, but all he could do was stare at her beautiful hair glowing in the morning light.

His woman straightened her shoulders and found the courage he lacked. "Why did you sleep in here last night?"

"I didn't get in until five, and you were sleeping so peacefully I didn't want to wake you."

She nodded as if to herself. Her cute little teeth bit into the corner of her lip, broadcasting that she struggled with uncomfortable thoughts.

"Why were you watching me sleep?" Sharp tried to make his tone teasing, hoping maybe he could undo some of the damage his violent act last night had caused on his delicate girl.

"We need to talk, but I didn't want to wake you, so I waited."

The words put a bitter taste in his mouth, even though they were true. Pixie needed to understand while he would talk and try to ease her mind, she was his and that wasn't going to change. Sharp sat up, the comforter dropping to his waist. He didn't sleep in clothes unless he had to and the spark of hunger in Pixie's eyes told him not all was broken by what she had seen last night.

He patted the bed next to him. "If we're going to talk, sit up here with me."

She stood, her bare little feet making no noise as she crossed the floor. She perched on the edge of the bed, barely sitting. Sharp tried to run a hand down her arm in a comforting gesture, but she scooted over to avoid the touch.

Fuck, she was terrified of him and, while he understood, it pissed him off. "You don't have to be scared of me, darlin'. I would never hurt you."

"I'm not scared." Her quick breaths and clipped tone told him a different story.

"Then why did you pull away?" He tried to control his anger, but the fact Tina could ruin something so critical with her bullshit infuriated him. The more he went over the previous night, the more he believed she had seen Pixie and set up the whole thing to play some sick game.

"I need to talk to you, ask you some things, but when you touch me I go all fuzzy, and all I want to do is touch you back."

Her words blunted his anger. He loved knowing he affected her as much as she did him. "You can ask me anything, darlin'."

He watched the soft green fabric of her dress rise and fall

over her beautiful breasts as she took a few deep breaths. "I know you were with another woman last night." Her words were like ice water on his thoughts. Every one of his muscles tightened in fury. Pixie didn't notice because she continued. "I would like... if possible... in the future... I would prefer to be present when you are with another woman." She finally looked at him and read the obvious anger in his glare. "Or not." Her body shook with fear, and for once Sharp was damn glad for it.

"You know I was with another woman last night?"

She nodded, her eyes glistening with unshed tears. "I wasn't trying to spy, but I saw you when I was at the Clubhouse."

"What exactly did you see?"

"Not much. I didn't want to be in the way and I wasn't sure what you would want, so I left."

A part of Sharp was relieved she hadn't seen what followed, but he was angry she believed he would do that to her. It was irrational. There were no promises between them, and only a week of history to go by. But if she felt anything close to what he did, she wouldn't easily give him up to another woman.

"Do you want me to invite you to watch or do you want to participate?" His voice had gone tight as his feelings ate away at him.

"Whatever you want. I know I'm not enough to keep a man like you satisfied. If that means sharing, then... Okay."

"A man like me? Does this mean you'll invite me when you're with other men?"

"No! I mean I would prefer it if you didn't share me with other men. I don't want anyone else." Her words and the single tear that dripped down her cheek barely softened his rage.

"You prefer. Really? Does the idea of me fucking another woman while you watch turn you on? Should I order her to eat you out while I fuck her until she screams into your pussy?"

Sharp had seen a few Brothers take on several women at once, and he had even participated in a few gangbangs, but that wasn't his thing. He liked fucking in public, watching while women wanted to be his partner and men wanted a piece of the woman he was claiming. He loved rough, wild, out-of-control sex in as many places and positions as he could think up. But the idea of sharing Pixie with another woman or man had red filling his vision.

"If that's what you want. I'll do it."

"I asked if it turned you on?"

"Sure." Her word was slow and stuttered, the lie obvious.

He grabbed her and dragged her face down over his lap, flipping her skirt up. He took a brief moment to enjoy the fact she had followed his request to go without panties. Then he spread her legs, running two fingers between her folds.

"Just what I thought. You are a little liar. Dry as a desert."

"No. I'm just nervous about our talk."

His hand came down on her ass in a slap that echoed in the room. "Don't fucking lie to me, darlin'. I will put up with a lot of things, but that isn't one of them." He smacked her several more times, loving the way her skin reddened, showing his handprint, and the way she wiggled against his cock, the thin, soft cotton of her dress a single piece of fabric between them. He emphasized every word with a spank. "Do you want me to fuck other women?" He made sure the last blow was hard enough she would be feeling it all day if she sat down.

"No!" Her answer was a screaming sob. The sound caused his dick to pulse against her stomach in arousal. He traced gentle fingertips over the red marks his hand had made.

"Better. Stand up with your arms up."

Sharp was a selfish prick. His point had been made. He should pull her into his arms and talk lovingly to her about the misunderstanding then make gentle love, but that wasn't what he wanted. After the stress of the previous day, he needed a wild release, and she was going to give it to him.

When she stood as he had instructed, Sharp pulled Pixie's dress up over her head tossing the material off to the corner.

"Hands behind your head."

She laced her fingers behind her head, pushing out her breasts just like he wanted. He sat on the edge of the bed, tracing the curves of her breasts, trailing his nails along the edges of her nipples, watching them tighten in response.

"Now what we have here is a misunderstanding." He took her nipples between his fingers, rolling them in alternating rhythms. "What you saw was a Club slut talking shit and trying to take something that wasn't hers."

Sharp watched as Pixie's eyes glazed over and soft sounds of need came out of her parted lips. He wanted to see his mark on her breast and focus her attention back on the crucial conversation. He slapped one breast, then the other her tiny cries of pain and pleasure causing his dick to throb.

Her legs pressed together and he growled out. "Legs apart." She gave a small whine of protest before widening her stance. "Now whose tits are these?" He gave each one a sharp slap.

"Yours."

"And whose pussy is this?" He slapped her hard between her legs, loving the wet sound that told him she loved this as much as he did.

"Yours."

He stroked his cock, watching her eyes follow his every movement. "And if she is very good and doesn't make assumptions, who is the only fucking woman who gets to play with this cock?"

Pixie's eyes shot up and locked with Sharp's, desire and hope so obvious he almost couldn't take it.

"Me?"

"That's fucking right." He stopped stroking his cock and ran his hand through the wetness that he could see glistening between her legs. Her clit was poking out, begging for attention, but he teasingly circled it slowly with one hand. With the other hand, he started gently rolling a nipple, an evil thought playing in his mind. He gradually increased the motions of both hands, watching as she struggled not to move and push against him.

"My girl is wet like the rainforests now. If you see something that bothers you or makes you question us, you ask me. Don't assume you know what's in my mind."

Pixie struggled, her head shaking back and forth. "You said not tonight. I thought that meant... ahhh."

"Don't you come yet, darlin', our talk isn't over."

Pixie bit hard on her lip, her muscles tightening. Sharp didn't let up circling her throbbing bud, twisting her nipple with increasing speed.

"That was just words to make an annoying cunt go away as fast as possible." He pressed down a little harder on his next circle. "Who do you belong to, Pixie?"

"You, oh God, Sharp, you! I can't, I'm gonna..."

"Who do I belong to?"

Her breath caught and tears flowed out of her eyes in beautiful trails. "Me."

"Come for me, beautiful." Sharp pinched down on her clit and nipple, watching how the pleasure and pain shattered her apart. Her screams were music he knew echoed even outside his house. When her knees started to buckle, he couldn't hold back anymore.

He tossed her face down on the bed, spreading her thighs with his own. He wrapped a hand in her hair and without even letting her get to her knees slammed himself deep inside. The walls of her pussy were still spasming in orgasm and he let out his own shout of pleasure as the tip of his dick slammed into her cervix.

Fuck, she was so tight and hot, the cream of her excitement against the bare skin of his cock was beyond amazing. He had never ridden a woman bareback in his life, but now that he had felt the sweet velvet of Pixie's pussy, he didn't think he could have anything between them again.

"You're mine!" He pulled up on her hair, forcing her to arch her back as he fucked her as hard as he could. He didn't care that his hand would leave bruises as it pinned her hips to the mattress. All he cared about at that moment was owning her entirely, because she already fucking owned him.

Chapter 18

Girl Power - (Adj) The feeling of having a stiletto stuck up your ass sideways.

Happiness fizzed through Pixie's veins, making her giggle with delight. Sharp's words made her able to let go of the old Phoebe and believe she could be anyone she wanted. And she wanted to be Pixie. Her arms remembered the comforting feel of him carrying her like something precious. The way he gently cleaned her up, the perfect balm to her nervous soul.

Her fear of being around his Brothers wasn't going to disappear tomorrow but for the first time she did believe it would happen one day. When Sharp went to work, she fell back asleep and got six hours of the best rest she could remember. She had cleaned up the house, then headed over to the Clubhouse to clean up breakfast and lunch.

Sharp wouldn't be home until after seven, so she made herself a sandwich and wondered what to do.

Pixie turned on her stool to the familiar voice at her back.

"I knew that dress would look good but honey, you look sweeter than a mint julep in July."

"Val!" Pixie turned, happy to see her friend and ran to give her a hug.

Val was dressed in tight jeans with rhinestones down the sides and a halter-top that said: 'Support your local Dark Sons MC' and a cute black leather cut like the men wore.

"You look like a mare who broke out and found herself a stallion."

Pixie blushed. "What are you doing here?"

"All right, I won't pry. Dozer wanted to hang out for a spell, so I came with him. A few of us old ladies still come on party nights though we don't stay too late. Why don't I introduce you around some?"

The idea of going out to the party without Sharp had her pulse racing, but she swallowed it down. "That would be great."

When Val turned around, on her cut was a patch much like Sharp's, but hers read 'Property of Dozer Dark Sons MC'. The patches on the Brother's cuts were fascinating, and she often wondered what some of them meant, but this one was self-explanatory. Many women would feel uncomfortable being called property, but to Pixie, it was a declaration of both love and protection.

Sharp had talked about putting his patch on her back when he tucked her back into bed; she hoped this is what he meant. Val took her around the room, introducing her as Sharp's girl. She hated how nervous she felt around the guys who were nothing but polite. The few old ladies she met were a hoot, as Val said.

She sat on a couch with Val and two other old ladies, listening to their stories as they tried to one-up each other with crazy shit they'd seen. Anna, a cute Asian looking woman who was Tick's Old Lady, was telling a story about one of the Brothers getting drunk and swearing he could break dance. She was in the middle of describing how he had thrown out his back in spectacular fashion when he had tried to do a handstand, when Maria hissed, "Damn, *Mamacita*, what did you do to piss off Tina? She's looking at you like you stole her favorite vibrator."

Pixie looked in the direction Maria nodded and the woman from last night was glaring death daggers her direction. She wore what might generously be called a bikini top on her obviously fake double Ds. Her ass cheeks peeked out below a scrap of leather that had probably been designed for a child. Pixie rolled her eyes and contained the urge to flip off the woman before turning back to the group.

"Sharp turned her down last night. Guess she isn't happy." Pixie shrugged, pretending it hadn't hurt. It had probably been a good thing in hindsight. If not for that slut getting overly aggressive, she wouldn't have had the best sex in her life this morning.

"That's a polite way to say it." Anna snorted.

"Spill girl. You know you can't clam up like that." Val's eyes sparkled, and Pixie had to laugh at the eager look on Val and Maria's faces.

Anna leaned forward as if about to impart the secret of life. "Tick told me when she wouldn't get off of him, Sharp pinned her by the throat to the bar until she was close to passing out and threatened to ban her if she tried that shit again."

Pixie wasn't proud of the fact he had done that, but the image made her wet and, without panties on, she couldn't deny it.

"Damn, Pixie. I'm glad my *Papi* is more the cuddly type than wild man."

Val choked on her beer, laughing. "You're talking about Smoke, right? The man who got his nickname because, after the explosion is over, all that's left of his enemies is smoke."

Maria waved it off with a gesture. "Men and their tall tales. He is just *Papi* to me."

Anna smiled. "And you love being his bratty *Chiquita*."

They all burst into laughter at the mock indignant look on Maria's face. The four of them talked and told Phoebe about the Sunday barbeque where everyone brought their family and spent the afternoon bonding. Pixie agreed to bring cookies and make lots of her French bread. They all decided to meet up and introduce her to everyone she needed to know.

"Well, dolls, it's ten o'clock. Time for prissy old ladies to leave so the whores can play," Anna teased.

Pixie was shocked at how late it had gotten and looked around. Sharp was still nowhere to be seen. Her current bodyguard, Puck, was drinking a beer at the bar and talking to a few Brothers she recognized. She hugged the women, whom she hoped would be new friends, goodbye, and headed over to Puck, planning to ask him if he knew where Sharp was. Pixie barely managed not to go sprawling when a shoulder knocked into her with such force, she was afraid it might leave a bruise. She was going to apologize when she caught sight of the smug look on bikini bitch's face.

Before she could curse the woman out, Puck was between the two of them.

"You think that's a smart move, Tina?" Puck crossed his arms, creating a wall of muscle, completely blocking the woman from Pixie's sight.

"What? It was an accident."

Pixie snorted but decided the woman wasn't worth creating a scene. She placed a hand on her bodyguard's back. "Come on, Puck. I'm fine."

"Yeah, Puck, wouldn't want Sharp's little Pixie getting a hangnail."

No matter how much she wanted to rip into Tina, she headed off towards the bar, figuring Puck would follow. She walked behind the bar because it would offer her the illusion of safety. Only prospects who were tasked with bartending went back there, so Tina wouldn't dare cause issue. She found her hidden six-pack of water in one of the refrigerators and pulled out a bottle.

She chugged down the entire thing, letting the water calm and cool her down.

"Damn, girl, you swallow like a pro."

Pixie recognized Max's teasing tone and turned toward him. Several Brothers were watching her curiously, and with the surface between them, she didn't feel her usual fear. She didn't know if it was her newfound confidence or the adrenaline from her encounter with Tina, but she decided to tease back for once. "It's a matter of opening your throat and letting it slide right down." She added a wink, feeling a rush of power. "Plus the practice not to gag."

Several of the Brothers chuckled, and Max choked a bit on his beer. "Sounds like you have hidden talents other than cooking."

"Wouldn't you like to know."

"You want a beer, *Chica*?" Dragon was the prospect currently working the bar, and he appeared amused by her presence behind it.

"I'm good." Pixie held up her empty water bottle.

"You don't drink, Pixie?" Puck seemed surprised.

"Not anymore. Besides, I don't turn twenty-one for another few weeks."

That had all the Brothers laughing and teasing her about being such a good girl.

"You got my woman working behind the bar now? Can't you assholes do anything yourselves?"

"Sharp!" Pixie scrambled up onto the bar, launching herself at him with a happy squeal. He caught her in his arms and kissed her smiling lips.

"It has been one hell of a day, darlin', but for a greeting like that I would do it all again."

Pixie was happy he was finally here and was mildly disappointed when he lowered her to her feet rather than carrying her off to somewhere private. She rested her head against Sharp's chest, soaking in his warmth. He exchanged joking greetings with the Brothers around her. It was fascinating how the Brothers deferred to him; you could tell he was held in deep respect.

She looked up at his incredible blue eyes and had to hold in a sigh of contentment. The world could be going crazy around them, but one look in his eyes and she felt the peace of safety.

"Sorry I was late, darlin'. Had some unwelcome auditors from the state and I couldn't leave until they were done."

"I thought Minetti was supposed to take care of that?" Max didn't look happy, and neither did Sharp.

"So did I."

"I'll let Hawk know." The Road Captain got up from his seat and headed towards the back.

Pixie was a little confused by the sudden high level of tension in the air and hoped that whatever this audit found it didn't cause Sharp any significant issues. "I understand. I hung out with some of the old ladies for a bit then went back there to wait." She waved to the back of the bar.

"You have fun with the old ladies?" Sharp smiled down.

"Val is always fun, and Anna and Maria told some of the funniest stories about your Brothers."

"They're some of the good ones. Glad you weren't bored." He leaned down and gave her a kiss that had her swaying against him. She wanted to climb back up his body and give him a proper welcome home, but he broke the kiss when a few men gave some enthusiastic catcalls. He wrapped an arm around her neck and leaned in to whisper in her ear, "I have to check in with some of the Brothers and then talk to Hawk for a few, but after that, I am going to take you home and fuck you until your legs don't work and your throat is sore from screaming."

Pixie's body heated and the dampness of her arousal started to leak out of her pussy. Right now, she would take a quickie against the wall if it would ease the ache forming inside her but for Sharp, she would wait however long he needed. "Yes, please. Do you want me to wait behind the bar?"

"No. I think I'll keep you by my side and make my Brothers jealous that I'm the one who gets to take you home and flip up that cute little skirt. Every one of them will wish it was their cock that was going to be sinking in that perfect pussy of yours."

From the growing bulge in his pants, she could see Sharp's arousal matched her own. "Sounds like a plan. But you are going to need to rethink this no panty policy. I can already feel myself dripping on my thigh."

"Fuck, darlin', you are killing me." He nipped her ear. "I will be as quick as I can."

Sharp led her through the crowds, his arm wrapped around her shoulders, keeping her close. Val had been right. The party had swung into full gear after they left. Pixie nodded politely to all the Brothers Sharp stopped to talk to, but her real attention was on the uninhibited partying.

It was like a mix of a frat party and a strip club where sex was on the menu. Mostly people drank, talked, and played pool, but at least half the women were dressed like they had a set on a pole coming up any minute.

Unenthusiastic blowjobs seemed to be the activity of the

hour while one woman getting fucked against a pool table drew more complaints about blocking shots than encouragement. Pixie was tempted to see what Sharp would do if she dropped to her knees and showed the room what a little enthusiasm could bring to the party.

She was pretty sure he wouldn't be able to continue discussing a custom shock job for a bike if she pulled out all the stops. Her daydream was spoiled when she caught sight of Tina rubbing up against a man right in Sharp's line of sight. Her tits had escaped the tiny fabric of her top, and she was working the guy behind her like a lap dance pro. The slut's eyes though were all for Sharp, hungry and inviting as she rubbed down her body and moaned.

Pixie glanced up at Sharp and smirked because he wasn't even noticing the show put on for his benefit. He was focused on the conversation in front of him. Pixie looked back at the pathetic woman and knew at some point she was going to have problems. Tina had noticed her show was having no effect and had switched to trying to kill Pixie with a look.

A little while later Sharp took her outside where even more Brothers were drinking and smoking. The mood outside was more relaxed, the music muffled and the women scarcer.

"Hey, Sharp, Pixie," Tek called over to them. The Brother's blond hair, fancy haircut and sleek good looks made him seem odd in his biker gear. She didn't doubt he was one of the Brothers, but something about him shouted boardroom instead of brawl. Like Dragon, his presence comforted her and made her feel safe.

"Hey, Tek." Sharp greeted him with a handshake and half hug that seemed standard among tough men everywhere.

"Sorry, Pixie. I need to steal your man for a minute for Club business. Promise to bring him right back."

Sharp walked her over to an empty picnic table and pressed her up against it. "Wait here for me, darlin'. I'll be a few minutes, then I'll find Hawk so I can get down to doing all the things I've imagined for the last hour." He ran a thumb over her lips, pressing his obviously hard dick against her. Pixie imagined what he wanted to do with her mouth and couldn't wait.

"I'll be right here."

Tek and Sharp stepped away from the side of the Club-house. She could still see him and the other Brothers who joined him, but couldn't hear anything that was said.

Could it have been less than a week ago that she had been ready to kill herself with a stranger's gun? Life had gone from hopeless to full of so many possibilities in such a short time, it felt like a dream. Let other girls dream of princes or rich wimpy men who gave them flowers. Pixie loved these rough men and their violent world that could keep her safe from the worst monsters.

Maybe Sharp would know a way she could help the other victims of Mitchel. She knew a lot about his organization, there had to be some way to find someone who could do some-thing about it. She would think on it. Sharp had never brought it up again so he must have done something. There was no way Mitchel would give up the money she represented. But if she brought up her captivity, she was afraid he would go back to treating her like a fragile doll. She would ask Val the next time they were together.

"Well if it isn't Shushie homemaker all by her lonesome." Tina's words were slurred from alcohol and filled with venom. Pixie wondered how much and how fast the woman had been drinking to get this tanked in under an hour. The woman was striding over with way too much purpose for Pixie's comfort. Trailing behind her were differing versions of brunette stripper Barbie who appeared as drunk as Tina and eager for a confrontation.

Pixie looked around. While a few Brothers were looking in

their general direction, no one from Sharp's group was, and none seemed to be paying attention.

"Go away, Tina." Sharp wouldn't want her to make a scene, but it was hard to keep her temper.

"You don't tell me what to do, bitch. I've been part of Dark Sons for years. No muffin baking little girl is going to act high and mighty like she's got a magic cunt or something."

Her friends laughed, and Pixie gritted her teeth as the conversations around them quieted and heads turned their way.

"You're embarrassing yourself. Just go back inside and play who wants to be my stripper pole. I'm sure you'll have plenty of volunteers." Her fists were clenching at the effort not to raise her voice to match the drunk bitch in front of her.

"You know I never thought I'd see the day when the Dark Sons would be pussy whipped, begging for a woman's cookies. It's pathetic." As the meaning of Tina's words sunk in, her friends stepped back with nervous looks on their faces. The drunk bitch herself didn't hesitate though. "But I know what they really want. When Sharp remembers he's a man and wants a real woman to fuck him dirty like he wants, he'll be fucking back with me and you will be nothing more than a weekend memory."

"You know what, bitch?" Despite all her effort to stay calm, she was now yelling. "Maybe it isn't my baking that's the issue. Maybe he got tired of fucking your overstretched cunt that's been used by so many men it should have a public health warning on it!"

"Cunt!" Tina lurched forward.

Pixie had become too used to being safe at the compound, so she didn't have time to react when Tina backhanded her. The strength behind it was surprising and sent Pixie sprawling to the dirt.

She blinked dust and dirt out of her eyes as rage tore

through her system. She wasn't Suzie homemaker; she was a fucked up foster kid who had spent nearly ten years going to therapy for her uncontrolled rage. The only good fucking thing that had come out of those sessions had been years of martial arts training to help channel her energy. This bitch was about to find out how well she'd learned those lessons.

Chapter 19

It is the quiet ones you have to watch out for.

"Sorry to pull you away from your girl but I have news I don't think you want her hearing." Tek walked Sharp over to the side of the Clubhouse. Hawk, Max and Smoke were waiting there all looking grim.

Sharp made sure he could still see Pixie before turning to his Brothers. "What's up?"

Hawk looked ready to chew someone up. "Minetti got the feds to back down but says the Staties are going to take a few days."

"I figured that when they showed up at the garage with a warrant today and trashed my shop. Does this mean the deal with Minetti is off?" Sharp sounded eager but he was pissed and wanted to take his frustration out on the rat who had started this mess.

"Not exactly. Breaker says if anything comes of this, we take out Caravaggio as payment. But until then we hold off."

Sharp smacked the corner of the building in frustration.

"All respect to our National Pres, but it isn't his shit he had to watch get tossed and sit on his hands like a pansy."

Hawk looked him in the eyes before talking. "We hold for now. We all know that moron is going to do something else, then we'll have the all-clear to erase him."

"Caravaggio isn't our only problem," Tek broke in. The ex-ranger didn't often come to party nights. The fact he was here gave Sharp a feeling of dread. Tek was a loyal Brother but he spent the majority of his days and nights as CEO of one of the fastest growing security technology companies in the US. He was a fantastic hacker in his own right but with the resources of his contacts and company, he made sure that Dark Sons were digitally secure from even the best hackers and better informed than most government agencies.

"What do you know?" Hawk asked.

"I still haven't been able to find even a single digital foot-print of Mitchel Thomas. The name has to be a front and a good one. But an hour ago the username 'Master_MT' put out a ten-thousand-dollar contract for the capture of your woman. Specified no permanent damage. The contract contained pictures and the address of the Clubhouse." Sharp had never seen his Brother so on edge.

"Shit!" Sharp bit off. Ten thousand wouldn't bring out any big players with the Dark Sons address attached but it would bring the stupid. He also had the feeling if the number got much higher, they might get some serious mercenaries trying their luck.

Tina's shrill, drunk voice throwing insults from somewhere nearby disturbed the quiet night and Sharp regretted not banning the woman last night. All he needed was to have to deal with some drama that bitch drummed up on top of every-thing else. He turned and stilled as he and all the Brothers around them heard her call them a bunch of pussies.

When his little Pixie's elevated voice was added to the mix, he spun around and realized he had been so distracted, he had let that bitch get near his woman.

Smoke chuckled. "Your woman has a mouth–"

All the Brothers let out a growl as Tina backhanded Pixie to the ground. Sharp moved, but not fast enough. His forward steps were halted by shock when Pixie pushed off the ground and, with three quick strikes, had the other woman face down in the dirt, her tiny shoe at her neck.

"Holy shit. Pixie's got some moves. That was one of the best axe kicks I've ever seen." Max's voice rang out clear against the silent night.

But Pixie wasn't done. Covered in dirt, her dress slightly ripped and a tiny bit of blood on her lip, she screamed down at the woman she held pinned. "I'm more than a cook you used up cunt! I'm whatever Sharp or the Dark Sons need. That's what it means to be a real fucking woman. So, if they need cookies, I'll ask what kind, and if Sharp needs someone to swallow every inch of his cock or ride him like a championship cowgirl in the middle of the Club, I'll say yee-haw, bitch."

Pixie pulled back her foot, obviously intending to kick Tina in the face. Sharp moved, amusement and shock warring for supremacy in his emotions. He had to stop her though, because there was one rule when it came to fighting at the Clubhouse: only family could fight. He hadn't thought he would need to warn Pixie and since he had been stupidly waiting for the family barbeque on Sunday to give her his cut in some romantic gesture, she wasn't family yet. Punishment for hangers-on fighting could be anything the Pres decided, but usually included at least a temporary ban.

Tina had started the fight but instead of waiting for help that was feet away, his Pixie had kicked some serious ass. Sharp caught his warrior woman around the waist and pulled her back, so her kick connected with nothing but air. Her elbow caught him in the ribs with a good sharp jab, making him laugh. If she had any muscle or weight behind the blow, it might have hurt.

"Calm down, darlin'. It's me."

She continued to scream and fight, and Sharp had to struggle to contain her without hurting her.

"Damn, Sharp. You sure that's your Pixie? Sounds more like a Banshee." Max's comment wasn't far off the mark. What had happened to the sweet, shy woman who opened up under his touch? Was it wrong he found this hellcat sexy? Sharp slapped her ass hard trying to break through whatever panic had seized her mind.

Pixie froze mid-thrash and looked around. "Sharp? Oh, I am so sorry. Did I hurt you?"

Sharp laughed harder as did many of the Brothers who were now surrounding the scene taking in the evening's entertainment.

Tina tried to scramble off the ground, her outfit no longer covering anything significant. "I'll fucking kill you!"

Hawk grabbed the drunk woman by the hair and hauled her to her feet. No amusement showed anywhere in his stance or expression.

"Hawk, sshhhe started it," the woman slurred.

"So, you're a liar as well as a stupid cunt." He threw her to the ground. "You stay there on your knees, bitch, until I'm ready to deal with you." He turned to the Dark Sons gathered around. "She moves, one of you shoot her."

Several guns were pulled and readied, but from the stunned expression of a woman quickly sobering up, Sharp didn't think she would move. Hawk walked over towards them. Pixie squirmed against his chest like she was trying to burrow through his chest and escape. But since he held her suspended off the ground, her efforts were useless.

Hawk looked at the woman in his arms who had finally gone still. "Can you stand, Pixie?"

Pixie nodded and Sharp put her down. He hated having to step back from her, but his Pres needed to make an example of both women. The common punishment for bitches fighting was cleaning duty or a fine. Either way, she would survive. Embarrassed but intact. He doubted his Pres would ban her with her life in danger.

Pixie stood, shaking and covered in dirt, but didn't flinch when Hawk took her chin in his hand.

"Looks like you have a small cut on your lip. Any other injuries?"

"No, Sir." Pixie's voice was so small, it reminded him of a small child. Sharp wanted to wrap her up in his arms, but couldn't.

"Tell me what happened." Hawk's voice held no sympathy or emotion other than the slight heat of anger.

Pixie told the story quickly with very few details. Hawk nodded, glaring at the woman cradling a limp arm in the dirt.

"Pixie might not know the rules, Tina, but you fucking do. Only family can fight on Club property. Or did you think we were too pussy whipped to enforce our rules?" His last sentence came out with ice on every word.

"No, Hawk, I didn't mean... I just was saying Sharp–"

"I never thought I'd see the day when Dark Sons were pussy whipped. I believe those were your exact words."

"I'm sorry, Hawk. I didn't mean it."

"You were banned from the Clubhouse for life the minute you disrespected the Club. But for fighting, lying, and being the worthless piece of trash you are, you no longer have a job, an apartment, or the right to breathe anywhere we claim. You have one week to get the fuck out of our territory, or you won't like what happens to you."

"You can't!"

"We own the Club you work in, the building you rent from, and no one will be stupid enough to cross us for a used-up cunt like yours. And if you decide to try and cause more trouble, leaving the country won't even be enough to hide you from me. Am I clear?"

Tina was sobbing, her words unintelligible, but she nodded.

"Have Doc set her shoulder before throwing her off the property. That is the last shred of kindness any Dark Son will ever show her."

Sharp wasn't surprised by Hawk's judgment. Disrespect was something none of them could tolerate and with the blow that swallowing Caravaggio's insult was doing to their egos, it was even more critical. He hoped that since Pixie had shown respect and not known she was breaking the rules, Hawk could find some pity.

Pixie wanted to throw up. Why hadn't anyone told her about the no fighting rule? Without Sharp's warmth at her back, she felt alone and adrift. They had banned a woman and blown up her life and she had been with them for years. What would they do to someone who had only been around for a week? And they had called her a Banshee. Was she really that bad?

She would have sat and taken the beating. Hell, she would let them all beat her if it meant she didn't have to leave Sharp. Would he allow them to send her away? Part of her was convinced he wouldn't but Pixie remembered Val's warning from early on; Brothers first, family second, and right now she was neither.

Hawk looked her up and down, shaking his head. "You came to us, Pixie with a metric shit ton of problems on your heels. We took you in and have kept you safe. I've had to juggle resources to watch over you and we are still cleaning up the mess that is your past."

"Pres–" Sharp's voice was protesting, but a hard look from Hawk had him closing his mouth.

"Up until now, I've been happy with you. You showed respect to my Brothers, cleaned up the Clubhouse and made meals that were better than my own mom's cooking. Did you know our rules about fighting?"

"No. I swear." Pixie was happy her voice didn't waver, but she couldn't help the tears that were running down her cheeks.

"You're not family–"

"I am making her my Old Lady." Sharp's voice was loud and held a tinge of anger.

Pixie's breath caught and hope flared up inside her. He had said I am, not I was going to. If that meant she was going to get to stay she could take whatever came.

"That's good. But she wasn't earlier and I think after tonight if you don't, several of your Brothers are going to be knocking down her door." For the first time, Hawk's voice had lost some of its blankness. "You stood up for the Club. But you fought when there was no need. Your man was one shout away. If you had called out for help when that bitch first approached you, we wouldn't be here."

"I'm sorry, Hawk. I let my anger get away from me. What do you need me to do to make it up to the Club?"

"You already cook and clean more than anyone ever has, and I know you have no money to cover a fine." He held up a hand as if others were going to protest. "Though I am sure you would have plenty of volunteers to give you the cash, I'm thinking of a unique punishment. You made some pretty bold claims when you had Tina pinned to the ground. Did you mean it?"

Pixie sort of remembered what she'd said after getting knocked to the ground. "Uhm, about baking cookies?"

"No, but my favorite is chocolate chip with walnuts." Hawk cracked a smile.

Pixie thought for a moment and blushed as her body unexpectedly heated, her nipples tightening. "You mean the stuff with Sharp?" She needed to be sure. Doing those things with him excited her but she wasn't sure if she could do them with anyone else and not feel terror.

"Since I don't want gunfire and bodies everywhere, yes, with Sharp. And it needs to be out in the center of the Club where everyone will see you are his and loyal to the Club."

"Hawk don't do this to her. She's been through enough already. I'll pay whatever fine you want."

Hawk's eyes hardened. "It's this or a fine and she's banned from Club property for a week. Rules don't bend for anyone."

Pixie loved that Sharp was trying to protect her, but nothing Hawk had suggested bothered her. Hell, she could feel herself getting wet thinking about it. "I'll do it."

Sharp spun her around, holding her face in his hands. "You don't have to do this, darlin'. I'll take you away for a week. Pay the fine."

She grabbed his hands, gently looking into his eyes. "I'll be fine. I feel safe here. As long as you are the only one who gets to touch me. Unless you don't want to." She hated that her last sentence sounded hurt, but she wondered if maybe he didn't want her that way anymore. If all his talk had been about protecting her, not because he actually wanted her.

Sharp touched his forehead to hers and gazed into eyes that were focused fully on him, not the insults and laughter around them. "The idea of fucking you while everyone watches has me hard as stone, darlin', but not if it's going to cause another episode."

"I'm good. I promise to tell you if something starts to bother me."

Sharp straightened and gave the middle finger to the crowd. It looked like everyone had come outside to watch the drama unfold. Pixie looked down at herself and winced. She must look like a wreck. She could feel her ponytail was loose, her dress was torn, and dirt spotted every part of her that she could see. She didn't want to put on a show looking like a victim.

Pixie looked over at Hawk and put her best-begging face on. "Can I get cleaned up and changed? I have clothes upstairs and I promise to be quick."

"I think I can allow that. In fifteen minutes, I expect you in the main room."

She nodded and took off at a sprint. Passing through the main room the only person she saw was Dragon who was on bar duty.

"You okay, *carina*?" he shouted as she ran for the stairs.

"No time! Be right back," she panted.

Pixie was determined to start running again; this winded thing was for the birds. She washed off quickly with a wash-cloth and brushed out her hair the best she could with her fingers. The ponytail was a bust without a brush, so she left it down. She opened the closet which still contained the rest of the clothing Val had bought her and considered what one should wear to get publicly fucked by their man. Her eye caught on a top made of red velvet and she smiled. Sharp hadn't seen any of the alternate dress options Val had provided. Pixie got wet at the idea. Maybe she would like to be Banshee as much as she liked being Pixie.

Everyone was back inside but it took a few minutes before Sharp could get a private word with Hawk. He made sure his voice was low. "I don't think she can do this."

"I think you underestimate your woman."

"She has nightmares that leave her shaking and crying and

only two nights ago she had a PTSD episode that had her catatonic for a time."

Hawk took a pull on his beer. "I thought you were just trying to keep her to yourself. She's shy but I didn't know she was having issues."

"I haven't asked her too many questions, but you saw the shape she was in. It's only been a week and some of the bruises are still there. Fuck, we were both soldiers. Imagine being captured and tortured for six months. We're lucky she's not a complete wreck."

"Shit. That long?" Hawk shook his head considering. "Okay, you make the call. I can't back down, but you can take your girl on a mini vacation–" Hawk's words were drowned out by whistles and catcalls from at least half the men in the room.

Chapter 20

Look at me I'm Sandra Fucking Dee.

Sharp turned and had to take a deep breath. His little Pixie was gone. Replaced by a woman who could star in wet dreams across the country. Her hair was loose and slightly messy, bringing to mind wild sex. She had makeup on and full, red, pouty lips that made a man envision them wrapped around his cock.

Sharp adjusted himself in his pants. Instead of her usual flats she had on black shiny fuck-me boots that went up so high they brushed the tiny, black, scrap of fabric that hugged her ass. The cherry on top of the cake was a crimson corset that showed off every inch of her curves and propped up her boobs, displaying them like precious pieces of art.

He caught her gorgeous green gaze and moaned when she bit her bottom lip, showing her hidden nerves. His Brothers were shouting something repeatedly and it took him a minute to realize they were chanting 'Banshee'. Unable to move and amazingly turned on, he stared as she walked up to him, giving him a perfect view of her cleavage.

Hawk smacked him on the shoulder. "I think your girl is good. Though I'm starting to think this isn't a punishment for her."

Sharp ran his hand over Pixie's shoulder and up to the base of her neck, locking his fingers in a tight grip in her hair. He pulled her back into an arch until he could see her nipples peeking over the edge of her top.

"That true, darlin'? Do you want me to show everyone what a talented mouth you have? Show you off to my Brothers and let them hear you beg me to orgasm, as I fuck you hard while they watch every expression on your gorgeous face?"

Pixie's eyes were half-lidded with pleasure, her short breaths causing her chest to rise and fall in a tempting rhythm. Her answer was a whisper that went straight to his cock. "Hell yes."

Sharp was starting to believe she was the answer to all his dreams. He had done dark and evil things in this life, but somewhere he must have pleased some higher power because Pixie was all his fantasies rolled into one unbelievable package.

He ran his fingers along the top of the corset, teasing her nipples and loving her gasp. He spun her around so her back was against his chest and he scooped her tits out, pushing the velvet down so they were on full display to the whole room. Her nipples were hard points and he pinched them, soaking in her sounds of pleasure as she closed her eyes and arched back into him.

"Open your eyes, Pixie. Everyone is looking at how fucking beautiful you are. All the bitches want to be you and the men want to be able to touch you, but they can't. Who do you belong to?"

"You, Sharp."

"That's right. No one gets to touch this body but me. Is your pussy wet?"

Sharp used his hand to drag up the front of her skirt and

run his hands through her smooth silky folds. She must have been lasered at some point because she always felt perfect.

"Fuck, Max, you win fifty bucks. I was sure she had curls." Highdive's complaining made him smile.

"Give you double or nothing she can't take him all without gagging."

"With that tiny mouth? That's a sucker's bet."

Sharp nuzzled Pixie's ear, enjoying the active betting and attention they were getting. He had fucked women publicly before – most of the Brothers had – but the feeling of putting on a show was practically intoxicating. "You hear that, darlin'? They don't think you can take all of me in that pretty little mouth."

She smiled, her green eyes sparkling. "I am such a tiny Pixie."

He nipped her ear. "I think you're loving playing the Banshee." He rolled her clit between his fingers until she pushed against his hand, her breath hitching. He pulled his hand away and wasn't the only one chuckling at her frustrated groan. "Show them what you can do."

Now came the part that would test every scrap of his self-control. He had felt what Pixie's talented little tongue could do and the urge to fuck her mouth with abandon would be a temptation. The little minx turned and slid her body down his, her hands pulling the magic trick that had his belt and pants undone by the time she reached her knees.

"How do you do that so quick?" With his woman's mouth so close to his cock it was hard to ask questions, but her maneuver was always impressive.

She ran her nails up his thighs, rubbing her face against his cock that strained to be free. She pulled back with a grin. "Nimble fingers."

Her right hand came up between them and she held his wallet between two fingers. The room burst into laughter as he shook his head and took it back from her. He shouldn't find that so damn sexy but as she used her nimble fingers to pull his cock out from his pants Sharp decided he didn't care.

Pixie's hand barely wrapped around him as she darted out her pink tongue, catching the first drop of pre-come. Her touch and licks were feather light, like a little kitten. He clenched his fists, wanting to grab her head and thrust himself down her throat, but decided to let her play.

This moment wasn't only about them. It was about putting on a show and paying her penance. So far Pixie seemed to be enjoying this as much as he was, and Sharp didn't want to fuck it up by pushing her faster.

When she took the head of his cock between her red lips, Sharp was afraid he was going to come from the view alone. Pixie sucked him in halfway, her cheeks hollowing and sending a jolt of pleasure straight up his spine. She moved up and down, using her hand to work the rest of his length.

"That's not every inch. Suzie Sunshine can't even take half of him," some bitch from the crowd jeered. Sharp was ready to have the woman thrown out for interrupting when Pixie winked at him.

She loosened her jaw and then excruciatingly slowly she moved her mouth forward. Her throat wrapped around the tip of his dick and pulled him in with ball tightening swallows. His nails bit into his hands as he fought back the orgasm that threatened to explode out of him. When her nose touched his belly, he wanted to take a picture. She looked so fucking perfect with her eyes glistening and his whole cock shoved down her throat.

His hand gripped the back of her head, giving in to the urge to hold her there for a minute to savor the experience. When he let go and pulled back her gasp for air was the sexiest sound in a room full of masculine shouts of encouragement.

Pixie felt alive and more turned on than she had believed was possible. Her whole body was focused entirely on Sharp, but the knowledge that over fifty people were watching, commenting and getting turned on gave her a sense of power she had never experienced.

Pixie barely kept from falling forward when he pulled back, suddenly stepping away from her. Brain fogged by lust, it took a moment for her to realize he had walked over to a chair someone had apparently placed in the center of the room.

She licked her swollen lips, Sharp slowly stroking himself as he sat. A small smile curved his lips as he looked at her on her knees, breasts bare to the room and lips swollen from being wrapped around his cock. "Yee-haw, Cowgirl." His teasing words reminded her she had one more boast to fulfill.

"Yippee-ki-yay." Pixie laughed and stood. She could feel her excitement dripping down her thighs as she stood and walked over to him. She started to straddle him face to face, but he spun her around.

"This is a show, darlin'. I want them to see my girl's tits bouncing as I fuck her mindless."

A slight high from the endorphins revved up her body. She lowered herself down and Sharp positioned himself at her entrance. Pixie arched her back as he slid in. With her legs pressed closed between his thighs, his cock stretched her in delicious ways. A tremor ran through her as his cock rubbed against her G-spot before sliding home. She gripped his knees, reveling in the feeling of being completely filled.

"God, Sharp, yes!"

She set a slow rhythm at first, rolling her hips like a belly dancer rising up until he was stroking that perfect place, then grinding back against him until he hit bottom. All the eyes in the room felt like extra hands stroking against her skin.

Someone turned on music and she lost herself in sensation and rhythm, entirely forgetting anything but her pleasure and his groans as she undulated to a classic Nine Inch Nails song.

Her orgasm grew like a tidal wave and she picked up speed. "Please, Sharp! Oh God!" She started slamming down to the beat of the music, trying to get the deep penetration she loved so much.

Sharp reached around, grabbing her breasts, using them to pull her down as he started to thrust up into her. Pixie screamed and an orgasm blinded her, making her convulse, unable to do anything. But his hold had them still moving, her orgasm riding higher as he piteously ground against both her cervix and G-spot, causing her to gush. Passing out was starting to become a possibility when he lifted her and stood, taking her to hands and knees on the ground.

He grabbed her hair and slammed himself so deep she swore he had reached her womb. Pain and pleasure mixed in a beautiful combination, pushing her right back to the edge of orgasm.

"You are mine, Pixie." Sharp's words were punctuated with every thrust, loud enough for everyone to hear. "My Old Lady. Say it!"

Her second orgasm hit as she screamed, "I'm yours!"

"Dark Sons for life," Sharp said, as his orgasm riding her own filled her.

"Dark Sons for life!" echoed voices through the room.

Chapter 21

The packaging may be pretty but it is what is inside that matters.

Pixie woke sore and more than a little giddy. She lifted her face off Sharp's chest. Warmth flushed her cheeks at the memory of last night. The teasing from the Brothers about her twin sister Banshee being a badass made her giggle. They hadn't shown her any less respect. In fact, Sharp received more teasing about being saddled with an Old Lady then she had about her little show.

She watched Sharp's sleeping face and couldn't believe he had made her the biker equivalent of his wife. She wanted to run outside and shout it to the world. She scooted up a bit and kissed his nose. Sharp's face scrunched up and he opened sleepy eyes.

"Mornin' darlin'. What time is it?"

She looked over his shoulder at the clock. "Oh my goodness it's eight o'clock!" She scrambled out of bed, looking for clothes.

"And we didn't get to bed until after four this morning."

"But breakfast!"

"Isn't happening on weekends, remember?"

Pixie flopped down on the bed, shaking her head. "I'm still getting used to things. Sorry, I woke you."

Sharp sat up and Pixie enjoyed the view of his muscled chest with the colorful tattoos. "You know you don't have to cook or clean at the Clubhouse. We might have a riot of Brothers looking for your bread, but they'll adapt back to drive through and delivery."

"What else would I do with my time? I had months of doing nothing. I can't do that again."

"You could get a job or a hobby. Whatever makes you happy."

"I don't have a high school diploma or even know how to drive a car." She shrugged and tried not to let it bug her. "Besides, I love cooking."

"Come here, Pixie." He pulled her up and onto his lap. "You have a photographic memory. How come you never graduated?"

She shrugged. "My last foster home wasn't a good place so I decided to go my own way. I was sixteen." A high school diploma didn't mean much if you didn't have ID. You needed both to get a job. Maybe if she had tried harder, she wouldn't have ended up chained in some basement for months.

"If you want to get your GED, we'll figure it out. If you want to go to college or cooking school, the same thing. You're mine, darlin', anything you want, I will make it happen as long as I get to come home to you smiling."

"I want to keep cooking for your Brothers but cooking school would be amazing. And can you teach me to drive a motorcycle?"

Sharp laughed, kissing the top of her head. "How about we start with a car? Only riding you need to know how to do is behind me."

"All right, but I kinda like riding you from the front."

"Brat." Sharp rolled her over and kissed her breathless.

An hour later Pixie skipped down into the kitchen to make her and Sharp breakfast. Old Lady, cooking school, it was all more than she could have dreamed when she had been picking pockets to get her next meal on the streets of Denver, living in and out of the shelters.

Whistling, she opened the refrigerator to scope out what supplies she could work with.

"Well, that is the sound of a well-fucked woman." Pixie let out a short squeak and turned around. Kickstand was sprawled on the couch looking way too smug about something. His glare and tone was off somehow, and it made her nervous. She caught movement and realized his hand was inside his pants and moving.

She spun back around, embarrassment flushing her face. After last night she didn't think knowing someone was jerking off would bother her, but something about the way he looked at her made her feel dirty. This was Sharp's home and she had believed they were alone. Why was he masturbating in Sharp's living room anyway? "I'm sorry, I didn't know you were down here."

"Pixie duty until six, bar bitch until midnight. The glamorous life of a prospect."

"I was going to make breakfast. Looks like Sharp has enough eggs and bacon, would you like some?" She had her head bent down in the refrigerator, trying to act like she wasn't creeped out.

"Amazing, you're still pretending to be an innocent homemaker even after he made you his Old Lady. That's cute." His voice came from right behind her and startled her so badly she came close to dropping the eggs.

She moved away from him, placing the kitchen island

between them as she laid out the materials for omelets. "What are you talking about?"

"Most bitches get what they want and show their true faces. After what I saw last night, I wouldn't give a fuck if you were a harpy if I got a piece of that every night."

Kickstand's words killed what little joy she had left. Last night she had enjoyed herself immensely, but his words made her feel small. A part of her brain wanted to flip him off and say he was never getting a piece of anything. But the other part felt guilty about being bitchy because he was one of the people stuck babysitting her.

Pixie was saved from replying by the sound of Sharp coming down the stairs. She plastered on a smile trying to hide the fact she was so uncomfortable. Her man came in for a kiss and she leaned against him, trying to find the strength and happiness she had felt earlier in the morning.

How could this man make her feel so safe by just standing near her? Thoughts of creepy prospects and insecurities floated away as his hands ran up and down her back. She needed to be stronger and with his silent support, it was possible.

Sharp was surprised to find Kickstand standing in his kitchen instead of outside keeping guard like he was supposed to be. While Pixie had been changing the night before, he and Hawk had decided it was a good idea to keep someone near Pixie until they shut down the bounty and dealt with both Mitchel and Caravaggio.

He decided to let it go. For now. Later he'd explain to Pixie that the people watching her needed to be outside where they could see people coming, not inside eating breakfast. That combined with the electronic security and the patrols of Brothers, watching the compound was more than enough to keep her safe. But Kickstand should know better.

His woman was withdrawn and quiet throughout breakfast and seemed uncomfortable with something.

"I've got to head over to the Clubhouse, pick some things up, and talk to some people. I'll be back around lunchtime."

Pixie's head snapped up. "I can come with you."

"Stay here and settle in. Watch TV and relax."

"But..." Pixie seemed nervous, the confident side he had seen last night entirely gone.

"Kickstand will be outside. You're safe on the compound. I'm taking you into town with me this afternoon and I have Club business to finish before we go."

"Where are we going?" A little excitement returned to her voice, easing some of Sharp's concern.

"You asked to come when I got more work done on my tattoo. Ink has an opening at one if you want to go. Or you can stay here if you prefer."

"No, I want to go. You said Kickstand will be outside. I'll be fine."

Sharp was surprised on the odd emphasis on the word 'outside'. He wondered if she still didn't feel comfortable with the prospect. She had warmed up to most of the people she had been in close contact with, but not Kickstand. After the prospect's crap attitude the last week, Sharp didn't know if the guy was going to make it to patching in. The man never precisely complained about the shit duties prospects were given, but he also didn't seem to appreciate the fact that every Brother had gone through the same process. Like boot camp in the military, it was a shared experience that earned their place and drew them together.

"Yeah, darlin'. He needs to be outside on watch. Unless something's wrong, you shouldn't be asking him inside, even for breakfast."

"But I—"

"I'll head back out now," Kickstand cut in, giving a nod as he headed out the front door.

Pixie looked confused and concerned between the door and him. "Sharp, I—"

"Don't worry about it." He leaned in and kissed her. "I'll be back for lunch and you'll get to watch Ink torture me for his art."

She smiled, the first real smile since he joined her in the kitchen. "What should I wear?"

Sharp shook his head. Only a woman would worry about what to wear to a tattoo parlor. He looked at her yellow-as-sunshine dress with the scoop neck and tiny straps that were so innocent and sexy all at the same time. They were going to be riding his bike and the image of her skirt blowing up, giving people a glance at her legs and ass, had his dick coming to full attention. "I like what you're wearing. In deference to that sweet pussy and the length of the drive you can put panties on."

Her nipples tightened, beautifully visible under the light fabric. "Okay."

Fuck, this was going to be a long ride.

Chapter 22

I licked it so it is mine!

It was hell but Sharp managed to finish up his work in just a few hours. He held the boxes containing the items he had ordered for Pixie as he walked into their house. Being nervous wasn't something he was used to. The boxes contained what were the physical representation of accepting becoming his Old Lady. Every Dark Son gave their women similar gifts after they received that title.

He wanted her to love each item and understand just how important they were. "Where are you, darlin'?" Sharp called out as he walked through the front door. He placed his packages on the kitchen counter.

He heard Pixie hurrying down the stairs right before he saw her. Like a sparkle of light, she was breathtaking. She hadn't changed out of her adorable as fuck sundress, but she had added short leggings that peeked out the bottom of her skirt. He couldn't resist wrapping his hand around her neck and pulling her towards him, taking her mouth with a hungry kiss.

"I'm ready." The breathiness of her voice told him she was ready for more than just the ride to the tattoo shop. He picked her up so she sat on the counter, putting them almost eye to eye.

"I got you some presents." Sharp kissed her nose and gestured to the boxes on the counter. The over-the-top shock on her face made him want to hurt the people in her previous life who had taught her never to expect anything.

"Really?" She clasped her hands tightly, staring hungrily at the boxes as if afraid to touch them.

He handed her the smallest box and chuckled as she tore open the cardboard. It was the least personal of the gifts, a new smartphone. It was pre-programed with all the Brothers' numbers and would allow her to have a way to communicate at all times.

"This is too much," Pixie started to protest. Sharp placed a thumb over her lips, quieting her.

He tipped her chin up so he was looking deep into her eyes. "Of all the things I ever want to hear from you about gifts, none of them will ever include cost or whether or not you deserve them." He planted a gentle kiss on her lips. "You are my woman and deserve everything under the sun."

Pixie blushed, her lips still slightly parted. "Okay."

Sharp leaned back a bit and handed her the biggest box. She giggled and lifted off the lid, her voice escaping in an 'oh' as she saw what was inside. A black leather cut was laying in the box, folded so the Dark Sons emblem was displayed. Sharp saw Pixie's hand tremble as she brushed her fingertips over the patch that read 'Property of Sharp'. His woman looked up, her eyes shining with tears.

"Can I put it on?" Her voice was quiet but full of such hope, Sharp knew she really meant it.

He pulled it out of the tissue paper and felt a wave of possessive pride as he saw the black leather slip over her innocent as shit little dress. His dick felt like it was trying to punch through his jeans. It fit her perfectly, her name on her chest and his on her back. He almost forgot there was one more gift to go. The cut was the most important gift to most Brothers, an open sign to the world that their woman was claimed, but to him what was in the last box meant so much more.

He grabbed it himself, opening the lid and tilting it towards her. Sitting on fluffy cotton was a titanium choker, the thick links almost bordering on masculine. A round pendant hung from the front engraved with a beautiful fairy on one side and 'Sharp's little Pixie' on the back. Instead of the usual clasp for the back, a small decorative-looking padlock made of the same metal as the necklace held the jewelry together.

Pixie's eyes widened and her fingertips were held against her lips as if she was trying to hold back her words. Sharp pulled his keys out of his pocket and unlocked it. He took the necklace in his hands, letting her study the pendant and take in the meaning of the unusual clasp. What he wasn't telling her was all three items he brought her today were altered by Tek to hold trackers that could be traced from almost anywhere. Only the officers knew every Old Lady was tracked this way and for safety reasons that was how it would stay.

Sharp cleared his throat. "This is it, Pixie. I gave you my Cut. When I put this on you, there is no going back." He knew his words were intense, but she needed to know how he felt. "I put this on you, you're mine and no one else can ever take it off but me." He moved the necklace forward a little before pausing, waiting for her acceptance.

She took in a shuddering breath. "I love you, Sharp. It's fast and messed up in so many ways but it's right. We're right. I want to be yours." Her eyes sparkled. "You're my Old Man, no going back." She lifted her ponytail, inviting him to lock the necklace around her.

The sound of the lock clicking into place fired his blood.

He leaned forward, sinking his teeth into the delicate flesh where her shoulder met her neck, needing to mark her. Pixie's moan was like a starting bell. His hands gripped the leather of her new cut and he pulled her close. He ran his tongue up her neck, nipping and sucking as he went. He gripped her earlobe in his teeth, growling the only word he could think.

"Mine."

"God, yes, Sharp!"

He reached under her skirt, pulling off her leggings and her underwear with a jerk, tossing them behind him. Sharp freed his aching cock and dragged her right to the edge of the countertop, pushing up her skirt so he could see the wet aching bounty that waited for him. Not willing to wait a second longer he lined them up, pulling her onto him as he thrust forward with a brutal stroke. She was so tight he groaned, the feel of her slick heat the exact thing he wanted.

Her cries echoed around him like sweet music as he controlled their motions with a firm grip, thrusting to the perfect rhythm of his heartbeat. He tangled his mouth against hers, needing and wanting to make every part of them as close as they could get.

"Please." Sharp didn't know what she was begging for, but his own need drove him to pound deeper, needing to feel the end of her. He had to become one with her. The tempo was frenetic and when he felt her tighten around him, he growled with the primal desire to match their release perfectly. This would not be long or drawn out. It was a claiming on the most basic of levels.

"You wait for me, Pixie. Don't you dare come until I tell you to."

Pixie gasped and her struggle played across her face in an exquisite display of conflict. Sharp pushed her back, laying her down over the countertop like a beautiful feast. Her dress, the cut, the necklace, and her soaking pussy all added up to his version of heaven.

He let off the brakes, slamming into her with a force and rhythm that should have broken her in half, but she met him stroke for stroke. Her moans turned to screams of ecstasy as she fought back her orgasm. Sparks of pleasure started at the base of his spine and he knew it was time. He wanted to hold back, make this last, but it wasn't going to be possible.

"Now, darlin'. Fuck... You're mine, love. I want you to come all over my cock."

With his words she bucked against him, her body going wild, and he lost all semblance of control, giving himself over to the animal pleasure that was the two of them becoming one. His orgasm ripped through him and he gripped her hips so hard he had no doubt that she would have bruises.

She was his and Sharp would never let anyone take her away from him.

Chapter 23

Now you see it... Then it's mine.

Kickstand and Max waved to Sharp as they pulled back onto the road. They would return in a few hours to escort Pixie and him back to the Clubhouse. It was unnecessary for them to stay since there were more than enough Brothers in and around Ink's shop. He took a moment to enjoy the feel of his Old Lady pressed against his back. Life was crazy but he couldn't be happier that he had managed to find someone who was so perfect and patch her as his own.

"Where are they going?" Pixie asked as she swung off his bike.

"Back to the Clubhouse." Sharp followed behind her and pulled her into his arms, loving her tiny and delicate body against his front. His cock stiffened and he wondered if he could convince her to spend some time with him at the back of the shop. Last night she had seemed to love fucking in public as much as he had but so far this morning the wild Banshee of last night was nowhere to be seen.

"Why did they ride all the way down here to then head back?" Her ponytail bobbed as she cocked her head in confusion.

"Security." Sharp bit back a laugh when Pixie started looking around as if someone was going to jump out at her. Sharp took her chin in his hands and placed a light kiss on her lips. "Just a precaution."

"I'm sorry. I should have stayed home." The fear in his woman's voice tore at him.

"You're safe. See those bikes?" He nodded to a row of five bikes lined up next to his. "All Brothers. They have customers, but this place belongs to the Dark Sons and no one would mess with you while we're here."

He wished she had more faith in his ability to keep her safe, but that would take time. Pixie gave him an unsure smile and he couldn't help but lean down and taste her pink lips again. Tension leaked out of her as he deepened the kiss and his cock pulsed against his zipper. He nipped at her bottom lip, loving the soft moan the action elicited, and wished he could find them somewhere private right at that moment.

"Sooner we get inside, the faster I can get you home."

Dark Ink had been in business almost as long as the Dark Sons had been in Colorado. Even more popular than his garage, Hannibal and Ink drew customers from around the country with their unique and detailed designs. The place was meticulously clean for what was considered a biker business. Five stations – the majority of them occupied at the moment – made up the front of the shop and two privacy booths were hidden at the back. Everything in Dark Ink was chrome and black, giving it a retro feel. The color in the place came from the people and large photographs on the walls. Each station had photographs of the artist's best work proudly on display. Up front near the register in a place of honor was a larger-than-life print of Hawk's back piece.

The tattoo deserved its own wall. Ink had done the main Dark Sons Logo, but every artist here had added to it, somehow keeping cohesion while highlighting their own styles. Pixie stood staring at the image like it was the Mona Lisa and Sharp couldn't hide his amused smile.

"Sharp, you tired old squid." Hannibal's deep bayou-accented voice cut through the classic rock that played over the speakers. The tattoo artist was cleaning up his station while a young customer slipped on his shirt over a bandage that covered his upper arm. From the look of the kid, he was either recently out of boot camp or about to head in.

Hannibal was a large, overly muscular, bald man with darkness dusting his skin. That combined with his sweet Louisiana drawl let no one doubt his Creole heritage. The man was a walking advertisement for his work with piercings and elaborate tattoos covering all but his face. Sharp stepped away from Pixie and clasped forearms with his longtime friend.

"Ink should be done in the back soon. Got a shy bird getting a flower on her ass." Hannibal nodded towards the closed curtain at the back.

"He must be in heaven," Sharp snorted.

"He does love a woman from the rear. Speaking of heaven, is this the woman who finally proved once and for all you are a shitty excuse of a sniper?" Hannibal winked before turning to face Pixie.

"Excuse me?" Sharp loved the indignant tone and look on his woman's face.

Hannibal flashed a charming smile her way. "Now don't get your feathers in a fluff, *cher*. Snipers are supposed to be observant and I hear you lifted his gun off his belt. If a bitty thing like you can pull one over on him what does that say about the quality of SEAL snipers?"

Pixie's face reddened and her eyes narrowed at his Cajun Brother. He might not like Hannibal using creole endearments on his woman, but it was freaking adorable; she looked like she might start swinging at the Louisiana man. "Don't mind him. Poor guy was a lowly Ranger Sniper and we all know grunts got the short end of the intelligence stick."

"Oh." The flame died in her eyes and was replaced by a strange glint Sharp wasn't sure how to read. He was sure he would learn all of her looks soon enough but this one was new. Pixie leaned in and began inspecting Hannibal's arms. "I don't see a Ranger tattoo."

Hannibal stood and turned his left arm, displaying his Death Before Dishonor black work. Pixie stepped forward, reaching out a hand.

"Can I touch it?"

His Brother nodded and she reached over, brushing her fingers over the tattoo. Sharp smiled, glad that Pixie was quickly relaxing around the giant man. It was important to him that she felt comfortable with his Brothers. She traced a few tattoos further down his arm and then her gaze caught on a picture high up on the wall.

"Is that one yours? It's beautiful!"

Sharp turned and looked along with Hannibal to the picture she indicated. The artist nodded. "The Phoenix? Yeah, that's mine."

"Did you do the sunset on Sharp's back? The style looks the same." Pixie's voice was filled with excessive excitement and Sharp started to wonder what she was getting up to.

"Good eye, *cher*. That's my work."

Then Pixie surprised them both by giggling and giving Hannibal a hug from behind that was strong enough to sway the bigger man. "I love that one." She released him and wandered a few steps away, playing with her skirt while she stared up at the other photos on the wall. She continued her slow stroll until she was on the other side of his chair and Sharp's instincts said something was not quite right.

"*Ou byen fè*! I see why you patched that one so fast. She's like sunshine in a tiny bottle." Hannibal rocked back on his heels shaking his head.

Sharp nodded, trying to figure out what she was up to.

"I would love to get a tattoo." Pixie swirled her skirt a bit and Sharp couldn't help imagining flipping the little cotton up and bending her over the chair.

"What would you get, darlin'?" Sharp asked, loving the idea of seeing ink on her skin. Maybe he could convince her to get his name on the small of her back.

"I always wanted to do the angel-devil thing on each shoulder. But now I think a pixie and a banshee fits better." Pixie fingered the pendant at the base of her throat and Sharp was once again grateful Tek had done something special for his woman.

"I think that would look amazing." Sharp smiled, trying to get his dick under control.

"You let me know when, *cher*. I would love to get my needles on you." Sharp would have been jealous at the flirting tone in Hannibal's voice, but the Cajun didn't mean anything by it.

Pixie seemed to think for a moment, then smiled. "How about a bet?"

"What are we betting on?" Hannibal smiled and looked interested.

"If I manage to lift your wallet," she paused thinking, "or any other item from your body, you do a tattoo on me for free."

Hannibal gave a deep belly laugh, getting the attention of everyone in the shop. "You're on, baby girl. One tattoo for every item you get, but if you don't manage to get anything by the time you leave, I get to pierce the body part of Sharp's choosing."

Pixie's eyes hooded and her lips parted as she imagined getting something pierced. Sharp was going to have to find out what picture was in her mind because it apparently had her turned on and he wanted to know everything that put that look on her face. To him, it was a win-win bet, though having to wait while any of his favorite parts healed wasn't appealing.

"It's a bet." Her voice was breathy with desire and she shook her head as if clearing out dirty fantasies.

Hannibal clapped his hand and several people chuckled. "Good luck, *cher*. I grew up in the bayou on top of being a trained–"

Hannibal's words were cut off as Sharp's devious, beautiful woman tossed a wallet down on the chair. The Ranger's jaw dropped when a string of condoms followed. A low cheer echoed in the front room followed by masculine chuckles as Pixie gently laid a .45 on the seat and dangled a chunky men's watch off one finger.

"A trained what?" Pixie's eyes twinkled.

Hannibal looked down at his wrist in complete disbelief. "Fuck!" Everyone in the room burst into renewed laughter.

Pixie tossed Hannibal his watch. She felt like she was on cloud nine. Not only had she been able to defend Sharp's reputation, but she had won at least four tattoos from an extremely talented artist. The pictures on the walls showed bright beautiful images which were amazingly detailed. Some looked more like photographs on skin rather than ink.

"What has y'all cackling like a pack of hyenas on a hunt?" A man wearing a Dark Sons leather cut stepped out from behind the curtained area in the back and turned down the music slightly. He had long, light-brown hair pulled back from his face in a ponytail. Unlike the Brothers Pixie had met he was well defined, but not bulky. His deep Texas accent had her picturing him with a cowboy hat selling out concerts while he strummed a guitar and sang about heartbreak.

As he came closer, she noticed among his many tattoos, he had a wolf head on his arm which was so realistic she swore it would turn and growl at her.

"My woman was just proving how the mighty Rangers can fall. Pixie, this is Ink. He was in Hannibal's Ranger squad and is the sadistic fucker who will hopefully be finishing my dragon today."

Deciding to make the gag complete she smiled and ran over to Ink, giving him a hug around the waist. "Ink! So great to meet you. I love your work!"

Remembering Sharp's earlier comments, she made sure to wiggle her ass a bit as added distraction. She started to lift Ink's wallet, but it was clipped to his jeans by a long-linked chain. It took an extra second to remove the clip from the wallet to one of his belt loops. She kept the pressure of her hug on the outsides of his hips to pull his focus. The long leather cut was perfect camouflage to her motions.

"She's adorable, Sharp. How did you ever get her to wear your patch?"

Pixie smiled up at Ink and made her way back to Sharp, hiding the wallet in the folds of her skirt.

"You won't think she's so cute when she picks your pockets clean," Hannibal joked, as he re-holstered his gun and fastened his watch back on.

Ink burst out laughing. "You lost your watch to a light finger, that is priceless." The Texan gave Pixie a wink. "I would be happy to let you put your hands in my pockets anytime."

Pixie held his wallet up behind Sharp's back, twisting it so Hannibal could see what she had.

Her new Cajun friend smiled. "You're so sure she can't get your wallet? Let's bet. If she lifts your wallet, you do one of the tattoos she won from me. She doesn't, I buy you a steak dinner."

Everyone in the shop was quiet, half of them able to see the wallet in Pixie's hand, the others probably wanting to see if she could do it again. Pixie did her best to look interested in the proposition instead of guilty. She studied Ink's body, pretending to look for valuables.

"You're on. But I'm no fool. I keep my shit locked tight." He rattled the chain on his belt that used to be attached to his wallet. Luckily since she had clipped the other end to a belt loop, he didn't realize he'd already been played.

His arrogance made Pixie a little greedy and she narrowed her eyes. "Increased difficulty—I think I should get two tattoos."

Sharp looked down at her. "For a girl with virgin skin, you have big plans."

Pixie had no idea what else she would get but with two world class artists she was sure she would think of something. "I've always loved beautiful art."

"You got a deal, darlin'." Ink hooked his thumbs in his pockets, smiling. Everyone in the shop who knew she had the wallet burst out laughing. Even Pixie couldn't help but add her giggles. The tattoo artist narrowed his eyes and reached behind him. The look of shock on his face had her laughing so hard she had to lean on Sharp.

She pulled herself together and tossed Ink his wallet with a wink.

"Son of a bitch!" Ink slapped the wallet against his thigh.

Chapter 24

I am responsible for what I say, not what you understand.

Two hours later Ink was deep into work on coloring Sharp's tattoo and Pixie was face down on Hannibal's chair with all the other artists hard at work around them. The man was a crazy good artist. He had spent over an hour drawing up a fairy pixie wearing a black leather cut like her own. He had sized it perfectly to fit on her shoulder, and used a cool machine to make a stencil he then transferred onto her right shoulder blade. They would have to wait on the other shoulder blade until the stitches she had in it were completely healed. He had asked if she wanted to wait on the other as well since she still had very light-yellow bruising, but she had told him she was fine.

Pixie gripped the edge of the chair, trying to contain her nervous energy. Hannibal patted her hand with his latex-covered one as he set up his supplies. "Don't you worry, *cher*. This is going to hurt, but we'll take as many breaks as you need."

Pixie wasn't worried about the pain. She was more

concerned about what he would think if it was obvious she enjoyed it. So far she and Sharp seemed to match in their sexual needs but he hadn't seen the full scope of the darkness she felt inside her. But she had hope. It was the Cajun's reaction that gave her pause. What did she know about Hannibal? He had been a good sport earlier and he must have seen plenty of different reactions to pain from people in his chair.

A conversation she had with Val earlier in the week bubbled up in her mind. "Can I ask you a personal question?"

"Sure."

She lowered her voice a bit, figuring with the music and the other people talking no one would overhear. "Is it true you like needle play?"

Hannibal paused in his preparations, his eyes twinkling. "Sharp tell you that to scare you?"

"He wouldn't do something like that."

Hannibal studied her face and she wondered what he saw there. "Yes, *cher*, with a willing woman. But you won the bet remember?"

"But are you a sadist?"

Heat flared in his gaze and Pixie tingled in response. "That too, but don't worry your little head. I won't make this hurt any more than it has to."

She wanted to tell him she would be okay; nothing could compare to the pain she had endured for much less pleasant reasons. But why ruin a fun afternoon with drama? She just said, "Okay," before turning her head back to face towards Sharp.

He gave her an encouraging smile. "Ready?"

"Yes."

The buzzing sound of the needle was immediately followed by lightning zipping across her nerves. She stifled a moan as the pain washed over her and, like always, slipped right into pleasure. It was a torturous dance that Hannibal began. The needle would snap her alive, making her hyper aware of every part of her body, then he would pause and wipe the ink away and endorphins would flood her system, pushing her closer to orgasm.

She wondered if Hannibal noticed or if he was caught up in his own art, oblivious to the effect he was having on her. Pixie didn't dare look at the man holding the tattoo gun but from the heat in Sharp's gaze every time she opened her eyes, he at least could tell how worked up she was. She hoped the desire in his eyes meant he knew she wasn't thinking about anyone but him as she slowly grew more and more turned on.

Pixie lost herself in sensation. Her nipples tight underneath her added their own pleasure every time she rocked when Hannibal wiped away ink. The feel of her satin underwear against her swollen pussy was its own form of teasing; she didn't dare move or she would push right over the edge into a screaming orgasm.

The waves of pain and pleasure crested and fell until they seemed to merge. She tried to breathe, tried to hold back, but after what seemed like an eternity, she didn't think she could hold back much longer.

"Thank Christ I'm done," Ink muttered to Sharp, as he cleaned off the last bit of the Dragon. "Do you have any idea what kind of torture it is bending over your ugly chest with my dick as hard as fucking steel?"

Sharp understood exactly what he meant. For the past two hours, without a break, he had listened to his woman's tiny whimpers and moans as Hannibal worked some kind of voodoo magic on her back. From the knowing glances and smiles of every man and woman in the place, they were aware his baby was deeply enjoying her first tattoo. It seemed as if she didn't just like pain in the bedroom, and boy was that going to make life fun.

The sounds she was making – and the fact every man here envied the shit out of him right now – had his own cock pressing uncomfortably against his zipper.

"You could have warned us she was a pain slut. Would have set up in the back and let you give her a break once in a while. Hannibal has got to be in heaven right now and I barely got to enjoy the show."

"I didn't know. But when she comes back for the color, I'm bringing a gag and we can give you guys a real show. You'll have to bring your own hands-on entertainment, though. I don't share like you fuckers."

"Damn, shame that. But we have Didi coming in fifteen and the way Hannibal's riled up that woman is in for a treat."

The two men chuckled, and Ink snapped a picture of his finished chest piece while Sharp took a moment to admire the outcome. It had taken three sessions to finish, but the dragon was a masterpiece. Ink put cream over the tattoo and taped on a bandage.

"I need a break." Pixie's voice sounded panicked, snapping Sharp's attention back to his woman.

"We need five more minutes to finish the outline, *cher*."

"I'm sorry, I've got to—" Pixie rolled off the chair, barely catching her top from exposing her to the room. She stumbled a bit and started sprinting towards the back of the shop.

Sharp stepped out into her path to catch her, determined to find out what went wrong. She slammed into his chest and he caught her as a familiar cry of pleasure ripped out of her throat and visible tremors ran through her body.

All the blood in his body raced straight to his cock as he watched Pixie, lost in her orgasm, standing in the middle of Dark Ink. Her lips were parted, eyes half closed, and her head was thrown back so he could see every emotion as it passed over her face.

"Holy shit, did she just come?"

Sharp didn't know who asked the question, but he needed to take care of his baby right now. He looked over to Ink and said, "We'll be in the back."

The man smiled and nodded.

"Lucky fucking bastard." Sharp recognized Hannibal's deep voice and agreed with him. He scooped up Pixie into his arms and headed into the curtained area at the back of the shop.

There were three stations in the back of the shop designed to offer privacy for shy customers or the more intimate tattoos and piercing. A few of his Brothers swore that there was nothing in the world better than getting a blowjob while getting a tattoo and the happy perverts who worked here had no problems with it at long as you could hold still.

Sharp sat Pixie on the edge of the first chair he came to and took her mouth with his own. Hours of her small moans tormenting him and the show she put on had him nearly wild with the need to fuck her.

Her hands gripped his bare arms with a need which was almost as desperate as his. Pixie's sundress was pooled around her waist, exposing her beautiful tits. He had to taste them, so he took one in a rough hand and the other he sucked into his mouth, enjoying the feel of the pert little nipple as it brushed over his tongue.

Pixie's body shook with another orgasm. "Please, Sharp, I need you to fuck me!"

Sharp had no intention of rushing this, though he feared his control might not last. He nipped at her breast, occasionally biting her nipples, reveling in her whimpers. He held her knees apart so she couldn't find the release she wanted.

"Shh, darlin', I'll give you my cock but only when I have

had my fill of this body. Do you have any idea how sexy it was to hear your little moans as he ran that needle over your skin? How much I wanted to come over and stick my hand up your skirt and see how wet your little pussy was. If I had sunk my fingers inside you, would your hungry little cunt have clenched around them, begging for me to make you come?"

"Yes. Please, I feel so empty."

The curtain swayed closed around Hannibal and Ink as they led Didi, their regular fuckbuddy, into the back private area stopping just across from where they were. Sharp ran his hand up Pixie's thigh, brushing against the damp fabric of her panties. He leaned in, brushing his lips against her ear. "See how fucking hot you made them both. They can't wait even a minute to get a woman between them."

Pixie thought she was going to combust; the two orgasms she'd had barely touching the edge of the need she felt. She watched as Hannibal grabbed the woman's dress by the hem and practically ripped the dress over her head. Pixie was fascinated by the different tattoos that entwined the woman's body.

Sharp's fingers wrapped around her panties and she gasped as the soaked fabric pulled away from her aching pussy as he dropped them to the ground.

"See how they're watching you? They may have Didi between them, but their cocks are hard for you."

The side view Pixie had of the three was perfect. Hannibal and Ink had the now naked woman between them. She had their dicks in her hands and was stroking them both slowly as the threesome watched her. Sharp ran a thumb over her clit, sending shivers up her back.

"Turn over. I want them to see your beautiful tits while I taste your gorgeous pussy."

It was exciting and surreal. Pixie stood and bent over the tattoo chair, bracing on her elbows so her breasts hung down. She watched as Hannibal swiveled the chair across from them and bent Didi into the same position she was in. Then he placed his cock in front of her mouth and the woman began licking and sucking him, all while his eyes were focused on Pixie.

Cool air blew against her pussy as Sharp held her open, his tongue lapping at her folds in teasing strokes. Pixie wanted him inside her so badly, a frustrated moan escaped her lips.

Ink had slipped a condom on and was now sliding slowly in and out of Didi, making Pixie jealous. Two men had never intrigued her but the sight and sounds of the two men fucking the busty blonde from both ends, just feet away, was erotic and adding to her aching need.

Sharp sucked her clit into his mouth and the orgasm that ripped through her bordered on painful. She needed something inside her to fill the spasming void that had been building for hours.

"God. Yes. Sharp, I hurt. I need your cock inside me, please!"

She clawed onto the edge of the chair, nearly feral with need. The sight of the two men now brutally fucking the woman in front of her, the sound of Didi's muffled cries of pleasure, and the feel of her man behind her, shredded her control.

Sharp's hand covered her mouth, muffling her screams, as he slammed himself inside her without warning. Pixie's mind blanked as she finally felt whole. There were no sights or sounds, just feelings of complete bliss as waves of orgasms blanketed her.

She floated in a dreamy place until the feeling of a warm, wet cloth between her legs started to rouse her. Someone else was rubbing something cool into her shoulder and the fear of a stranger touching her brought her back down to earth. She took stock and realized she was face down on a soft padded surface, the sounds of two men talking above her.

"You are one lucky son of a bitch." Hannibal's voice came from near her shoulder.

"Don't I know it." Sharp pulled up her panties over legs that felt like jelly. Knowing she was safe with her man helped slow the rising nerves.

"No wonder Caravaggio is willing to sacrifice his men and risk war with the Dark Sons to take her from you."

"Not going to happen."

"She's special and she's your property. Dark Sons will have your back."

Dark nightmares swirled in Pixie's mind, destroying the peace that had started to settle moments before. "Caravaggio is trying to take me?" Her words were slightly slurred, but she was quickly coming back into focus.

"Don't you worry about that, darlin'."

Terror washed away the last of the drugging bliss. She sat up, slipping her arms into the straps of her dress, angry and needing to be less vulnerable. "You don't think I should worry about a man whose idea of fun is slicing up a screaming woman for hours then fucking her dead corpse? I mean, silly me, worrying that he wants me."

"*Fout tonère!*" Hannibal cursed under his breath.

"He's not going to get to you."

The urge to run and hide itched under her skin. She had met a lot of Dark Sons, but how much power did they really have? Caravaggio was the freaking Mafia. He had enough power and money to be one of Mitchel's frequent customers. She had to make Sharp see how terrifying this man was. "Him getting his hands on me is the reason I found the courage to ask you for help. The only reason I'm here." Did he understand the level of fear it had taken to override months of brain-washed hopelessness?

Sharp's face became ice. "Yeah, babe. I get that you tried to kill yourself rather than go to him. Glad you think fucking me for protection isn't a worse fate."

Pixie's stomach clenched like she'd been punched. "That is not what I meant."

He shoved her new cut at her. "Max and Kickstand are outside. Go wait by my bike."

"You should have told me, that's all I was—"

"Shut the fuck up and go wait by my bike." His words were like daggers ripping into her heart.

She clutched the leather to her chest and ran out through the front of the shop, not acknowledging any of the words thrown her way. She stood by the bike, ignoring Max's friendly greeting as she slipped on the leather cut.

She barely remembered the ride home or being left there with Kickstand as her guard. She barely noticed the prospect's lewd come-ons and snide remarks, remaining completely silent as she unbandaged her new tattoo and washed and cared for the gorgeous pixie now permanently on her shoulder. Nothing Kickstand said nor did was important enough to break through the wall of worry and anger that had her locked inside her own mind.

Pixie decided to lose herself in baking cookies for tomorrow's family barbeque. Try to find some order in her life which was once again spinning out of control. How had the day gone so sideways? She had the start of an absolutely gorgeous tattoo and amazing sex that morning but she was beginning to feel the sense of safety she had experienced was a lie. Sharp had kept from her the fact that a psychopath was actively trying to get to her. That the man with the Mafia behind him had obviously done something that sacrificed men and risked war. If her being safe was a lie, what else was he keeping from her?

The hateful confrontation played like a loop in her brain. Maybe her word choice earlier had been poor. But the way he had acted… did Sharp believe she could solely want him for protection? She had done everything she could to show him how she felt. He had made her his Old Lady and she thought that meant he loved her too. She hugged his leather cut around herself, not caring she got flour on the black leather. How could she prove she wanted him for no other reason than he made her heart happy?

Her mind ping-ponged between anger at being kept in the dark and terror he was going to leave her. Add in the underlying fear that she had two rich and dangerous men wanting to torture or kill her, and her nerves were on hyperdrive. Four hours and several hundred baked cookies later, she was no closer to knowing what to do. She did know, even though it was after midnight, sleep would be impossible in her current state.

Seeing Dragon walk past the front window gave her an idea. She opened the front door and yelled out to him. "Can we go for a run?"

He looked down at his phone. "It's one in the morning, *carina*."

"I know."

Dragon studied her and she knew she looked a wreck. She had cried as much as she had baked, and her face probably showed it. "You have good shoes this time?"

"I have something that will work. I'll get changed."

Chapter 25

Stop whining, put on your big boy pants, and suck it up.

Sharp woke up hungover and still pissed in one of the flop rooms of the Clubhouse. He wanted to calm down before talking to Pixie, but Hannibal and Max started riding his ass and then he found out that Grinder was in the hospital. He'd been jumped somewhere in Denver and left unconscious with a note pinned to his chest that said, *I want my property back—MT*.

After he met with Hawk and Highdive he'd settled in with a bottle of Jack to get some sleep. Now it was almost noon and he wasn't any closer to calming down. Brothers and their families would be showing up soon, if they weren't already here, to enjoy a relaxing family barbecue. How was he supposed to plaster on a smile and pretend he wasn't torn up inside?

Pixie consumed his every thought. She had gone with him that night to escape a fucked-up situation, but it pissed him off that she still felt that way. Would she take off the minute she was safe?

His stomach roiled and he chose to blame it on the Jack.

He showered quickly and headed down to the kitchen to get some water. He would get through today and hopefully by tonight he would know what to do with his Old Lady.

Sharp drank the cool bottle of water, looking out the window at everyone setting up tables and games. He caught sight of Pixie setting up a food table, her golden hair shining in a ponytail that swung every time she moved. She was still wearing his cut which he guessed was a good sign.

"You up for talking or do you still have your pink panties on?"

Sharp turned to see Hawk leaning against the doorway with a handful of cookies and a serious expression on his face.

"Fuck you, Pres. What do we have to talk about?"

"How about a little fluff that bakes like a goddess, screws like a demon, and looks at you like you hung the fucking moon? I think she even has your patch on her back, but I could be wrong." He popped a cookie in his mouth.

"She bake you those?"

"Chocolate chip with fucking walnuts. Left me a box of them on my desk so I don't have to share with you assholes."

"She knows how to suck up really well. I will give her that."

"I see you still got lacey panties on, whining like a little bitch with hurt feelings."

"Excuse me?" Sharp's temper rode him hard. Hawk and he had been friends a long time but he wasn't going to roll over like a prospect, taking insults because the man was President.

"You got your dick hurt. Your woman said something that hurt your pride and instead of manning up you tossed her aside and treated her like trash. And I'll warn you, you had better fix that shit quick, there are at least five Brothers willing to replace your patch with theirs. I'm fucking one of them."

Sharp got up in Hawk's face. "I did not toss her aside. She's got my fucking patch on her back and it's staying there. But the minute this shit with Caravaggio and Mitchel is done, you think she's going to stay?"

Hawk raised an eyebrow, not appearing even phased by the ex-SEAL screaming in his face. "I think your tampon is showing."

Sharp punched the wall and stepped back. "What the fuck!"

"Men don't sit around worrying about some bullshit that might happen. They make sure their woman knows who they belong to and if she starts to forget it, they fuck her until she's screaming their name to remind her. You and your Brothers are the one thing that stands between her and a gruesome death. Most women would crumple under that pressure but instead she is out there trying to make a place for herself in our world. Doing it right, too. She hasn't said one word of complaint and shows everyone she knows the meaning of respect, all while making calf eyes at no one but you. You're the only one who even questions how that girl feels. So yeah. You need to find your balls and get over whatever bullshit is in your head."

Hawk turned and left Sharp standing stunned. His friend never laid him out like that. He questioned if his Pres had a point. Were his own insecurities and feelings getting in the way of seeing things clearly?

The door to the outside opened and Dragon walked in carrying a bunch of empty Tupperware containers. From the scowl on the big prospect's face Sharp could tell the man wasn't happy. Unlike the rest of his Brothers, Dragon had formed a big Brother relationship with Pixie which meant Sharp trusted him to give him honesty about what was best for her.

"How is she doing?"

Dragon dumped the Tupperware in the sink and took a deep breath. "Fine."

"What does that mean?"

"She's alive and safe. I'm doing my job, Sir."

Sharp recognized that 'Sir' from years in the military. It was the word you spit out when you wanted to say mother-fucker but couldn't. "We have a problem?"

"You're a Brother and I have to show you respect. And with all due respect, you are a *pendejo*."

"What did she tell you happened?" He was curious to hear her side of things.

"If you think your woman would say shit about you, you haven't been paying attention to anything above her neck."

Sharp reined in his desire to lash out at the prospect. Talking to this man was his best bet at finding out what was inside his woman's head. "What happened last night?"

"I got a call from Kickstand asking if I could take over early because he couldn't deal with your woman's zombie crying bullshit. When I got there, she didn't even acknowledge me. She moved around the kitchen making cookies, not looking up, tears pouring down her face that broke my heart."

"Jesus."

"I tried to talk to her, but it was like she couldn't hear me."

"Why didn't you call me?"

"I was going to. But, according to Max, who was outside when I stepped out to call you, you were the one to break her. So, I changed my mind. She did that shit for four hours. I've never seen so many cookies in one place. Around one o'clock this morning I stepped out to do a perimeter check and she followed me out asking if she could go for a run."

"A run?"

"Apparently she wanted to tire herself out."

It had been a long damn day; the fact she was still awake at one o'clock was a miracle, forget asking to go for a run. "What did you do?"

"We went running. Used the road that runs around the interior of the compound."

The road was about two miles long, circling the compound. The majority of the compound was old farmland and woods with about five acres of it developed with houses and buildings. "How far did she run?"

"We circled the compound five times when her legs gave out and I carried her back to the house. She ran for two hours, sobbing for the first half hour, then completely silent until she collapsed."

Sharp wasn't sure he was hearing Dragon correctly. "You ran with her for ten miles?"

Dragon nodded. "Then watched all night as she whimpered in her sleep with nightmares because she didn't want to leave the couch in case you came home and didn't want her in your bed."

"Shit."

"I have seen this too many times. Men fucked up after years in the sand pit. PTSD eating away at their souls. Your woman needs help, not more trauma."

"I need to figure out what the fuck I am going to do."

"I don't know, man, but you had better do it quick. There are only so many times a tree can bend before it breaks."

Chapter 26

Fairies Rock!

Pixie was amazed by all that went into the family barbecue. There was a bounce house for the kids along with every portable outdoor game she could think of, from disk golf to horseshoes. Everyone brought large helpings of sides and desserts to contribute. Two large grills were set up and Brothers were already cooking on them.

She had learned that this chapter of Dark Sons had fifty-three members who lived on the compound or nearby and another thirty or so either active-duty military or living elsewhere in retirement. She got to meet Sax, the eldest local Brother, who was seventy-six and could still pinch an ass with enthusiasm.

The sense of family and belonging was nearly overwhelming to a woman who had never had a family. Pixie wished she could relax and enjoy the party, but she still hadn't seen Sharp. She wondered where he had slept last night and if he was still pissed.

"There you are, girl. I have been huntin' all over for you." Val's voice cut through the happy chatter around her.

"Well, you found me." Pixie pasted on a smile for her friend.

"Now don't you go giving me no beauty queen Vaseline smile. What's wrong?"

"Rough night's sleep, that's all."

Kickstand snorted from his post, uncomfortably close by. "That's one way of saying you blubbered all night because your man put you in your place."

Pixie's cheeks heated and she clenched her fists. Her and Sharp's business wasn't something she wanted tossed around like cheap gossip.

Val snorted. "No one asked you. Go stand your watch over there and stop hovering over the woman like a boy trying to rub against his first set of pantyhose."

"When I'm a Brother—"

"You'll have maybe earned my respect. Until then, shoo." Val made flicking motions with her hands.

Kickstand stormed off towards the grill and Pixie swore she could almost see the steam coming out of his ears. She appreciated the break from the jerk but worried for Val.

"You know he is going to remember this when he's a Brother."

"Honey child, if that man makes Brother, I'll eat crow. But I would bet he bails within the month."

"How do you know?"

"My daddy and my grandpappy are bikers and I grew up among them. It takes dedication and a deep sense of loyalty to make it through prospecting and I doubt he has either. He's one of the idiots that sees the easy pussy and hard partying and thinks that's all that being a Brother is about."

"I'll take your word for it."

"That little piece of road rash made me nearly forget why I

was looking for you. Deep's Old Lady Cheryl is looking for you. She's with her little girls by the bounce house."

"Why's she looking for me?"

"Her and her husband are the Club's lawyers. She said Sharp asked her to do something for you and she needed some information." Val headed off towards the area all the little kids were playing in.

"Lawyers?"

"Don't be shocked. Bikers aren't all mechanics and construction workers like our men. Dark Sons come from all walks of life. We have accountants, lawyers, and even a billionaire playboy."

"Oh my God, who is that?"

"Have you met Tek?"

"Sure."

"He's the owner and CEO of Vallier Technologies."

Pixie was shocked. Even she had heard of Vallier Technologies. They were famous for donating time and resources to missing person's cases. After finding an A-list actor's kidnapped daughter, they became the security system of choice for the rich and famous.

They were approaching a woman with waist-length raven-black hair who wore the black cut that marked every Old Lady. On her shoulder was a sleeping baby maybe a year old and running around her a little girl of around four, in a fairy princess costume whose messy black hair gave no doubt as to who her mother was.

The little girl shocked Pixie by sprinting right at her and coming close to knocking her over with a bear hug that wrapped around her legs.

"I love you. I love you. I love you!" the little girl chanted as she danced around Pixie, never letting go of her legs.

"Why, thank you." Pixie laughed, not sure of what to do with her new wiggling accessory.

"Tayla, that woman is not your personal jungle gym."

The girl let go and ran back to her mother, pouting. "But Mama, she's wearing a princess dress like me!"

Pixie smiled and couldn't help but swing her skirt a bit. While it wasn't a princess costume, compared to the jeans and t-shirts the majority of the women were wearing, she could see where a little imagination might turn a sundress into a princess outfit. Val laughed and scooped up the little girl in a twirling swing. "Yes, she is, but she's not a fairy like you. Only fairies with wings can fly." She spun the girl a few more times and put her down.

"Maybe her wings are inbisible."

"Invisible, dear," her mother corrected.

"That's what I said."

The raven-haired beauty reached out her free hand to Pixie. "I'm Cheryl. You must be Sharp's woman. Do you prefer Phoebe or Pixie?"

"Pixie."

"She's a pixie and pixies are fairies, so she is a fairy princess like me!" The little girl's proclamation was so enthusiastic and cheerful it broke through some of the melancholy that had wrapped up Pixie's heart.

Val smiled down at Tayla and then swept her up in another flying spin. "Well aren't you the smart one. Why don't I take Sasha and Tayla over to the dessert table and let Tayla try one of Pixie's cookies?"

Cheryl handed over the sleeping baby. "One cookie."

Tayla clapped her hands and sprinted off towards the food, leaving Val to follow behind.

"Val is so amazing with kids." Cheryl sighed.

"Does she have any?"

"No, but I think her and Dozer are trying."

"She would make a great mom."

"I agree." Cheryl reached into her back pocket and pulled

out a smartphone. After playing with it for a moment she looked up. "I have a couple of questions."

"What about?" Pixie didn't mind answering questions but wondered what a lawyer would want to know.

"Sharp didn't tell you?"

"No."

"I swear, our men think we're mind readers. My husband and I are the primary lawyers for the local chapter."

"Val told me."

"Well my husband deals with any criminal or Club specific things and I deal mostly with family needs or real estate. Sharp said you didn't have any ID and asked if I could get you what you needed so you could get a driver's license or go to school."

Pixie was shocked Sharp had already put things in motion to get her what she would need to follow their barely hatched plans for her future. "Wow, that would be amazing."

"Is there any reason we can't use your real identity? If we have to get you a whole new one it will take some more time."

"You could do that?"

"Sure, but it will be expensive, so if we don't have to, we won't."

"No. I mean there is no reason to. I've never been arrested or anything."

"Great. So, any details you could give me would be helpful. No matter what Sharp thinks, 'twenty-year-old Phoebe no last name who was at some point in foster care' is not a lot to go on."

Pixie laughed. She took a moment and searched through her memory until she found a picture of the front sheet of her foster care file. She rattled off her vital statistics including the foster case number. "Phoebe Smith. Though I don't know what my birth name was. My mom was a drug addict who OD'd when I was four. Caseworkers never found ID on her or me, so

I was placed in the system. I was a foster kid until sixteen. Is that enough to go on?"

"A social security number and your case file is more than I could have hoped for. Any jobs or taxes filed?"

"No."

"You want me to see if I can find your bio family? With the new DNA tracing it might be possible."

Most foster kids dreamed of reconnecting with some magical family, but she hadn't considered it since she gave up on her imaginary brother when she was six. "I don't think so."

"You change your mind, you let me know. Tek is amazing at finding people. I should have your birth certificate soon. The rest shouldn't take much longer."

"Thank you." The words weren't nearly enough. She would have options she never had before. Maybe she would go to cooking school like Sharp had suggested—that was if he still wanted her Remembering that conversation drew her mood back down.

As if her thoughts had summoned him, Sharp was walking towards her, the look on his face matching her sudden sour mood. Pixie both hoped and feared he was ready to talk. The uncertainty of everything was making her stomach hurt but she didn't think she could handle it if he was cruel to her again.

Pixie gave herself a kick. She had survived much worse than a misunderstanding. Last night she realized a broken heart might feel worse than a broken body, but she wasn't going to give up no matter what.

Tayla skipped up with Val and the baby trailing right behind her just as Sharp reached her.

"I told everyone you had to be a fairy princess like me because your cookies have fairy dust on them. But you don't have wings and that was sad. But Hannibal said you have wings on your back. Is he lying?"

The little girl's words ran together making Pixie laugh. She looked over towards the food table and at Hannibal smiling over at her. She shook her head. "He wasn't lying. Would you like to see?"

"Please!"

Pixie slipped her arm out of the leather cut and pulled down the strap of her dress so her new tattoo was visible. She squatted down so the little girl could get a good look at the very realistic outline drawing.

"You have a whole fairy on your shoulder!" Tayla whirled around in a circle. "I want one, Momma!"

Cheryl looked down and admired the artwork. "That has to be Hannibal's work. Are you getting color or leaving it like it is?"

"This was all he had time for, but he said he would do color in a few weeks."

"Can I get a fairy too?" Tayla interrupted. "Please!"

"We will discuss it when you're eighteen." Cheryl shook her head in amusement and gave Sharp a nod of hello. "I got all I needed from Pixie. I'll get started on things tomorrow."

"Thanks, Cheryl." Sharp's voice seemed distracted. Pixie slipped back into her cut, hesitating a minute before standing and facing him. The two of them locked eyes and Pixie felt the chemistry between them flare to life.

She pushed down her desire. Chemistry wasn't enough. She had said one thing he took wrong and he completely shut her down. He wouldn't want her to make a scene and she could respect he needed to maintain face. Now wasn't the time or place to talk, but she couldn't stand there silently wondering what he wanted.

"Hey, Sharp." Her words weren't elegant, but they were something.

He wrapped his arms around her, pulling her in for a hug. With her face against his chest, Pixie didn't know if she should sob or punch him. Sharp pulled her around so his arm was over her shoulders. "We'll see you later, ladies."

Pixie struggled a bit as he pulled her away, fluctuating between embarrassment and fury at leaving so abruptly. She must not have hidden either expression well because both women laughed and waved her off. Giving in to the inevitable, she followed without comment as Sharp led them away from the party around to the back of a secluded building she had noticed before, but had never asked about.

"Where are you taking me?"

"Somewhere we can talk."

"What is this building?"

"It's the gun range. Kids aren't allowed near it and no one will come here during family time."

That answered the where, but she still couldn't tell his mood. She was afraid he was going to yell at her for something and she was at the end of her patience. The old Phoebe wanted to cower and take whatever he was going to give her so he wouldn't send her away. Pixie wanted to fight for what they had and wouldn't accept being treated like shit and Banshee wanted to beat the shit out of him for being an asshole then fuck him hard.

Pixie wondered for a moment what her old psychiatrist would say if she admitted to thinking she was three different people. Maybe she was headed for the funny farm. Sharp had obviously found the spot he was looking for because he stopped next to a picnic table completely hidden from view and far enough away from the party that it was quiet, with occasional shouts in the distance.

"We have to talk." Sharp stepped away and paced a few steps. He looked frustrated and angry, but still didn't say anything more.

Pixie threw her hands in the air. "I got that when you dragged me away from Cheryl and Val."

He paced some more, not looking at her. After another minute of silence, an emotion Pixie wasn't expecting won her internal battle for control: fatigue. She didn't want to fight. She needed to know where she stood so she could take her next step. If he was done with her, it would destroy a huge part of her, but for once in her life she knew, without a doubt, she would find a way to survive.

She was bad at a lot of things, but if her hell of a life had taught her anything, it was how to keep breathing. Exhaustion laced her voice as she spoke. "If you're going to yell at me, just do it. If you want your cut back—" Her throat closed on the last words, but she managed not to sob.

"I'm fucking this up. God, Pixie, I can't think when I'm around you."

"What does that even mean?"

"It means every time I'm around you I want to lose myself inside you, forget the rest of the world exists and only be with you. I want to make you laugh and kill anyone who makes you sad. I want everyone to know you're mine, and the fact you don't feel the same way destroys me."

Pixie's heart almost burst with happiness at every shouted gruff word that came out of his mouth. "But I do feel that way, Sharp."

He gave a mocking huff. "The reason you're here is because you're in danger. What happens after the danger is over?"

She wanted to smack him and kiss him all at the same time. "Yes, the reason I had the nerve to ask a scary-as-shit biker for help was because a sadistic asshole was going to sell me to a psychotic necrophiliac. But that's not why I'm with you. I've done everything I could to find my place in your weird ass Dark Sons world. I do that because I fell in love with a man who talked to me for hours after I freaked out in the middle of really hot sex. A man who, when not being a dismissive asshole, makes me feel happy and safe for the first time in my life."

"You love me?"

"When you aren't treating me like I'm too fragile to know what's going on, yes."

He stepped close, taking her face between his hands. "You are one of the strongest women I've met. What you've survived would break most men."

"I need you not to keep things from me. I'm not talking about your super-secret boys' Club things, but you have to tell me the stuff that directly affects my safety."

"Boys' Club?" He raised an eyebrow.

"I'm sorry – your very manly, badass motorcycle Club."

"I'm going to spank that very impertinent ass of yours."

Pixie shuddered, her nipples hardening instantly. "Stop trying to distract me."

"Would you like that, darlin'? I thought you enjoyed it the other night. Do you want me to turn your ass red so you have to think of me every time you sit down?"

Pixie's body softened and her core started to get wet. "Sharp! You have to promise me to tell me about things that are about me."

His hand cupped her breast and his thumb played back and forth over her nipple. She moaned, biting her lip, trying to keep focused.

"I won't add to the burden you already carry. It is my job to keep you safe." His other hand cupped her other breast and Pixie's knees weakened as he pinched her nipples.

"I can handle it."

He pinched harder and she gasped, loving the shot of pleasure that came with the pain. He pinched tighter and Pixie's core clenched in a mini orgasm.

"God, I love how your body reacts to me."

"Sharp!" she gasped, trying to keep her focus. "I'm serious. Keeping things from me does not help anyone."

"I will try, darlin'. But I have to do what I think is right." He leaned down and bit hard at her neck.

The small orgasm turned into something bigger as his teeth sank into the muscle at the base of her neck. No one had bitten her before, but the action spoke to something primal inside her. He licked gently at the spot and she whimpered.

"Do you know how hard it makes me knowing I never have to hold back with you? That as rough as I want to get, your pussy will be soaking wet."

He moved a hand down and under her skirt, running fingers through her drenched folds, proving his statement.

"You don't think I'm a f-freak." She wanted to believe her stutter was caused by his thumb circling her clit, but her insecurities hadn't disappeared with a few days of acceptance from him and the Club.

"Watching you moaning and rubbing your thighs together in that tattoo chair was probably the hottest thing I ever saw. I can't wait until you go back so I can see how many times I can make you come before he's finished."

"But it's not normal." Her old insecurities were slowly killing her desire.

"Is it normal to want to fuck you in front of my Brothers every chance I get? To feel my dick harden at the sight of my handprint on your ass or my teeth marks on your neck?"

He twisted her nipple and thrust two fingers into her wet pussy. "Yes!" she shouted, not sure if she answered his question but needing him not to stop.

"Fuck normal. All that matters is what works for us."

He fucked her with his fingers and the wave of pleasure was so intense she clutched at his shoulders trying to keep herself upright. Sharp used his thumb to press down against her clit and his mouth clamped over hers, swallowing her screams of pleasure as an orgasm blew through her body.

He kissed her until she relaxed into him, aftershocks slowly ebbing. Then his hands were on her hips, lifting and carrying her over to the picnic table. He nipped at her neck and Pixie loved the prickling shocks it caused.

"I love your screams of pleasure, darlin', but I need you to be quiet this once or we'll have parents complaining."

He flipped up her skirt and rubbed teasingly along her clit while he freed himself from his jeans. Heat ran across Pixie's skin, half embarrassment for forgetting where she was and half in desire for him to bury himself inside her.

He pulled her hips forward and slowly teased at her entrance. The feel of him so close, yet not inside her, drove her crazy, making her whimper and pull at his hips. Sharp chuckled, pulling further back and brushing his cock against her clit with maddeningly light strokes.

Deciding two could play the teasing game, Pixie leaned back flat on the table. She played with the top of her breasts, slipping her fingers under the fabric and playing with her nipples. They were sensitive from his earlier rough treatment, making her body shudder with each pass of her fingertips.

"Show me your tits. I want to see you playing with them." Sharp's voice was rough with desire, but he continued to tease Pixie.

She pulled the top of her dress down, letting the straps slide over her shoulders, exposing her breasts to the afternoon light. She cupped them, pinching at her own nipples and losing herself to the sensation. Her pussy clenched in response, achingly empty.

Sharp thrust into her and she barely remembered to stifle her cry. Pleasure built up as the two came together over and over, the leather of her cut the only thing cushioning her back from the wood table. He lifted her feet onto his shoulders, the new angle letting him reach her depths.

The feeling of him filling her completely, pounding against her cervix, was too much for her to hold back anymore. She used her own hands to muffle her cries of pleasure as her whole body clenched with an orgasm.

"Christ, you feel so amazing. Say you're mine, Pixie, 'cause I'm never fucking letting you go."

"I'm yours, Sharp. I love you."

A final thrust and Pixie felt him coming deep inside her. Peace settled over her as he leaned forward and kissed her gently. He brushed his lips against hers, his eyes gentle. "I love you, too. No going back. You're mine."

Chapter 27

It's not a biker family barbeque unless pig is on the menu.

Sharp wanted to steal Pixie away for the rest of the day and imprint his love into every cell of her body. Maybe they could make a short appearance and then disappear into his house for at least the rest of the day. He checked his pockets for his phone and realized he must have left it in the room he crashed in.

"Let's get you back to the party, darlin'. I need to find my phone."

Pixie nodded, looking wonderfully fucked and sleepy. How had he gotten so lucky? Flashing lights near the front of the compound caught his attention as they walked towards the party which was no longer very festive. The women had gathered up all the kids and had them moved to the back of the open yard. All his Brothers were in various groups looking toward the front gate.

"Shit." He looked between Pixie and where some sort of action was going on, blocked from sight by the Clubhouse.

"I'll go find Val and stay with her. You go deal with whatever is going on."

The fact she so quickly understood what he needed without question was yet another reason he loved her. With a quick squeeze of her shoulder he strode off to the front of the property.

When he rounded the front corner of the building Hawk's voice bellowed across the distance. "Sharp!"

He kicked into a jog and was at the president's side in seconds. Max, Highdive and Deep, the Club's lawyer, were talking to two state cops by the front gate. Across the street sat three other state cop cars. A man with a dog was the center of a second group of five state cops standing on the front lawn of the Club's guesthouse.

"Why weren't you answering your phone?" Hawk sounded pissed.

"Forgot it upstairs this morning."

"You get your shit sorted?"

"Yeah. What the fuck is this mess?"

"At least one thing is going right today. They've got a warrant to search your property."

"What the fuck for?"

"Illegal drugs and guns. Apparently, you're now a suspected heroin dealer."

"You have gotta be shitting me."

"Wish I was. Oh, and you're holding a woman hostage."

"Fucking Caravaggio. Did you talk to Minetti?"

"Yup, apparently his nephew has dropped off the radar and ditched his babysitters. He's recalled his men and has let it be known if his nephew wants to disregard family, then he is on his own. He did remind me that the original deal still stands."

"So, it has to look like natural causes."

"Yup."

Sharp was glad to finally be free to act. Hopefully Tek would have better luck finding this asshole because he had a lot of pent-up frustration to vent. "Grinder conscious yet?"

"He's in and out. You and I are heading over there after this shit is dealt with."

"Fine. Usual play?"

Hawk nodded.

The conversation between Deep and the lead officer was getting heated when they finally headed over.

"You expect me to believe that the Vice President of your little gang doesn't live within your compound property?" the officer, whose name tag read Volker, screamed.

Deep shrugged. "Your warrant is for that property over there. It doesn't matter what you do or don't believe."

Sharp made sure to keep his face blank. All the Brothers who lived on compound property listed the guest house as their residence for just this reason. The compound was owned by a corporation that rented the property to another corporation both owned and operated by Dark Sons after many cut outs. They knew they weren't fooling anyone. It did give them time if needed while legal loopholes were navigated.

"You Sean Oliver?" The State cop looked like he was moments away from an aneurysm. He didn't look like a cop who got out into the field very often. With more than a couple of extra pounds around the middle and the pasty look, he was definitely someone who spent more time indoors than out.

"That's me." Sharp stepped up next to Deep and crossed his arms.

"And where is the girl?" The smile that Officer Volker turned on Sharp was definitely not friendly.

"What girl would that be?"

"The one you kidnapped and are holding against her will."

Deep spoke up. "We do not know of any girl being kidnapped nor is anyone being held against their will."

"I was talking to him."

"I'm his lawyer. You want to talk to him, you go through me."

"You don't look like a lawyer."

Volker was obviously blinded, as most people were by the cut and comfortable clothes everyone was wearing. Deep's expensive haircut and the courtroom tone he was using had been perfected by eight years as a JA in the Marines as well as seven years practicing law in the civilian world. "Well, luckily the Bar Association of Colorado disagrees."

"You let him do all your talking?" Volker tried to taunt Sharp who shrugged and remained silent. Sharp had enough experience with the law to know not to say anything but your name and 'I want a lawyer' when confronted by someone who so obviously wanted to arrest you.

For several minutes, the overweight desk jockey tried to bully, threaten, and harass them into saying or doing something stupid. He finally gave up and sent his men in to toss the place, though they all knew it was a waste of time.

As the officers ripped apart the house across the street, Volker apparently decided he was alone enough to deliver the real reason he was here.

"I'd heard Dark Sons were smart, military types, but how smart is it to get your whole Club under the microscope for one piece of stolen trash."

Sharp hadn't even realized he had started forward before Hawk was in his way. The insults to him earlier hadn't even raised his blood pressure. Apparently, the dirty cop had found his weak spot. He needed to lock it down or he would be spending time in jail for sure.

"She must have some sort of magic pussy if you all are willing to have your business fucked up over and over. This isn't going to go away. Her fiancé wants her back. I can't imagine why he would after you all took a turn. But I guess some guys like used-up pussy."

Hawk tightened his grip on Sharp, keeping him from decking the arrogant man. Deep, who had been busy typing on his phone through the majority of the exchange, perked up. "Fiancé? I thought you got an anonymous tip about some random woman."

"We did and it included a picture of the girl and the fact Anthony Caravaggio was willing to pay $50,000 for the return of his fiancée."

"Seems odd don't you think? If this woman is his fiancée that you have a picture, but no name?" Deep raised an eyebrow.

"Must just be one of those oversights." Officer Volker looked around nervously. Sharp wondered if this man even had a scrap of guilt over the fact he was trying to assist a known psychopath get his next victim.

A shout from down the road caught their attention. A uniformed officer holding binoculars had stepped out from behind one of the cars and pointed dramatically towards the compound. "She's in there! I see her by the bounce house."

Hawk shook his head and snorted with disgust. "You know if we had kidnapped a girl, jumping up and down shouting 'I see her' would ruin any surprise you hoped to gain."

"The woman is coming with me," Volker snarled.

Deep stepped up into Volker's space. "Since you don't have a warrant and you haven't told us a name or shown us the supposed picture you have, you aren't getting shit. Whoever your man saw outside standing by a kid bounce house is obviously not in distress so if you step one foot further onto private property, we will be suing you personally as well as the State police."

Sharp wondered how Deep could keep his shit together so

well. If he was up in the pudgy fucker's face the urge to strangle him might be too great to resist.

"I am taking her into protective custody."

"Which she can refuse unless you have a court order, which I am sure you don't have since you would need a name to even try that," Deep shot back.

Two local cop cars pulled up at that point and Sharp needed to step away before his temper completely exploded. He trusted Deep to make the right moves. They needed to get these cops gone as soon as possible and start the hunt for Caravaggio. He needed something to vent his anger on and that man would do nicely.

Pixie tried to hide her concern, but something about the whole situation made her stomach knot. When one of the cops started shouting and pointing at her, she hurried over to Val hoping to get some insight.

"Does this sort of thing happen often?" She looked over her shoulder to the cop beyond the fence who was obviously looking at her through binoculars, though he had stopped shouting and pointing.

"Well, our men aren't choir boys, so it isn't exactly unusual to have the police stop by." Val looked worried.

"But?" This had something to do with her and she hated that her problems caused the family barbeque to be ruined.

Val stepped up and put a hand on Pixie's shoulder. "But if the men knew it was coming, they would have cancelled the picnic today. Plus, with captain obvious over there using his junior spy kit to stare at you, I'm guessing you know more about what is going on than we do."

"I don't know how much of my story you know."

"That Sharp got you out of an abusive situation and you needed help establishing a new life."

Bile rose, burning the back of her throat, but she pushed it down. If her problems were going to affect these women, they had a right to know. If they were going to be her friends, she wanted them to hear the truth from her. All the kids were busy playing, oblivious to the drama. Anna, Maria, Val and Cheryl had moved in around her as if to protect her from the watching cop.

She could do this. "A year ago, I was living on the street picking pockets or working under the table to feed myself. 'Usual runaway foster kid does bad' story. Then six months ago I was drugged and sold to a man who found, trained, and sold high-quality slaves to men around the world."

Maria snorted. "'High quality slaves'. You make it sound like he was a car dealer."

Pixie shrugged. "That was what Mitchel called himself. He found beautiful women who wouldn't be missed, broke their will, and trained them like dogs to follow orders before auctioning them off." Pixie's throat closed up and she took a shaking breath, remembering face after face of each of the women who came in terrified and left with soulless eyes.

Val looked like she was about to cry. "You don't have to say any more, sugar."

"No, let me finish so you understand. Mitchel kept me as his personal pet because he said he couldn't break me. I was broken long before he got me but I don't think he could tell." Pixie took a deep breath and waved off the comforting sounds the women were making. "Either way, Caravaggio saw me and tried to buy me, but Mitchel refused. He told me he kept some lower end merchandise around because Caravaggio didn't want class, just a girl to scream and die for him. I was more valuable than a toss away, but Mitchel did let him help break me on occasion for a price. Most of my scars are from him."

Even though Pixie had been trying to keep her emotions out and just give the basic facts, the women all looked horrified, some with tears leaking from their eyes.

"The night Sharp brought me here I guess Mitchel had decided that six months with me was enough and accepted whatever price Caravaggio offered. When I asked Sharp for help, I was just trying to distract him long enough to get his gun."

"To kill that motherfucker?" Anna spit out, fury lighting her eyes.

Pixie laughed, enjoying the feeling of having friends who cared about her. "No, but it didn't matter. His gun was broken or jammed; it didn't fire."

"Who were you going to shoot?" Horror crossed Val's features as she realized the truth. "Oh, honey child, don't you ever think that way again."

Pixie found herself in the middle of a group hug with tears wetting her cheeks that had more to do with happiness.

"I found out yesterday Caravaggio still wants me and has been trying to get me. Mitchel would never work with the police, so this has to be him."

"You are a Dark Sons' Old Lady. That *bastardo* will never get his hands on you," Maria said with such conviction that Pixie wanted to believe her.

Cheryl's phone rang and she stepped away.

"Thank you, Maria, but Caravaggio is a powerful man. Part of the Mafia."

The women all seemed to roll their eyes at once and laugh as they stepped back. Val was the first to speak. "Mafia Smafia. This isn't a Godfather movie."

"Pixie. The guys need the two of us up front," Cheryl said while pocketing her phone. "Val, can you watch the kiddos? Sasha is asleep in the stroller and Tayla is in the bounce house."

"Sure thing."

As Cheryl walked Pixie around the side of the Clubhouse, she explained the police had received a report that she was being held against her will.

"You need to tell them I am your lawyer so they can't separate us. You can give them your name and say you are here of your own free will, but don't say anything else. These are dirty cops, but we have enough local police and witnesses, they won't be able to do anything unless you give them a reason. I want you to let me answer for you."

"Okay." Pixie was terrified that somehow this was going to go badly, but she had to trust Cheryl knew what she was talking about.

Chapter 28

I'm not a fucking mind reader but I do have a mean right hook.

The scene they approached didn't fill her with confidence. The five police officers standing and staring at her by the gate made Pixie uncomfortable. Their expressions ranged from disgust to pity and she had no idea what she had done to trigger those feelings. Max, Highdive, and a Brother she didn't recognize were standing facing the police, arms crossed with hostile expressions on their faces. Fear rushed through her body, causing tiny tremors to clench her fists, and she tried to draw strength from Cheryl who displayed nothing but cool professionalism.

Sharp and Hawk were off to the side talking and across the street Puck and Kickstand were watching other police going in and out of a small house she had never noticed before. The fact Sharp wasn't moving toward her had her nerves skyrocketing.

"Sharp is the one they are accusing of kidnapping you. I'm

sure they said he couldn't be next to you for the questions." Cheryl tried to comfort her.

Pixie's feet wouldn't move any closer to the police. What if they took her away and arrested her for something? Gave her back to Mitchel or Caravaggio? Could these men really stop it? "Do I have to do this?"

Cheryl stopped, taking in Pixie's terrified expression. "No, you don't. But we can make them go away a lot faster if you do."

The cop in the middle was giving her looks which reminded her so much of the men who passed through the training center, she wanted to throw up. Her knees were weak, and memories started to flicker through her. She couldn't go back; she couldn't leave Sharp. She tried to look over to him for strength, but the expression on his face was so angry it made things worse. Was he angry her problems had brought trouble to his Club? Would they ask her to leave? She didn't think she could survive on her own.

"Hey, Banshee!" Pixie's head snapped up, startled by Max's loud yell. He was fifty feet away, but he had yelled like she was across a stadium. His usual teasing smile comforted her and he winked, letting her know they weren't mad at her. "Come tell the clueless brigade what they want to hear so we can get back to the party."

Something about his cavalier words and relaxed stance gave her strength. She had faced a room full of bikers and beat up a Club slut. She wasn't helpless. Not with all these men and women at her back. No dirty cop was going to take her away from her new family.

She straightened her shoulders and walked the rest of the way with her head high. Banshee was a strong bitch who wouldn't let some scum's creepy look or scary eyes bother her.

"You're going to come down to the station and answer some questions," the scum in question declared.

Arguments broke out between everyone and Highdive had to join Hawk who was now physically restraining Sharp. Every one of the Dark Sons were on her side and most of the cops looked uncomfortable with the arrogant stance their fellow officer was taking.

"No, I won't," Pixie said so loudly it cut through the sound of everyone else's voices. She let it quiet down a bit, then finished telling them what she had been told to say. "I am here by choice, of my own free will. Cheryl is my lawyer. I will answer any questions unless she tells me not to."

The out-of-shape cop reddened and glared at Pixie. "You expect me to believe anything you say while you're standing in the middle of the people who are holding you hostage?"

"I am not being held hostage." Pixie tried to think of a way to convince the other police because this jerk had no intention of listening. "See this cut?" She spun, giving a view of the back to anyone who cared to look. "It means that man over there is my old man. He chose me and I chose him."

"Pretty quick, leaving your fiancé and shacking up with another man," her new least favorite cop sneered.

Surprised anyone had claimed a relationship with her, she forgot she wasn't supposed to be saying anything. "Mitchel said I was his fiancée?" The urge to rip apart the slaver who had stolen the last six months of her life overwhelmed any fear she used to have.

"Who is Mitchel? I thought her fiancé was Anthony Caravaggio," the young cop at the end of the line asked.

Pixie took a step back as if she had been punched in the stomach. "I wouldn't willingly be in a room with that man. If he says I agreed to marry him then he needs to get his meds checked." Not that she had wanted either man to pretend a relationship with her, but the idea that Caravaggio had made this claim when his plan was to torture and kill her took psychotic to a whole new definition.

The low laughter of some of the Brothers helped her get her poker face back on. She looked over at Cheryl who had both pride and sympathy on her face. "Do I need to answer any more questions?"

Cheryl turned and faced the men. "Do you have any further questions for my client?"

"I need her name and identification. Then we'll see."

"Officer Volker." The Brother whose name Pixie could now see was Deep spoke up. He must be the Club's other lawyer, Cheryl's husband. "As you should know Colorado law says unless you have reasonable cause to believe that Banshee has committed a crime or is about to commit a crime, she does not have to self-identify." Pixie studied the man standing up for her. She preferred Sharp's rugged looks, but Cheryl was still an incredibly lucky woman to have a man with such classically tall, dark, and handsome features.

Pixie marveled she found it comforting to have lawyers around. Sharp had calmed down and his look was now gentle and full of pride. How had she gotten so lucky to find a man and friends so perfect for her screwed-up self.

Eventually the lawyers and the cops finished arguing. Her relief was like a cool breeze when they left and Sharp swept her up into a crushing hug. His arms around her felt like home and pushed away all the doubts and lingering fears, even if for a moment. Across the street the police still gathered around the house pretending to investigate, occasionally harassing Kickstand or Puck, but her part was over for now and she could relax and hope no one was angry at her for ruining the barbecue.

Sharp took a deep breath, enjoying the pure scent that was Pixie. Watching her stand alone against Volker had been one of the hardest things he had ever had to do. He had to remember to thank Max for helping her out when he had been ordered to step back and remain silent. He knew deep in his gut if that dirty cop got his hands on Pixie, she would vanish.

"You okay, darlin'?" Sharp studied Pixie's sweet features. She looked tired but no longer scared.

"Yeah."

He leaned down and kissed her tempting lips. The way she immediately softened made him groan. There wasn't time for more, although his cock disagreed, wanting round two of what they had been doing earlier.

Hawk strode up to them, eyes softening as he watched them. "Hate to interrupt, but we need to check in with Grinder. See if he has any info on where we can find that fucker Mitchel. Tek should be getting back to us on his search as well. There will be plenty of time to enjoy your woman once we neutralize the threats."

Sharp pulled away from the nirvana that was Pixie's lips knowing Hawk was right. He looked down into her eyes, expecting the sleepy satisfied smile she always wore after a kiss, but was startled to see fury snapping out of her eyes. She shoved at his chest and he let her push him back a step.

"What's wrong?" he asked, annoyed by her whiplash change of mood.

"What's wrong? You're looking for Mitchel!" Her voice was a hiss as she planted her fists on her hips. It was adorable and he fought to keep a smile off his face. Was she worried about them?

"Yeah. But he is a hard man to find. Don't worry about it, we'll find him."

"Men," she growled in frustration. "Do you have something to write on?"

Max and Highdive had joined Hawk and appeared as amused by his spitting little kitten of a woman as he was. What she could possibly want to write down was beyond him. "No. I left my phone inside. Where is your phone?"

She made a sweeping gesture that took in her outfit. "No pockets."

"Your cut has a pock–"

"Do one of you have a phone?" Pixie cut him off, turning to his Brothers.

Max held out his phone and didn't hold back the chuckle when she snatched it and stepped away a few steps. Her muttered curses about stupidity and the male race had Hawk smirking and lifting an eyebrow.

"As amusing as your tiny Banshee is, this shit needs to get settled. Max, you keep an eye on the guesthouse and our unwelcome visitors while Sharp and I head over to the hospital."

It was hard for Sharp to stay focused when Pixie kept looking up at the sky muttering some more curses, then typing furiously on the screen of Max's phone. Max didn't seem to have the same problem and nodded his agreement.

Highdive seemed irritated by everything. Ever since they received the news that Grinder was hurt, the sergeant at arms had been a complete asshole. Pixie's actions definitely didn't amuse him as he gave her an angry glare before saying to Hawk, "I am going to tell the men to get their families home. I think we should have church when you all get back and let everyone know the state of things. We need to shut this shit down. We've lost enough face. Soon we're going to be back to proving ourselves like some no-name Club."

"We will have payback for Grinder, Brother. Don't you worry," Hawk said, as Pixie stomped back up and shoved Max's phone in Sharp's chest. When he took it, she crossed her arms, pushing up her chest in a wonderfully sexy way, which was probably the furthest thing from her mind right now given the situation at hand.

Sharp smiled and looked down at the screen, not sure what he expected to see, but this definitely wasn't it. She had created a list called 'Mitchel' containing several locations including training center, home, clinic, auction house, and three different entries for random storage buildings. Each entry was followed by a GPS coordinate that, from his limited knowledge, he guessed were somewhere close to the Colorado border, either in Wyoming or Nebraska. He couldn't believe what he was seeing.

"Why didn't you tell us you knew where he was?" Sharp's tone was made harsh by his surprise as he passed the phone over to Hawk.

Pixie's glare was impressive, even on her small frame. "You never asked. In fact, I believe you said it was all under control and not to worry about it."

She was right, and he was immediately sorry for his harsh tone. Sharp realized in wanting to protect her from having to think about the horror she went through, he had thrown away a possible asset. To his defense, he had thought she might only have minimal details which probably wouldn't help, so he wanted to protect her from the memories that trying to remember details might dreg up. Never did he think she would have GPS coordinates which could lead them right to the elusive man.

Highdive managed to look both pissed and skeptical at the same time. "If you were actually a prisoner like you said, how did you get this kind of information?"

The hurt and anger in Pixie's eyes made Sharp want to punch his Brother for his offhand remark. It was torture to stand back and watch her body practically convulse from emotions, but if he touched her, he wouldn't be able to stop there. If things weren't so on edge, he would sweep her away and keep her safe and isolated until she forgot everything bad. He would spend years replacing every nightmare with wonderful dreams fueled by endless days and nights of the type of pleasure that was only possible between the two of them.

Instead, he had to stand by while his own Brother triggered Pixie's flashbacks with his careless words. Sharp had to give her space but if Highdive kept pushing or attacking her the gloves would come off. Pixie's quick recovery surprised him as she straightened her shoulders and faced off against Highdive.

"I wasn't just a prisoner. I was a sex slave." Emotion choked her voice but Sharp was proud of how Pixie was holding it together. "Mitchel liked getting blowjobs while being driven around for work. He would chain me to the back seat of his fancy SUV which had a nav system on the center console."

"And you remember all these coordinates?" Highdive's doubt turned his words into a sneer. Sharp's control was near its end, his knuckles cracking as he tightened his hands into fists. Pixie had done nothing to deserve his Brother's attitude. If his Brother wanted to lash out at random targets, he was about to find out that sometimes you got hit back.

"Yeah," Pixie snapped. "Photo-fucking-graphic memory. I remember everything. *Ev-er-y-thing* I have ever seen. From the nightmare-inducing image of a girl barely old enough to vote being stabbed twenty-three times then literally fucked to death, to the stupid number on your driver's license that I saw for two seconds when you pulled out the picture of your niece." She was panting, her breath coming too fast, but she wasn't screaming or acting hysterical. After a few seconds all the light and life seemed to drain out of her. The broken tone in her voice almost took Sharp out at the knees. "Forget it. I'm done. You all do whatever. I am going to help clean up since that is all I am apparently good for."

She spun and practically ran for the Clubhouse without a hint of the sobs which were right below the surface. Sharp knew he should call out to her, go comfort her, but Hawk's grip held him in place.

"What the fuck, man?" Sharp's rage was evident in his voice.

Highdive's sneer was ugly. "Don't you think it's a bit convenient? She shows up and we got cops on our doorstep, a war with the Minettis, and a man even Tek can't find is taking out hits on the Brothers. Yet she had his home address in her back pocket. She's no victim. She's a honey trap bringing down this Club and you're falling for it!"

Highdive was ready for a fight, but he didn't see the punch that knocked him to the ground because it didn't come from Sharp. It came from Max, the funny and calm Road Captain who was now standing over the downed man with a terrifying light in his eyes. "Don't get up until I've said my piece, or you will regret it." The usually calm and cheerful Brother's voice was gone; these words had ice on every syllable.

"Her body was covered with so many knife wounds and bruises that I don't think there was an inch of her back or legs unmarked. I've seen men bedridden for days from injuries half that bad. But she rode for hours on the back of Sharp's bike until her clothing was soaked with blood without complaint. She hasn't been complaining or planting dissent within the Club. She doesn't bitch. Instead, she does everything she can to help. That girl has done nothing but survive the shittiest life any of us could imagine and still manages to bring light into the world. You're pissed Grinder got hurt and you're taking that bullshit out on her. Sharp made that woman family and you just shit all over her."

Sharp's own anger was cooled by the shock of Max's aggressive reaction. Highdive was an ex-Marine, their sergeant at arms, and a brutal enforcer who had never been knocked down in a fight. All they knew about Max was he was into motocross and had been patched in ten years ago in LA. He had been made Road Captain because of his quick mind and level temper. This cold scary side made Sharp wonder what other secrets he might be hiding. He knew without words not to push the man right now because death might be a real possibility.

But Highdive wasn't giving up so easily. "If she hadn't lured Sharp in–"

"Lured? You weren't fucking there, but I know Sharp told you what happened. She said two words: 'Help me'. And I was never fucking prouder to be a Dark Son than when Sharp stepped up. You think you know hell having been in combat? You don't know shit. Women who survive that asshole for even a few months are rare. Mitchel is known within certain communities for his ruthless brutality. If I had known who that fucker was back at the bar, I would have slit his throat."

"Something you need to tell us, Max?" Even Hawk was being wary of this new scarier version of the Brother.

Max stepped back from Highdive, letting him stand. He ran a hand through his hair and seemed to come to a decision. "Mitchel Thomas is a ghost known as the Recluse. He isn't just a slaver. He is an information broker with dirt on important people throughout the world. He sells women to the rich and twisted of the world, but the price isn't primarily money. He uses the information and power he gets to keep him and his inner circle untouchable. To think he's been hiding in Wyoming and not some tropical private island is a joke."

"How do you know this shit and why didn't you tell us earlier?"

"I didn't know at first. When Tek started searching, a few of my old contacts reached out. They made it very clear that if we find and take out this guy under the radar, parties will be thrown in our honor. And if we can turn over any information we find, we can set the price. Hell, I didn't think we had a chance. The recluse has had a three-million-dollar price on his head for over five years and no one has collected. I tried to find the fucker myself when I was still active after encountering firsthand some of his handiwork. Honestly, I was happy we were able to save one of his victims before she became another empty shell. The women he turns out—well, they're broken dolls both physically and mentally that no glue can put back together."

Max's words hit Sharp on a visceral level. The possibility of his Pixie being one of many broken women was almost more than he could handle.

"What now?" Highdive rubbed his jaw. He didn't necessarily seem contrite, but he had dropped the attitude.

Hawk looked them all over and Sharp wished he was inside his friend's mind. He never envied Hawk's position of having to balance the needs of the Club as a whole over the needs of his Brothers.

"The Dark Sons are going to erase two motherfuckers from existence."

Chapter 29

I'm more confused than a chameleon in a bag of Skittles.

Pixie stood in the Clubhouse kitchen trying to work out her frustration, punching and kneading the bread dough in front of her. The last twenty-four hours had been confusing to say the least. These men were enough to drive any woman insane. After insulting and attacking her they believed halfhearted apologies where the words 'I'm sorry' that might as well have been replaced with 'suck it up' would make her feel better. She had hoped and expected more from Sharp; the quick kiss he had thrown in before leaving was lackluster at best. Highdive's apology had been unexpected and sounded more like a sullen teen being forced to mumble the words.

Then the men had disappeared into their secret meeting all night and pulled in all the women and children. Now they had everyone on lockdown in the Clubhouse with no explanation. They had all left except for a few Brothers and the prospects. The single clue she had as to what was going on was a quick kiss from Sharp and muttered promise that it should all be over soon.

She slammed her fists into the dough with a frustrated growl.

"Ah, the war cry of the worried woman." Val's southern twang was comforting and teasing.

"How can you deal with it?" Pixie set aside the last loaf she had been working on to rise.

"A lifetime of practice. What has a burr in your britches? That we're on lockdown or is it something else?"

"This whole thing is my fault. And God only knows what they are out there doing right now. Grinder was hurt because of me. What if someone else gets hurt? Or worse?" She flattened the bread again, the angry punch emphasizing her words. She would give almost anything to have Mitchel get his due and the women trapped in that hell to be free. But she would give up her vengeance if it meant Sharp would be home safe with her.

Val pulled up a stool to the large island where Pixie had a few dozen loaves of bread dough laid out and sat. "You know, this isn't the first time these men have been in danger. It won't be the last time either." She leaned forward and smiled. "I grew up in my daddy's Club – Soldiers of Fury – and all I saw was gruff men who liked to ride motorcycles. But that was a childhood fantasy. When I was nineteen a rival Club got angry because they wanted SoF to merge with them and my daddy, as president, said no. Apparently the SoF sold arms and ran protection for the local prostitutes but had no interest in getting into drugs. They were a small Club, maybe sixty members in all of Georgia."

Pixie paused in her baking. "What happened?"

"I was going to school to be a nurse and had no idea what was going on. They snatched me as I was heading to my car. The plan was to force Big Daddy into doing what they wanted."

Pixie sat down next to her friend. "So, your father saved you?"

"In a way. The SoF had been friendly with the Dark Sons for years and Dozer and I had been flirting. My daddy called Breaker and got the Dark Sons to ride down to help."

"I haven't met Breaker."

Val gave Pixie's hand a squeeze. "He's the Dark Sons' National president—he lives in Texas. All the SoF and about seventy Dark Sons rode in to save me. Dozer was there and claimed me that day. But my blinders were well and truly gone. Our men may have jobs, pay taxes, and do amazing charity work but they are laws unto themselves. For each other, for us, their women and children, they will lie, cheat and kill and damn the consequences."

"But–" Pixie struggled with what to say.

"But nothin'." Val made a zip it motion. "You put that patch on your back, so you have to choose. Pretend you don't know what kind of man you have," Val gestured at Maria and Anna, "or embrace you have a badass man who loves you. Either way, you have a life no civilian woman can understand and a lot of scary men at your back whenever you need them."

Val's story hit home with Pixie. Knowing the woman had her own experiences with darkness made her feel less alone. She loved Sharp and if that meant living in a dangerous world, he was worth it. She couldn't pretend she didn't know about the danger but maybe she could accept it.

"Thank you. I'm still going to worry, but I think I get it."

Val clapped her hands together like she was cleaning off flour. "Well, my work here is done. Now to check on the rest of the ladies and make sure the kids believe this is all a grand adventure."

"I guess you're the den mother?"

"Well someone has to be and since God hasn't seen fit to give me babies of my own, I figure it might as well be me."

Val's words were tinged with a longing that Pixie wished she could do something about. At twenty-nine Val wasn't old but since her and Dozer had been together for more than ten years, Pixie assumed there must be something more to the story.

She checked her phone to see if Sharp had texted, but her screen was blank. The Brothers had left this morning without any indication of when they would be back. She slipped the first three loaves into the oven, setting the timer. Impulsively she picked up the phone and sent off a quick text:

I love you. Be careful.

It was a few moments before she got a response:

Love you too, darlin'

His words made her feel like she was floating, and she decided she had moped enough. She was going to take a shower to wash off all the flour in her hair from her vigorous beating of the dough. She asked Maria to pull the bread out if she wasn't down in time and headed upstairs.

Her shoulders itched and she knew without looking Kickstand followed her. Even though the prospect was doing as he had been told, it still set off some primal part of her brain. He looked at her differently than the others, always stood too close when they were alone, and the image of him jacking off while looking at her was burned into her memory. It wasn't the act itself, but the disgust and hunger in his eyes.

Pixie tried for polite. "You don't have to follow me. There is no other way down. I'm going to freshen up, nothing else."

"There are other ways down. And you're the prize everyone wants, so it would be stupid to leave you unguarded."

Other ways? She had cleaned this entire floor and there was only the one staircase. Did the man think she was going to jump out a window? When they got to the door of the bedroom she and Sharp used when staying here, he was less than a half step behind her, making her feel like prey.

He needed to back off and when Sharp got back, she would beg him never to leave her alone with Kickstand again. Rational or not, the prospect made her uncomfortable. She slowed to tell him he couldn't be in the room when she showered. She would use a chair to block the door to be safe.

When she tried to stop, he pushed her forward, his hand wrapping around and covering her mouth. She started to struggle and bit down on his hand, right as a sharp pinch at her neck was followed by fire running through her veins.

He spun her around and tried to hit her with a backhand that she dodged before her legs buckled out from under her. She tried to scream, but the muscles in her chest were like lead and it came out so weak she doubted anyone would hear it. As darkness closed over her, Kickstand's voice chased her into nightmares.

"If you weren't worth fifty-thousand-dollars untouched, I would make you pay for that, bitch. Maybe Caravaggio will give me a go at you before he fucks that pretty body up too much."

Chapter 30

Violence may not be the only answer but sometimes it is the right one.

S
weat rolled down Sharp's neck and onto his black BDUs as he crouched outside the one-story warehouse. Being dressed in black, full-combat armor including a helmet and skull painted faceguard meant all of them were feeling the afternoon heat. The gear would help keep them and their identities safe but it was far from comfortable. Sharp led thirty Brothers who were ready to wipe out every piece of scum in this so-called training center while Hawk led fifteen to take out the location Pixie labeled 'home'. They had split up to reduce the chance any of the slavers would escape the hard justice that was coming their way.

The outer guards had been taken care of earlier and the external surveillance disabled. The Dark Sons needed to move soon before the gap in security was discovered.

"I've got eyes inside," Tek said over their coms. "Twenty-two hostiles roaming ground level. Five hostiles in the basement with over twenty lambs. Bravo Plan in thirty seconds on my mark."

Sharp did a quick check of his weapons and felt Rooster's hand on his shoulder, signaling his readiness to move. Two of his Brothers quickly moved off to get into position for the secondary infiltration plan they had designed. Five men with him would take the front while the back, sides and loading dock area would be taken by the others. Smoke had already set up the water charge with a thirty second timer.

"Mark."

Max started the timer as the five Dark Sons crouched behind a blast shield Smoke had given them. The explosion reverberated through the air, echoed in the distance by four other explosions. The smell of gunpowder kicked Sharp's senses into high gear and on the adrenaline rush he entered the building with his Brothers at his back.

Sharp sighted left and fired, killing the first man before he had time to raise his gun. Six more men who were scrambling for cover looked like they had been seated at a card table in the middle of the large room. Cages and crates lined the walls and posts stuck out of the floor with chains dangling from metal rings. A naked woman was manacled to the one closest to the table.

Moving quickly, Sharp took out another man who managed to give off a single wild shot. Max fired from his right and Smoke from his left, taking down two more. Sharp moved quickly, pulling his unit to the left, trying to reduce the chance of the woman getting caught in the crossfire.

Sharp succeeded in taking out the leg of another hostile when the idiot didn't fully get himself behind cover. Pain punched his shoulder blade as a bullet impacted with his Kevlar vest. Smoke and Max kept firing as he spun to see a hostile less than five feet away coming out from between the crates. Before he was fully turned around, Rooster smashed his AR into the man's face, then fired twice as he fell.

"Fucking Breachers." Max shook his head teasing. "A gun is for shooting, not bashing."

Rooster flipped him the middle finger before shrugging and bringing his gun back to the ready. "I shot him."

"Focus, boys," Dozer growled, as he and Colt broke off to the right, their goal now to secure the terrified woman curled up against the floor.

Sharp rolled his shoulder, letting the sharp ache roll through him. The bruise would be spectacular but not anything that would hinder his movement. Using the clutter, they moved in on the remaining three men.

"Zone three clear heading to Zone one ," Ink's Texan drawl came over coms.

Sharp and his men fired at the boxes their targets were hiding behind.

"Zone two clear lambs secure." Sharp felt relief at Gear's calm words.

"Zone four clear minor casualties."

Bullets sprayed towards Sharp and his men and they ducked behind a large crate. He keyed his mic.

"Zone one still hot three hostiles remain in northern quadrant one lamb."

Smoke pulled out a flashbang, holding it for second until Sharp nodded.

"Zone one bang." Sharp let Dozer and Colt know to be ready.

As soon as the noise and light exploded in the room, Sharp and his men sprinted towards the location of the last three men. They rounded the corner and Sharp felt satisfaction watching the last of the assholes jerk as the bullets ended their existence. Until he saw one of the motherfuckers start to crawl for his dropped weapon; Sharp strode to him, pointed his Sig at his head, and pulled the trigger.

"Zone one clear."

Chapter 31

Karma's only a bitch if you are.

Pixie's arms and back ached as the vehicle she was prisoner in pulled to a stop, causing her to roll further under the tarp into the motorcycle lying in the truck bed next to her. Fear and rage played ping-pong inside her stomach as she waited to find out what would happen next. Whatever that prick had given her had worn off a little while ago and had given her too much time to think about how she wanted to kill Kickstand and what was going to happen to her if Mitchel got his hands on her.

Female laughter echoed against the tarp. "I can't wait to see that bitch's face." Pixie clenched her hands as she recognized Tina's voice.

The tarp was pulled off and the harsh bright light of the afternoon sun hurt Pixie's eyes. Kickstand and Tina stood at the back of the truck bed, smirking down at her. Kickstand lowered the gate and grabbed for her foot. She kicked out at him, but the asshole still managed to drag her out of the truck and dump her on the gravel on the side of the road.

The small road had no traffic or houses anywhere in sight. Trees lined both sides of the road like evil guardians trapping Pixie in her current situation. The rope holding her wrists together burned as it twisted when she moved to push herself to her feet.

Tina snuggled up against Kickstand like a bad imitation of a Bond girl. "Not so tough now, are you? Dark Sons think they are so special, but they couldn't even keep one of their precious old ladies safe." The black eye the woman had badly hidden under an excessive amount of makeup made Pixie smirk.

The knots holding her wrists together were well done and it would take a lot of time, or a sharp knife, to get her untied. "Guess being with a traitor who drugs and ties up women is a different kind of special."

The backhand from Kickstand that sent her banging into the tailgate wasn't a surprise. Tina walked up and tried to punch her in the stomach, but Pixie used her bound hands to block the blow. The crazy woman stepped back and pulled a small but sharp looking knife out from behind her.

Kickstand grabbed Tina by the back of the neck. "We can't damage her if we want our payday."

"Fine." When he released her the woman got a sly look in her eyes and walked over until Pixie could feel her breath on her cheek. Tina slipped the knife under her cut and Pixie wanted to cry as she felt the leather vest slipping from her shoulders.

Of all the things the woman could have done to her, this was the most painful. The sound of the leather hitting the dirt felt like it stripped her of Sharp's protection. No, he will come for me. Pixie just hoped it wouldn't be too late. Tina tried to rip off the necklace that Sharp had given her, but the thick metal held and the violent action caused Pixie to stumble back to her knees.

The sound of an approaching car stopped whatever

remaining humiliation Tina had planned for her. Pixie raised her head and whimpered involuntarily at the sight of the familiar metallic-black Mercedes Benz. The car slowed and stopped as bile rose and burned against the back of Pixie's tongue.

Mitchel's bodyguards stepped out of the front doors and one opened the back-passenger door for their master. He stepped out onto the deserted road, his perfectly styled blond hair and immaculately tailored suit the perfect camouflage for the monster behind his ice-blue eyes.

"Ah, good, you do have her." Mitchel's cultured voice sent chills racing down Pixie's spine.

"I want my money." Kickstand grabbed the back of Pixie's ponytail and pulled her to her feet.

"Of course." Mitchel nodded to one of his men who stepped back and grabbed a briefcase out of the front passenger seat.

This was it. The devil was here to drag her back into Hell. Pixie prayed for salvation, but a lifetime of unanswered prayers gave her little hope. Tina clapped her hands like a small child about to get a gift. Didn't this woman understand the evil that stood in front of her? That any one of these men would kill or abuse the stupid bitch for nothing more than a moment's amusement?

The bodyguard strode over, holding out the briefcase. Time lost all meaning as Pixie saw the gun a moment before it fired straight at her. The explosion rang painfully in her ears, but the only discomfort she felt was a slight tug against her ponytail. Her body shook with renewed adrenaline. Tina's scream echoed into the trees and Pixie turned, not caring she was giving her back to the man with the gun. Kickstand was motionless on the ground, his shocked, sightless eyes seemingly looking directly at her. The clean red wound was just off-center on his forehead, his blood soaking into the dirt behind him.

Tina was shrieking, her arms fluttering like a baby bird while the bodyguard calmly turned his gun towards the terrified woman. Mitchel walked up in that unhurried way which had always unnerved her. He cupped Pixie's cheek with a clammy hand in a mockery of a caring gesture. "I will enjoy watching him slice you into bloody pieces for all the trouble you have caused me. If I didn't want the information he is giving me so badly, I would keep you for myself and spend months punishing you." He looked over at Tina whose screams had turned to whimpers. The woman hugged herself as if any comfort could be found in this situation. "Normally I wouldn't waste such a pretty piece falling into my lap but unfortunately we only have the one trunk and time is short." He sighed and gave a curt nod.

The explosion of the shot echoed into silence as Tina fell backwards, joining Kickstand in death. On the edge of the now reddened dirt, her destroyed cut lay with the words 'Property of Sharp' taunting her of what had almost been hers.

Chapter 32

There are some actions for which an ass kicking isn't nearly enough.

Sharp stared at the twenty-seven zombie-like women huddling in blankets against the wall and had to fight the urge to wretch. Only four of them looked around as if they had minds of their own. The rest were cowering like broken animals, or were flat out catatonic.

Max walked over to Sharp after handing the last girl a bottle of water. His eyes were blazing blue over the skull face-mask that all the Brothers wore. Sharp wanted to rip his off and get some fresh air, but he couldn't in front of the women.

"What's the plan?" Max asked, pushing up his sleeves in frustration.

"Clean's crews already have the bodies and we aren't bothering with anything else. We found money, computers, and enough prescription drugs to start our own pharmacy but Tek says there is no sign of Mitchel at either location." Sharp caught the Road Captain up.

"And the girls?"

"Any of them sane enough to call the cops after we're long gone?"

"I can." A very curvy woman with auburn hair stood. She had a sheet wrapped around her body like a toga, making her look like a Greek Goddess in a low budget film. Some bruising was visible but Sharp guessed she must not have been a prisoner long.

His Brother studied the woman like he was trying to memorize every detail of her body and reached into his pocket, handing her one of the cellphones they had gotten off a dead guard. "Screens locked but you can hit the emergency call after we've left."

"I'm Trisha," she said, as if expecting the two of them to respond. Her eyes were filled with what seemed to be hero worship as they took in what she could see of Max.

Sharp studied the two, who both seemed caught in some sort of fucked up attraction. "Wait as long as you can—an hour would be great, but ten minutes is enough if you can't." His words must have interrupted the connection as Max spun and left the room.

Trisha nodded, clutching onto the phone. "Can I ask you something?"

"You can ask." Sharp didn't want to traumatize the woman anymore by cutting her short, but they needed to be going if they were going to hit the auction house tonight.

"Are you guys FBI?"

Sharp burst out laughing but tried to reel it in at the woman's hurt expression. "No. Just concerned citizens."

Sharp took his exit and once outside whistled to pull everyone in. Most climbed on their bikes; the rest got into the two nondescript vans they had brought.

Sharp sent off a text to Pixie:

Won't be home tonight. Miss you.

He waited a minute but when he didn't get a text back, he

put his phone in his chest pocket and started off towards their next location. Fifteen minutes later his phone vibrated, signaling an incoming call. He pulled out his phone, the display flashing Dragon's name. He cursed; he didn't have a Bluetooth earpiece in. He waved to get Max's attention before pulling off the road. The first call had ended before he stopped, and he had pulled down his facemask and was about to dial Dragon back when the phone started ringing again.

Sharp's stomach dropped as he hit accept. "What's wrong?"

"Pixie and Kickstand are missing. No one has seen either of them for over an hour. His bike and truck are gone."

"Shit."

"Puck was on the front gate. He says Kickstand said he was going on a grocery run and so he didn't stop him. Kickstand had a bunch of stuff in the bed of his truck, but it was covered up by a tarp. Could have been his bike on its side."

"And it could have been my woman. Fuck! I'll call you back."

Max had gotten off his bike and was walking up when Sharp dialed Tek.

Tek's voice was crisp and to the point. "Hey, Brother. I've sent the blueprints of the next place to your phone."

"I need you to put a trace on Pixie, she's vanished along with that cocksucker Kickstand." Sharp wasn't proud of the pure fear evident in his voice.

Max cursed and pulled down his face mask. "Are you fucking kidding me?"

"On it, one second. Her phone is at the Clubhouse."

"Yeah, well she isn't."

"Her cut is on a small road off of twenty-five, close to Colorado Springs."

"We're three hours from there. Do we know anyone in the area who can get there faster?"

"Rex and Javelin are stationed in Colorado Springs. I'll get someone to... wait. Her personal tracker pinged on eighty-five, a little north of Denver."

"God bless you and your paranoid triple back up." Pixie's necklace was thick titanium and locked to her neck. It would take special tools to remove it. "See if you can get someone to track down the cut. We're going to head west on eighty down to eighty-five. Text me when we're close or if anything changes. Dozer is driving a cage, so call him with details."

Sharp hung up without another word, kicking his bike into gear and circling his arm so that everyone would follow him. Max grabbed his arm. "We'll find her."

"Yeah, but will it be in time?"

Chapter 33

If you put my back against the wall you had better be about to kiss me or ready to fight.

B y the time the vehicle stopped again Pixie had pulled herself together. Somehow, someway, she would find the strength to not let Caravaggio break her. Sounds were muffled outside the car and she promised herself she would keep a level head and escape if at all possible.

"You'll get the slut when you give me the information you promised." Mitchel's icy tone was unmistakable.

"I'll give you nothing. Your incompetence has cost me more than you can imagine." The sound of Caravaggio's voice was enough to make Pixie break out in a cold sweat. She tried to move but found herself bumping her head on the metal roof of the trunk.

"Incompetence?" Mitchel's voice came from close by. "If you hadn't insisted on going after this particular girl none of this would even be a problem. I'm going to have to move my operation because of all the pressure that motorcycle gang is putting on the local talent. No information, no girl."

"Fine. It's inside."

Dim light illuminated the area as the trunk opened, revealing the early evening sky. Large, strong hands roughly pulled her out and dumped Pixie on the ground. She blinked, trying to take in everything she could. They were on a dirt driveway in front of a large cabin. Woods surrounded them on all sides with no other buildings in sight.

Caravaggio, Mitchel, and two of his favorite bodyguards were the only people she could see. What little hope she had of being rescued vanished as she realized they weren't anywhere she recognized. Did Sharp realize she was missing? Movement near the trees revealed guards patrolling with what looked like fully automatic weapons.

Considering the living nightmare the rest of her life had been, it was fitting she was going to find her end like some bad horror movie actress in the middle of nowhere, at the hands of an out-of-control psychopath.

"Get up, slut," Mitchel snarled, and Goon One pulled her to her feet. She stumbled into the man, her hands catching for a moment on his pocket. The movement gave her an idea. It would be hard with her hands tied together but it might work.

They all marched up to the front door and when they paused for a moment, Pixie threw herself at Mitchel, sobbing for all she was worth.

"Please, Master, don't give me to him." The words were bitter in her mouth as her hands did their work quickly. She pressed her head against the slaver's chest. "I'll do anything, please don't let him have me." She found what she was looking for in the second pocket she checked: Mitchel's switchblade that he loved tormenting her with. She had barely slipped it between her bound hands when a blow sent her tumbling down the steps.

Unable to catch herself or risk revealing her prize, the edge of the step caught her on the face and shoulder. Her lip split and she tasted the salty copper of blood. Goon Two had her back on her feet in a moment. Her sobs were real now as pain flashed through her system, the sharp jolt in her ribs indicating one was probably cracked.

She waited for the embarrassing rush of pleasure to follow but it never came. She started to laugh as they dragged her inside. The pain wasn't pleasurable, only painful! That knowledge was freeing despite the injuries.

"Crazy pain slut." Goon One's muttered slur stopped her laughing but didn't kill the strange sense of happiness she felt.

"Put my property in the back bedroom," Caravaggio said as soon as they were inside. "The files on my loving uncle are in my office. He chose to back scum bikers over me; it will be nice to watch you play him like a puppet."

Goon One dragged Pixie by her elbow down a hallway, shoving her inside the last door. When he didn't follow her inside the spacious bedroom, she couldn't believe her luck. Working quickly, she got the switchblade into her hands.

The steel blade sprung out and Pixie studied the sharp edge, dark thoughts swirling in her mind. The knife could free her forever. She could use it to kill herself. Bleed out before any of the men in the other room even knew something was wrong. A guarantee she would never be a victim ever again.

The image of Sharp suddenly filled her mind. She touched the pendant he had given her. The love and happiness he made her feel was more than she had dreamed was ever possible. She didn't know whether she would ever see him again, ever feel his strong arms holding her, but she did know he would do everything he could to find her. How would he react if she just gave up and took the easy way out?

But if Caravaggio started torturing her, would there be anything left for him to love? A strength settled in her gut. She survived before and for Sharp she could do it again. Even if she didn't survive, he would know she tried.

Pixie sat on the edge of the large bed and clamped the knife between her knees, cutting the rope holding her hands together. Within five minutes her hands were free. Ten minutes after that she was sure she couldn't sneak out a window with all the guards patrolling and she wondered how long she would have before Caravaggio came for her. Twenty nerve wracking minutes after that, the door slammed open to reveal an enraged Mitchel. Pixie was as ready as she could be for whatever was to follow with the switchblade concealed in her hand behind the skirt of her dress.

"How did they find my house?" Mitchel's eyes were wild and showed the man was completely out of control. She'd never seen him like this. Pixie didn't bother to hide the smirk on her face. Sharp and his Brothers had obviously acted on the information she had given them. "It's off the grid completely, self-contained, and the name on the property isn't connected to me. I don't even let my own men know where it is, yet somehow a bunch of muscle head bikers found it, and the training center, without tripping any of the cyber alerts I have in place."

"Guess taking me there was a mistake then." Pixie taunted him and stood. Mitchel had been careful almost every time he brought her to his house by blindfolding her, but one time the bag had been loose, and she had managed to get a glimpse of the nav system as he parked.

"You fucking bitch!"

Mitchel charged at her and she spun, kicking him squarely in the temple. The momentum of the larger man's body knocked her off balance and onto the floor. He tried to shake off the blow and lunged at her again on the floor. She did the only thing she could. She stabbed up with the switchblade.

He fell backward, grabbing his groin, a quickly spreading red stain around the knife buried there. She needed another weapon. She would survive. She would not be this motherfucker's victim ever again. She grabbed the lamp off the bedside end table, the metal biting into her hands, and let out all of her fury with a scream.

Chapter 34

*Every man has a breaking point and unfortunately for you I
reached mine ten minutes ago.*

"Four perimeter guards confirmed. Two more on the door," Smoke's deep voice whispered in Sharp's ear. They were up in a tree looking over the location that held his Pixie inside.

As his spotter rattled off the distances and wind conditions Sharp lost himself in the rhythm of his heart. Every good sniper had his calm place where adrenaline and random thoughts wouldn't affect their shot. It was harder than usual to find that place, but years of SEAL training overrode the chaos and worry of the moment. After a thirty count, all four men were in his line of sight. He began a rhythm that lasted twelve heart beats: squeeze... aim... settle... squeeze...

"All four down, front team go," Smoke's voice called out.

Sharp dropped down out of the tree leaving his MK11 sniper rifle for later retrieval. He might not be busting down the door with Max, but damn it all if he was going to be far behind. Pixie had been in this location for over half an hour and it had been torturous for the last ten minutes to not charge in right away, but instead pulling together a plan.

If Pixie was dead because Max had insisted on waiting, Sharp didn't know what he would do. He sent a prayer up as he sprinted across the lawn, *Please darlin', hold on for me.*

Sharp crossed the doorway, avoiding the two bodies sprawled across the hall. To the left, three of his Brothers had Caravaggio pinned to the ground, guns ready. A familiar scream had him running down a hall and dodging to avoid bowling through Dozer and Rooster.

Pixie's wordless scream echoed through the room and Sharp didn't understand why his two Brothers were standing staring instead of helping, until he took in the scene. He saw what he assumed to be Mitchel Thomas' body, sprawled lifeless on the ground, a metal knife jutting out of his crotch like some macabre codpiece.

Mitchel's face was unrecognizable. Pixie's eyes were wild as she repeatedly smashed a metal lamp into the pulp that was her tormentor's head. Blood covered her like tossed away paint, creating a picture straight out of a horror movie. Her beautiful blonde hair and pretty white sundress was now a patchwork of browns and reds. Her voice was cracking from the screaming, but she didn't seem to notice them, or be ready to stop any time soon.

Dozer looked between the screaming woman and Sharp, his look of disbelief being replaced with a smirk. "You got this?" Sharp nodded and both of his Brothers backed out of the room.

"Pixie?" Sharp tried in a gentle, but loud voice. His woman didn't even pause. "Darlin', you can put the lamp down." Nothing. His ears were starting to pound. "Banshee! He's dead. You can stop," Sharp shouted, finally breaking through.

The transformation was surreal. She paused with the lamp held over her head, eyes glassy, but no longer screaming. The woman he loved turned and looked at him with empty eyes. Seconds ticked by before sanity slowly seeped into her expression. Pixie's muscles relaxed and the lamp fell, forgotten, to the ground. Recognition clicked in her eyes and the spark of awareness returned.

"Sharp!" Her voice was raspy from vocal cords over-abused by screaming. She ran at him with such joy he could almost forget she looked like a *Carrie* stunt double when he caught her in his arms.

Deciding he didn't care about the blood, Sharp pulled her up into his arms, happy she appeared to be intact. He carried his bloody little prize out of the room, not sure what her reaction would be if she saw what she had done now that all her cylinders were firing.

When they reached the main room, Max rushed over with a med kit. "Where is she hurt?"

"I don't think any of the blood is hers." Sharp looked her over as much as he could. "Are you hurt anywhere, darlin'?"

She pulled her face out of his chest, shaking her head. The blood was now smeared across her face like body paint and Max widened his eyes as he took in how much of the stuff covered her. "I think I have a cracked rib and a small split lip but nothing worth..." She looked down at herself and a slightly hysterical laugh bubbled out of her lips. "I'm covered in blood."

"Yeah, darlin', you are." Sharp was careful to keep his tone neutral.

"I'm getting it all over your clothes." She looked around and giggled a bit. "You all match."

Max smiled a bit. "Black doesn't stain."

She nodded as if that made sense. "Are they all dead?"

Max looked to Sharp, who nodded once. "All but Caravaggio."

"Let's get you cleaned up, darlin'," Sharp coaxed Pixie.

Something was still slightly off with her and they couldn't travel with her or him covered in blood.

"You are going to kill Caravaggio?"

His woman was looking at Max, but Sharp answered, "He won't be a problem ever again."

"Okay." Her voice sounded tired but Sharp loved how she curled into his chest.

Pixie closed her eyes, letting the hot water of the shower wash away the evidence of what she had done. Something had snapped inside her back in that room. Months of rage had poured through her and she remembered everything she had done but it was like a movie, not something real.

While looking for a bathroom to get cleaned up in, they had found a room filled with pictures of her taken over the last six months. Hundreds of outfits in her size had filled the space, ranging from erotic lingerie to a snowsuit. If her own clothes hadn't been completely ruined, she wouldn't have touched any of them.

All the Brothers, even the ones she knew well, looked at her oddly and she didn't know if it was because she had killed Mitchel or because they saw her as a victim again. Even Sharp had started using his careful tones again. She wanted to rewind time, go back and not ignore her feelings about Kickstand. Then she wouldn't be back to freak status with the men who were quickly becoming her family.

She threw her head back in disgust and met a muscular chest. She let herself press back against the body she loved so much. Sharp chuckled and wrapped strong arms around her shoulders.

"I was wondering if you would even notice me."

She turned, resting her cheek against his heart, letting the warm water run over her shoulder and onto where their bodies met.

"You're hard to miss, even in a shower this big."

The shower was big with several showerheads and bench seating for the sauna settings. The master bedroom had turned out to be on the opposite side of the cabin from where she had been held. If it hadn't been for the rush and large amount of blood on her body, she would have opted for a swim in the jacuzzi.

Sharp picked up the shampoo and began rubbing it into her hair. Pixie tried to ignore the pink tint to the water and relaxed into his gentle touch. She arched her back trying to rinse out the soap, causing a sharp twinge of pain from her ribs. The pain morphed into pleasure as Sharp's hands ran down her shoulders and she moaned. Apparently, her body now rejected unwanted pain, but she was still a freak deep inside.

Sharp's cock grew, sliding against her stomach, and her body responded by getting wet. She moved her hands up his thighs but before she could wrap her hands around the part she wanted, he grabbed her wrists and gently pulled his body back from her.

"I came in to help things move faster. Not to seduce you."

His rejection hurt and embarrassment colored her cheeks. She turned around, pulling her hands free of his, and quickly scrubbed to get the soap out of her hair. "I understand." She was glad the shower covered what might or might not be tears forming in her eyes.

He moved quickly and pinned her up against the tile wall. "Don't turn away from me like that. What is it you think you understand?"

Pixie's mixed-up desire ratcheted up and the feel of his rock-hard cock against her back proved her next statement to be incorrect. "You don't want to have sex."

His hand fisted in her wet hair, pulling her back so his fingers could pluck lightly at her rock-hard nipples. "I want to fuck you so bad, I can taste your cream on my tongue. I want nothing more than to hear your cries of pleasure echoing off the walls." Pixie moaned, pushing her ass back into him, wishing for once she was about a foot taller so that he could slide right in. "So why do you think I stopped? What thought went through your mind that had you turning away from me like I slapped you?"

Both of his hands were playing with her breasts now. The pleasure of him twisting her nipples had her unable to think, so she spoke the unguarded truth. "I killed Mitchel."

"You think that bothers me?"

"Or you think I'm too broken."

He growled and bit her ear. "I find it sexy as fuck that you can do what is necessary to survive."

"Then why?"

She found herself lifted and placed kneeling on the tile bench, chest pressed against the cold tile. A second later Sharp slammed deep inside her. The pain morphed quickly into ecstasy and she began orgasming around his cock as it hit the depths of her with brutal blows. Warm water misted them, and Pixie felt the first orgasm building into a second with the steady thrusts rubbing against that spot deep inside her.

His rhythm sped up and his hand reached around her. Sharp's fingers found her clit and with a few flicks she was rocketing over the edge, screaming her release. Pixie clenched around him as his own orgasm chased hers. For several seconds nothing could be heard but the gentle rain of the water and their panting breaths.

A loud banging on the door was followed by Dozer's chuckled shout of, "T minus ten, get your ass in gear, Sharp."

Pixie groaned as Sharp pulled out and quickly cleaned

them both up. He shut off the water and handed her a towel. "That was why, darlin'."

Pixie took the towel, careful not to bend too much as she dried herself off. "Why what?"

He handed her the clothes she had laid out. "Why I pulled away. Smoke is currently setting this place to go up like a bonfire. I didn't think we had enough time for shower fun."

Pixie felt weird slipping on the jeans and shirt she had chosen. She had grown to love the free feeling that being in a sundress gave her, but the dresses in the creepy shrine wouldn't have worked on the back of a bike. "Shows what you know." She smoothed down the top and quickly braided her wet hair since there wasn't a brush and she didn't think there was time to find one. "I'm burning these clothes when we get home."

Sharp wrapped her up in a hug, wearing another set of bad guy, black, combat clothes. "I like the sound of that."

"What, burning my clothes?"

He gave her a smack on the ass. "No. Home."

Pixie smiled, enjoying the sight of Caravaggio gagged and tied up in the living room when they walked out of the door. His many victims were about to finally get justice. The flames were barely starting to lick out the windows when Sharp kicked his bike to life. Pixie hoped that all Caravaggio's victims were looking down right now and enjoying their long-deserved justice.

Sharp turned, and their gazes caught. Raw emotion poured out through his tough-as-nails, biker's eyes. "I love you, Pixie."

"I love you too, Sharp."

Epilogue

I'm going to ride you into the sunset.

Three weeks later

Sharp took a swig of his beer, enjoying the wild party around him, celebrating Dragon patching in as a full Brother. Hawk sat in the next recliner over, savoring his own beer. The President nodded over to where two of the Club's sweetbutts were giving an X-rated lap dance to a very drunk Dragon.

"Feels like a lifetime ago when that was us," Sharp laughed.

"It was. I don't know about you, but I have zero memory of the night I patched in."

"Nope. I drank so much, don't think I sobered up for three days."

"I'm surprised your woman isn't here. I thought her and Dragon were close."

Sharp looked down into his bottle, concern twisting his gut. "She's got a stomach bug that has been bringing her down for the last two days." If she was still sick tomorrow, he was dragging her ass to the doctor no matter what she said.

"She better be ready for the bash the women have cooking up for her birthday on Sunday. I have never seen so much fuss."

"I'm sure she will be. You've been quiet. Is all the blowback from a few weeks ago done with?"

Hawk smirked. "You could say that. Going to be announcing it at church. Max and Clean finished divvying out the metric shit ton of blackmail material we picked up to the various alphabet agencies. Tek set up a fund for the girls we rescued with the cash we found and has started operations to help any others still alive from the records he got. The pharmaceuticals and guns all had buyers within hours of us letting it be known they were available."

"Anyone grumbling that we gave away the cash?"

"A few idiots but they'll shut up when they get the cut from the other deals."

"That good?"

"Let's just say the investment dividends for even the newest Brother will be enough that if they live slim, they don't need a job."

"Damn, didn't think the government would pay quite so well."

"We may not want to get into the extortion business, but the different alphabet agencies don't have the same problems. God Bless America and its love of dirty little secrets." Hawk took a swig of his beer, his eyes caught on something across the room and a big smile broke out on his face. "Looks like Banshee is feeling better.

Sharp followed Hawk's gaze, and the sight before him had his dick jumping to attention. His Brothers called his woman

Banshee when she was putting someone in their place or when she broke out the leather, and he was hoping and praying it was the latter.

He had to hold in a groan as he took in his sexy woman. She was wearing her property cut with nothing but a sexy red lace bra under it. The sexy combo covered the necessities but offered perfect black and red framing to her luscious cleavage. She had on an honest-to-god Catholic schoolgirl skirt and shiny patent leather heels. Her hair was pulled up into pigtails, putting the cherry right on top of his fantasy.

Catcalls echoed through the Club but, like the good girl she was, she kept her eyes locked on him. Sharp's cock was going to punch right through his jeans, but he held still, letting her walk across the entire room towards him, enjoying how all eyes were on his woman.

She climbed up on his lap, straddling his legs, giving him a quick peek at her bare pussy as she settled the checkered fabric. He couldn't resist a second longer, grabbing the back of her neck and devouring her mouth in a kiss that left both of them short of breath.

He traced the edge of her bra with his fingertips, loving the contrast of the rough lace and her smooth skin. "What does my little Banshee want?" Sharp loved every aspect of this woman, from the sweet homemaker to the raunchy slut. Every part of her brilliant, twisted mind called to the very core of him.

Pixie smiled, running her hand down her abdomen to where her body rubbed against his hard cock. "I want you to fuck me, Daddy."

Sharp quirked an eyebrow. "This a new game, darlin'?"

She giggled, the sound cut right to his heart. She held her hand over her abdomen and looked him right in the eyes, taking his hand and placing it over her own. "You're going to be a daddy."

Sharp looked down, the exquisite joy building up in his chest. "You're sure?"

She bit her lip and nodded. He jumped up and swung her around, his kiss promising so much more.

Sharp leaned back and roared to the room, "I'm going to be a father!"

The End

Coming Soon

Dark Sons Motorcycle Club - Book Two

Lost in the Dark: Dragon's story

Ann Jensen

I'm a snarky Jersey Woman who dreamed of one day becoming an Author. I write Romance with bigger than life characters who have to dodge every obstacle I gleefully throw in their paths. Somehow my characters also find time for steamy fun on their way to their HEAs.

I'm an avid reader, engineer, photographer, and a proud Bi woman. My life is a journey that I hope never stops in one place too long. I fill it with love and laughter whenever possible and when I can't, I pull out my clue by four and use it with deadly precision.

https://annjensenwrites.com/

Dark Sons Motorcycle Club
Saved by the Dark
Lost in the Dark

Blushing Books

Blushing Books is one of the oldest eBook publishers on the web. We've been running websites that publish spanking and BDSM related romance and erotica since 1999, and we have been selling eBooks since 2003. We hope you'll check out our hundreds of offerings at http://www.blushingbooks.com.

Blushing Books Newsletter

Please join the Blushing Books newsletter
to receive updates & special promotional offers.
You can also join by using your mobile phone:
Just text BLUSHING to 22828.